SO-AXR-471

# DARKWATER SECRETS

Center Point
Large Print

| Books are produced in the United States using U.S.-based materials | Books are printed using a revolutionary new process called THINKtech™ that lowers energy usage by 70% and increases overall quality | Books are durable and flexible because of Smyth-sewing | Paper is sourced using environmentally responsible foresting methods and the paper is acid-free |

Also by Robin Caroll and available from Center Point Large Print:

*Torrents of Destruction*
*Weaver's Needle*

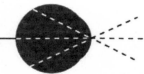

**This Large Print Book carries the Seal of Approval of N.A.V.H.**

# DARKWATER SECRETS

## DARKWATER INN SERIES

### BOOK ONE

# ROBIN CAROLL

CENTER POINT LARGE PRINT
THORNDIKE, MAINE

This Center Point Large Print edition
is published in the year 2018 by arrangement with
Gilead Publishing LLC.

The text of this Large Print edition is unabridged.
In other aspects, this book may vary
from the original edition.
Printed in the United States of America
on permanent paper.
Set in 16-point Times New Roman type.

ISBN: 978-1-68324-953-5

Library of Congress Cataloging-in-Publication Data

Names: Caroll, Robin, author.
Title: Darkwater secrets / Robin Caroll.
Description: Center Point Large print edition. | Thorndike, Maine :
    Center Point Large Print, 2018. | Series: Darkwater Inn series ; book 1
Identifiers: LCCN 2018034476 | ISBN 9781683249535
    (hardcover : alk. paper)
Subjects: LCSH: Murder—Fiction. | Homicide investigation—Fiction. |
    Louisiana--Fiction. | Large type books.
Classification: LCC PS3603.A7673 D37 2018 | DDC 813/.6—dc23
LC record available at https://lccn.loc.gov/2018034476

For Colleen

I'm so very thankful that He sent me you
as a mentor and friend.
I can't imagine any of this without you.

# ONE

## ADELAIDE

Surely that wasn't . . . it couldn't be . . .

Adelaide froze, squinting into the crowd. Her heart sputtered, then pounded. Her eyes had to be playing tricks on her. Here? No way could—

But it was.

Her lungs held her breath captive. At the same time, hot and cold washed through her chest. Nausea slammed over her. Her knees weakened, her legs locked, but the muscles yearned to run. To get as far away as possible before—

"Ms. Fountaine? Ms. Fountaine?"

She jerked her attention to the fire chief's face and demanded her legs support her.

"Are you okay, Ms. Fountaine?" Concern laced his words.

"What? Oh, sorry, I'm fine." No, she wasn't. Her heart lodged in the back of her throat. Thumping. Pounding. She couldn't fall apart here. Not now.

The chief continued to stare at her with widened eyes. "There's no evidence of any threat. Someone must have pulled the alarm as a prank."

7

He frowned, the deep lines digging further into his face. "I'll need to check any security footage near where the activated alarm is located."

"Yes. Yes, of course. Let me find our head of security." She glanced around the crowd, looking for Geoff but also for—

"It's clear for everyone to go back inside. I usually just stand in support when hotel management makes an announcement." He glanced at her. "In case there are questions or something."

"Of course." She cleared her throat. Her mouth felt as if she'd eaten a wad of cotton, but she had a job to do.

"Since we'll work to find out who's responsible for pulling the alarm, I'd appreciate you not giving too many details. If you can avoid it."

"I understand." Probably one of the sales reps in for the convention—goodness knew they'd been a handful—but she would let the fire department do their investigation for the truth.

"Adelaide."

She turned at the sound of Dimitri's voice, letting out the breath she hadn't even realized she'd been holding. He wore jeans and a button-down shirt. The warmth in his look pulled her shoulders back and straightened her posture.

"The chief says everything's all right." Adelaide smiled. "We're about to make an announcement and allow everyone back inside." She looked around to include the chief, her training and experience kicking in. "This is one of the hotel owners, Dimitri Pampalon. Perhaps you'd like to say something to our guests, Dimitri?"

"My father's the owner." Dimitri shifted his weight from one foot to the other but shook the fire chief's outstretched hand. "Nice to meet you, please forgive my attire." His smile came so easily, it was automatic. He nodded at Adelaide. "You go ahead and make the announcement. You're the GM."

His grin was so contagious that she smiled back, even though her world had been tilted on its axis. She gestured to the chief. "After you."

Together in the dusk light of New Orleans, the chief and Adelaide made their way up the front steps of the Darkwater Inn. Adelaide loved her hotel, despite its location in the backdrop of the gritty underbelly of Bourbon Street. She fixed her smile as she faced the people spilling into the street. "I'm Adelaide Fountaine, general manager of the Darkwater. I apologize for your inconvenience." She gestured to the fire chief. "The amazing and quick-responding fire department of New Orleans has given us the all clear. Please feel free to return to your rooms."

People flooded the doors in groups. She kept her stare focused on the faces that passed her, forcing herself to smile at the hotel guests. Some nodded at her as they flowed through the massive glass doors. Maybe she'd been mistaken. Maybe her eyes had played tricks on her.

Maybe, but not likely. Not *that* face.

Adelaide spied the head of security and motioned him over. She led the chief and Geoff toward the security office. Once inside the room filled with monitors, she made the introductions. "Chief Wesley, this is Geoff Aubois, head of security for the Darkwater."

Quickly, Chief Wesley rolled out a blueprint with the alarms marked and showed Geoff what areas of security footage he needed to review.

The vibration of her cell phone nearly made Adelaide jump out of her skin. She glanced at the caller ID and excused herself. Was it after six already? She answered the call as she stepped into the business offices hallway. "Hi, Daddy."

"Are you still at the hotel?"

She made her way to her office. "I am." Her day had been one upset after another, going from bad to worse. And it wasn't over yet.

"Good, glad I caught you before you headed out. I figured you'd be running late." Vincent Fountaine chuckled. "Can you pick up a loaf of garlic bread on your way? Or whatever you want to go with the spaghetti. I forgot to grab some when I was out today."

Adelaide Fountaine pressed the cell phone to her cheek, shut her office door, then sat. The well-worn leather contoured to her as she leaned back in her executive chair.

She let out a long breath and bent her head. "Daddy, I'm so sorry, but I'm not going to be able to make it tonight."

"It's Thursday."

She pinched the bridge of her nose and closed her eyes. "I know, but work's just been crazy today. Mr. Pampalon is out of the country, we've had a high number of staff call in sick, my in-house group is more than a little on the rowdy side, and we have just now been let back into the hotel after a fire alarm." She took note of his quick intake of breath. "Don't worry, there was no fire. The alarm was pulled as a prank, probably by one of my boisterous group, but nevertheless, I can't leave tonight."

She ignored the strong impulse to rush to her father's house and tell him all her problems so he could make everything better. But she knew better. He couldn't fix everything—anything— even if she could find the nerve to tell him. Instead she pinched the bridge of her nose harder.

"Doesn't matter. You still have to eat." No mistaking her father's authoritative tone.

But Adelaide was the general manager of the Darkwater Inn and, as such, was just as authoritative. "This *is* a four-star hotel, Daddy. I'll grab something here before I go up to my apartment."

"You need to get out of there. You work there, you live there, you never leave. That's not good for you. It's not healthy."

She forced a laugh. "Hi, pot, meet kettle."

"It's different for me."

"No, it isn't. You're a total recluse."

"I have to be. I don't have a choice. You do."

She didn't have time to argue with her father. Not now. "Can we talk about this later?"

A knock sounded on her door, followed by her assistant, Vicky, sticking her head in the office. Adelaide waved Vicky inside. What now? "I've got to run."

"Are you okay, honey? You sound a little off."

A little off? She was way off today in more ways than one. Just like him to pick up on the change in her, however slight, she thought. "I've just got a lot going on right now. I'm sorry I can't make it tonight." For a moment, she couldn't push away the wave of guilt rushing toward her.

Vicky, gripping a folder that most likely held a guest folio, leaned against one of the chairs facing Adelaide's desk and stared out the window, clearly trying not to eavesdrop. Or at least not be obvious about it.

"I worry about you, honey." Her father's softened tone almost unraveled her careful composure. And it assuaged her guilt.

A little. "Why don't I make a big pan of lasagna and bring it out Sunday after you get back from church? I can help you take down your Christmas tree and put it up in the attic." She held out her hand to Vicky, who passed her the folder. She opened the paper binder over her desk. It contained the pharmaceutical convention group folio. The number for the breakfast meal guarantee had been crossed out in red ink.

"Adelaide, are you really okay? I know you're busy and have a lot going on, but there's something in your voice that sounds really . . . You don't sound like yourself, and it's more than just being distracted."

"I'm fine, Daddy." She could barely force the words past the lump in her throat. "I've really got to go now. I'll call you tomorrow, and we're set for Sunday. I love you." She disconnected the call before she blurted out everything. Now wasn't the time, and this surely wasn't the place.

She couldn't let the fear and memories wash over her right now, but later tonight, when she could get out for a stress-relieving run . . . then she'd deal with the emotional mess threatening to strangle her.

Her assistant moved to the edge of her desk. "I'm sorry to bother you right now, Adelaide, but Kellie had to leave for the day. Now the group wants to reduce their breakfast guarantee by almost fifty, and that's not policy. I told Kellie I'd bring it to you." Vicky chewed her bottom lip. "I was supposed to bring it to you earlier, but with the fire alarm and all—"

"I understand." Adelaide glanced over the notes in the memo that Kellie, one of the hotel's best convention services managers, had listed about the group. "I'll take care of it, Vicky. Thank you."

"Adelaide, are you okay? Can I get you anything?"

Was she really that easy to read when she was upset? "I'm fine, Vicky, thank you. Just trying to get everything back on track." Like she'd carefully done with her life after . . .

"Yes, ma'am. If you need anything, you know where to find me." Vicky made a silent exit, closing the office door behind her.

Giving herself a mental shake, Adelaide studied the notes for a moment, taking in all the details. Poor Kellie had her hands full with this group, that was clear. She made a mental note to give Kellie a few extra days off next week. With pay.

A knock rapped against her door, followed by Geoff stepping inside, the fire chief behind him. "We've confirmed the alarm was pulled without any threat of fire," the chief stated.

Adelaide stood, crossing her arms over her chest. "I guess I'm not surprised."

Geoff nodded. "Security camera showed two men pulling the alarm, after checking the hall to make sure it was clear."

Great. Pranksters. And these were grown men.

Supposedly respected in the pharmaceutical industry. She shook her head.

"The men are easily identifiable on the security feed, and they pulled the alarm closest to their rooms. The police are on their way to bring them in." Geoff rolled his eyes. "I'll assist as needed. The *guests* were wearing their convention badges."

Lovely. "Thank you, Geoff." Adelaide smiled. Geoff was a good man. Protective.

"Thank you for your assistance, Ms. Fountaine. It's appreciated." The chief held out his hand.

She shook his hand. "No, thank you. Your response time was impressive, and I appreciate your thoroughness."

"We're going to wait for the police, then I'll be out of your hair. Nice meeting you, despite the circumstances." The chief turned.

"I'll let you know if there is any issue. I don't expect any, not with the police, but I'll handle whatever, don't worry." Geoff smiled, then ducked out of the office behind the chief.

Alone again, Adelaide sank into her chair and closed her eyes, digging her thumbs into her temples. The pressure hurt but then immediately soothed. Oh, what she wouldn't give to be able to climb into a hot bath with lots of bubbles and soak for an hour or so.

Her intercom buzzing interrupted her daydream. So much for even a moment to catch her breath. She pressed the button. "Adelaide Fountaine."

"Adelaide, this is Barb at the front desk. We have a guest checking out who claims he's supposed to be on the pharm group's master account, but I can't find any notation of that. Kellie's gone for the day, so . . ."

"I'm on my way." She snatched up the folder from her desk as she headed to the lobby area.

As she made her way across the marble-outlined floor, she flipped through the notes in the folder for the name and number of the planner for the group. She got in contact with her almost immediately, explained the situation with their guest, and asked her to verify with Barb regarding the master account. "Also, Ms. Parsons, I received a notation of a request to reduce the amount of guarantee meals for tomorrow's breakfast. Unfortunately, at this late date, we can't reduce the number. I'm sure you can understand. Kellie will be back in the morning and will work with you the best we can, but the guarantee number is firm."

After ensuring Barb had heard from Ms. Parsons and the guest was satisfied, Adelaide stood off to the side, watching the lobby area. Good flow. Ease of entrance to the streets of the French Quarter, yet a private courtyard for quiet evenings. Adelaide loved the Darkwater. Always had.

The hotel boasted a history almost as old and rich as the Crescent City itself. Records of the Darkwater dated from the 1840s, and several of the original structures had survived the ravages of time and hurricanes, such as Isle Dernière in 1856, Audrey in 1957, Camille in 1969, and most recently, Katrina in 2005. Adelaide loved the history and nuances of the old building as well as the fact that it'd endured so much, yet still stood proudly.

Across the lobby, familiar zydeco beats filtered from the bar as someone opened the door. A man and a woman wove and wobbled their way toward the elevators. Adelaide frowned. She should probably have a security officer in the area. The group had proven over the course of the last couple of days that they believed in playing hard. And loudly.

She checked her watch—closing in on nine. She should grab something to eat and head up. There was a department meeting scheduled for eight in the morning that she had to oversee. She headed toward the kitchen. An enticing aroma hit her before she pushed open the swinging doors. Her stomach growled in appreciation and in demand.

"Good evening, Adelaide."

She smiled as she turned. "Dimitri."

# TWO

## DIMITRI

Part of her beauty was that she wasn't even aware of the effect she had on most men. Something about Adelaide Fountaine's smile did more than a number on Dimitri's gut.

"I should have known you were cooking up something when my stomach growled." She closed the space between them, moving with the grace and poise he'd admired in silence the last couple of years. "What are you concocting tonight?"

"A new recipe: eggplant casserole with red pepper pesto, topped with a Cajun bread-crumb crust."

"It smells heavenly." She sniffed, closing her eyes.

He resisted the urge to tap the end of her nose. "Want a piece?"

"Oh yes, please. I'm starving." She dropped to one of the stools across the workstation from him.

He reached for a plate and knife. "Don't you usually go out on Thursday evenings for supper?"

He cut a generous piece of the steaming casserole and slid it expertly onto the plate, then added a fork before handing it to her. "Isn't that your night with your dad?"

She nodded as she took the offering. "Usually, but with everything going on today . . ."

He took in her drawn expression. Her normally sparkling eyes were reserved tonight. It was more than just exhaustion chasing Adelaide Fountaine today. Maybe he could get her to open up about what was bothering her. Give them something to really talk about instead of just the hotel and problems relating to it.

Like the constant issue of his father.

Adelaide slipped a bite into her mouth and closed her eyes as she chewed. "Oh, this is amazing, Dimitri. Perfection on a fork." She took another bite.

He chuckled and turned to the refrigerator, using the time it took to get her a bottle of water to hopefully clear his facial expressions. So far he'd managed to keep how much her praise meant to him a secret.

How much *she* meant to him a secret.

He let out a quick breath before turning back to her and handing her the bottle. A glimmer of the sparkle had returned to her eyes. Maybe he should just let her enjoy the meal.

"I'm serious, Dimitri, this is going on the menu immediately." She swallowed and wiped her mouth before drinking a sip of the water. "It's one of the best things I've ever eaten in my life." She took another big bite.

Heat filled his face. "Maybe you're just really hungry. It *is* rather late."

She shook her head. "That has nothing to do with it. You're a master in the kitchen. A true artist." She took the last bite, then wiped her mouth with the napkin he'd handed her with the water bottle. She waved her hand from his head to his feet. "Even your dress. In here, you're in jeans and a tee with a chef's jacket instead of the very expensive but very attractive suits. Much more relaxed."

She was right, but if his father ever saw him in jeans, he'd be livid. How many times had he heard his father's tirade? *A Pampalon must always look professional, Dimitri. Our appearance and name is our reputation.*

Adelaide lowered her voice. "Have you said anything to him yet?"

Dimitri didn't need to ask whom she was referring to. He shook his head.

"Are you sure he wouldn't understand? I mean, I know this hotel has been in your family for generations and you're—"

"I'm sure." How he wished he were wrong. Prayed it, even.

"I can understand your hesitation to say anything, knowing him, but Dimitri"—she reached across the space and laid a hand over his—"you love this, and you're so good at it. I've never seen anybody so born to be a chef."

"I do love it." He gave her hand a squeeze, then pulled away. "I'll figure it out."

She finished off the casserole. "I hope you do. You are amazing in the kitchen."

Time to change the subject. Dimitri leaned against the counter. "I was almost late today too. Guess what I found in the mailbox?"

"I doubt it was a past-due notice." She chuckled. "A request for a donation."

"How about a small boa constrictor?"

Her jaw dropped and her eyes widened. "Are you serious?"

He chuckled. "Very. Luckily, I'm not scared of snakes, so I took it out and dropped it off at a pet store on my way in to work."

"How did it get in your mailbox?"

He shrugged. "I'm guessing kids put it there." But that didn't explain the little cloth bag that he'd found in the back of the mailbox that contained leaves and what looked like rodent bones with ashes.

"Where would kids find a boa?"

"Probably one of their pets."

She shook her head. Her cell vibrated on her hip. She checked the caller ID before answering. "What's wrong, Geoff?"

Dimitri pulled her empty plate out of the way

as he listened to her side of the conversation.

"Well, that's good. Grown men acting like children. They deserve to be arrested."

She paused and took a drink. "Let the front desk know in the event they are late to check out of their room. We should bill them for an extra day." She chuckled.

Dimitri leaned on the counter, resting his chin in his hand and not bothering to hide his staring. Even as lovely as she was, there was something off about her tonight . . .

"Thank you, Geoff, for everything. I'll see you in the morning." She set the phone down and sighed.

Dimitri straightened. "About the fire alarm . . ."

The frown furrowed her eyebrows. "The police arrested the two men on the security footage for pulling the alarm without cause. Geoff thinks they might spend the night in jail because they didn't seem too inclined to call their wives to explain."

Silly men. "Will they be released tomorrow?"

"Geoff said it depends on what the judge thinks, but most likely."

"See, this is why you are much better at handling hotel business." If only his father could see—could understand.

The warmth of her hand covered his again. "You should talk to him, Dimitri. I think he'll understand."

He could only hope, but he knew his father too well. Knew what a proud man he was, and how he expected his only son to follow in his footsteps and take over the family business. "I've been praying about how I should handle the situation."

Her lips formed a thin, tight line and she gave a curt nod. She stood and pushed in the tall barstool. "I guess I'd better call it a night. I'm pretty beat and have a meeting in the morning, then the departments meeting at lunch. Don't forget—1:00 sharp."

"Of course." He always seemed to say the wrong thing to her when he wanted to know her better, wanted to know her heart.

But she smiled at him. "Thank you for the casserole. It truly is a wonderful creation, Dimitri."

He watched her leave without saying anything. Every time he brought up praying, she'd turn and retreat. What had happened to her? She'd never opened up about that part of her life. Well, there were a lot of parts of her life she kept to herself. That just made her all the more mysterious to him.

And Dimitri loved a good mystery.

## BEAU

The full moon cast a deceptively soft light over the Big Easy, aptly named for its easy-going way of life. Even though the French Quarter still pulsated with laughter and dance at the nearing midnight hour, the moonlight gave the appearance of romanticism along the brick-lined pathways leading into the dark alleys.

Beauregard Savoie stared out into the city streets. His city. He'd lived in New Orleans all his life and had no desire to be anywhere else. Yet just because he loved the area didn't mean he was unaware of the harshness hiding behind the slower, simpler way of life. Monsters could—and often did—hide in the dim back alleys and passages. It was Beau's job to find the monsters and put them away, but not tonight. After the discussion with his captain about the possibility of him being promoted . . . no, he wouldn't fight monsters tonight.

Tomorrow.

He slipped out of his car and headed toward Jackson Square. Something about being near the hub of the Quarter made Beau feel alive. Inhaling deeply, he drew in the essence of the crescent city. His steps were sure along the path as he noticed a woman ahead. Jogging. Alone.

Shaking his head, he sped up to move beside her. Tourists. She shouldn't be out here alone at this time of night. Not with the festivals so close.

He finally reached her. "Ma'am, I—" He touched her arm. "Addy!"

"Hi, Beau. What're you doing here?" She slowed to a walk and smiled, but it didn't quite reach her eyes as it usually did.

"No, what are *you* doing out here? And by yourself too."

She chuckled softly. "Yet here you are, out here all by yourself as well. I've lived here just as long as you. I'm well aware of how to make my way around here."

"I'm armed, are you?"

"Well, no. You've got me there, but I don't think I need to be armed out here for a run." As if to emphasize her point, she started walking faster again.

He fell into step with her. "Addy, it's a full moon, it's after midnight, and Twelfth Night is this weekend. You know that brings the crazies out. Almost as bad as Mardi Gras."

She nudged him. "Beauregard Savoie, are you honestly worried about me?"

All moisture left his mouth. If she only knew. Images fast-forwarded through his mind: sharing PB and Js on the back porch of her parents' cottage when they were no more than seven or eight, camping in her backyard with her dad when they were barely ten, countless Thanksgivings and Christmases and Easters . . . A knot lumped in the back of his throat as he remembered watching her leave with her homecoming dates, then her prom dates. Staying up late to wait for the car lights to pass his house on the way to her dad's when she was out on a date.

"Beau?" She tilted her head and stared at him.

He balled his hands into tight fists to keep from running a finger along her defined jawbone. He could do many things, but risk her friendship wasn't one of them. "I do worry about you. I worry about any woman out at night alone. You forget, *sha*, I see the worst of the city, and Twelfth Night seems to bring out some of the very worst."

Twelfth Night, twelve days after Christmas, was the official beginning of Mardi Gras season. Traditionally, the private krewes—groups who came together for the Carnival season with balls, parties, and parades—presented their kings and queens, complete in their fabulously outrageous costumes. The Twelfth Night carnival filled the New Orleans streets, especially in the Quarter, with the parades, music, and some of the spiciest and best food south Louisiana could offer.

It also brought out the demented, depraved, and desperate in just-as-bold living colors as the krewe costumes.

Normally, Addy would continue arguing with him. It was almost a thing with them. That she didn't now concerned him. He softened his tone. "Why are you out here so late?"

"Just wanted to go for a run to clear my head. It's been a long day."

"So I heard."

"Dad?"

He smiled. "I got the details from the scanner." But he'd tuned in when her father called to see if he knew about the problems at her hotel. "Heard we made a couple of arrests."

"Yeah. Don't know for how long, though. I'll be glad to see this group leave. They've been quite the headache."

"I told you, it's the coming carnival."

"We have one of the krewes booked for their party this weekend. I'll bet you they don't give us nearly the problems this pharmaceutical group has."

He chuckled as they stopped in front of the statue of Andrew Jackson on a rearing horse. "What happened to the good ole' days when tourists came to the city for its history and culture? Now it's for festivals and parties."

"Fun over facts, my friend." She stared up at the statue and cleared her throat before continuing in a stiff voice, "Did you know that Jackson Square is the site where the Louisiana Territory was turned over to the United States from France in 1803?"

Beau smiled and, in just as formal and stiff a voice, continued the spiel, "See these redbrick buildings that flank the square? They are called the Pontalba Buildings, were built in the 1840s, and are the oldest apartment buildings in the United States today."

Her laugh warmed him to his toes. "I think we might've heard the guide's lecture one too many times."

A breeze kicked an empty paper cup across the sidewalk in front of the statue.

Adelaide closed her eyes and inhaled deeply.

Beau understood. He liked to breathe in the city too. It centered him. Gave him focus. Another thing they had in common.

One of many.

She shivered. "I guess I should be heading back."

"Let me walk with you." He looped his arm through hers, not giving her the option to decline.

He didn't miss her little sigh. "So, was Daddy really put out that I didn't make it to supper tonight?"

"He was more concerned about you." They both were.

"Sometimes, my job has to come first. He should understand that." Addy's posture slumped just a little bit. A fraction of an inch, but Beau felt it.

"He does, he just worries about you." He drew her arm close to his side. "Can't fault him for loving you."

"I know. I know. I just think he sometimes forgets I'm not his little girl anymore, and that I have a job where people depend on me and the decisions I have to make." The timbre of her voice came out heavy, as if the weight of the world rested on her shoulders.

It was all Beau could do not to pull her into an embrace, but he knew he couldn't. The older he got, the harder his secret was to keep. So much time had passed. Still, he knew Vincent and Addy would feel the sting of his betrayal.

Pushing aside his own guilt as was his habit, he led her up to the Darkwater Inn and stopped. He faced her. "Vincent's proud of you and your work here, Addy. Don't ever think that he isn't."

She smiled, but it was weighed down with . . . he couldn't quite tell. "I know. It's just hard to tell him no."

Beau laughed. "Isn't that the truth? He has me signed up to help take down his Christmas tree Sunday afternoon."

Addy joined in, her laughter ringing truer than her smile had. "That stinker! I volunteered to come help him take down the tree then."

"Let me guess, you're bringing lasagna?"

She shook her head. "That man is incorrigible."

He waved toward the grand entrance to the hotel. "Then I guess I will see you Sunday afternoon. Should I bring the garlic bread?"

"I guess you should. I ought to make Dad spring for dessert."

"King cake?"

"Oh, yeah. I'm calling him in the morning and telling him to order one from Gambino's."

"Cream cheese/pecan praline, of course." Beau nodded, already tasting the rich sweetness, making his mouth water.

"Most definitely." She leaned up and pecked a kiss on his cheek. "Thanks, Beau. Just hanging out with you always makes a bad day better."

"See you Sunday." He forced the words out past his cotton-filled mouth as she climbed the steps to the hotel and disappeared behind the doors with a quick, final wave.

Beau headed back to his car. Tomorrow he'd get lost in the business of keeping the good citizens of New Orleans safe and sound, but tonight . . .

Tonight, Adelaide Fountaine would haunt his mind and make his sleep as restless as the spirits in the St. Louis Cemetery.

Just as she had for many years now.

# THREE

## KEVIN MULLER

What were the chances of seeing *her* again?

Finally alone, Kevin Muller sank back into the hotel room's chair. He kicked his loafers out of the way and propped his feet on the edge of the ottoman. He ran a finger over his top lip.

It'd been almost a decade since he'd seen her—years since he'd even thought about her, but now . . .

He closed his eyes and recalled the first time he ever saw her. It'd been a fluke that he'd been there that night. He'd just graduated—barely—but all that mattered was he actually got the degree and was starting out in the pharmaceutical industry. He'd had a date that ended badly and had needed a cup of coffee. He'd been annoyed that a poetry slam was in progress. Until he got swept up into the raw emotion of the poets.

She was one of them. He could see her as she was back then. Younger. So alive. Full of hope. Full of trust. He remembered she'd worn a black T-shirt featuring Edgar Allan Poe's face and one of those silly newsboy-style caps. A red one, but not a bright red, more of a deep crimson. Like the color of dried blood.

The poem she'd recited had been so filled with angst. Worry. Fear of failure. Her voice had even cracked at the most perfect places in the sonnet.

Slinking lower in the hotel chair, Kevin caught his bottom lip between his teeth. The next week, he'd gone again, looking for her there. She came in late, wearing a white shirt made of that gauzy material. He smiled at her and pointed to the stage where a stiff jerk whined in prose about being dumped. She shook her head but joined him at his table. She'd worn a heady perfume that drowned out the chicory smell permeating the campus coffee house. It was almost as intoxicating as the husky edge to her voice.

Kevin straightened in the hotel room and reached for his glass from the side table. The ice clanked as he downed the drink.

She'd been older today, of course, but the gut-level draw still pulled at him. Her eyes seemed guarded now but just as bright. Her face had flushed slightly as her gaze had swept over him in one defining moment. Had she recognized him? Had she realized who he was? She'd been such a draw to him that he almost gave her his real name. Yet in the back of his mind, even then, he knew what he intended to do.

Did she remember?

Glass empty, he set it on the table beside the

hotel chair. He sat up, then hunched over, resting his elbows on his knees. Seeing her again, while exciting, could hurt him. He had a career now. A pregnant wife. A promising future.

But there was still something about her—

*Creak.*

Kevin straightened and stilled, waiting a second. Another. Then another. A door banged shut from somewhere down the hall.

His thumb rubbed his wedding band. It was nothing. The convention had concluded tonight. He was set to check out in the morning and drive home after lunch with his regional team. Maybe he should skip the lunch and head home in the morning. Play it safe and get out. That'd been his motto for years and had served him well. His wife would be thrilled that he'd hurried home because he missed her. Yeah, that'd win him some points for sure.

*Creak. Creak. Creak.*

Every hair on the back of his neck shot to attention. Kevin jumped to his feet and stared at the closed room door. He squinted to make sure he'd pushed the hotel's night lock into place. Yep, he'd flipped the metal security bar over the door's catch.

Kevin shook his head. Seeing her again had made him jumpy. Nervous. He wasn't the type to be either. Maybe he was just tired. He tried to laugh at himself—a grown man wearing nothing but boxers and his tee from earlier tonight that still smelled like expensive whiskey and cheap perfume, getting jumpy alone in a hotel room.

He flipped off the lamp. Only a sliver of light from the moon slipped in from behind the closed curtains. From the corner of his eye, a shadow moved.

What?

Freezing, he stared into the dimness of the doorway, his heart hammering. He held his breath as his eyes adjusted to the desk and armoire partially outlined by the splinters of light teasing in from the windows of the courtyard below.

Nothing.

He let out a slow breath and chuckled. Now he was seeing things? Man, he needed to get some sleep. A shower first, though. He had to wash the smell of the woman off him or he'd never be able to sleep.

Kevin stomped around the bed and into the bathroom. He flipped on the lights.

And froze.

The shadow faced him.

"H-how did you get in here?" He barely managed to get the words out. Random facts assaulted his mind all at once. The door was locked. He was on the second floor with no stairs down from the slim balcony, only the rickety fire-escape pole.

Kevin had only a split second to register the

glint of silver flashing. Then it was buried into his chest.

Hot pain. He stumbled backward a step.

The blade came again. And again. And again.

He slumped to the floor against the shower stall. He couldn't get his legs to support him. His own pulse pounded in his ears.

The room spun.

He pressed his hand to his chest, pulled it back. His vision blurred, barely able to focus on the red staining his palm. It was wet . . . and warm. Nausea washed over him in waves. He couldn't breathe. He sputtered.

"W-wh—" He couldn't even get the words out.

"Rapist." Hate embodied that one word, filling his head, echoing over and over. And again.

Darkness took him.

# FOUR

## ADELAIDE

"You made some really good points in there." Dimitri held open the door, allowing her to precede him into her office. "You're an amazing general manager."

Adelaide set her folders on her desk, sat behind her desk, and took a sip of her sweet tea, a bring-away from the department heads' meeting. "You would be just as good if you ever had the inclination."

"Ah, there's the rub, right? I've found my passion in the kitchen." Dimitri slumped in one of the two chairs facing her desk.

"You're not telling me anything I don't already know." She set down her insulated tumbler and flipped the page in her planner. "Since you refuse to discuss this subject any further, can you at least tell me when your father will be home?" Even as general manager, she wasn't told of the owner's arrival date.

He shrugged. "Maybe Monday or maybe Tuesday. He likes to act vague to keep me guessing."

36

Adelaide's heart ached at the brokenness of his voice. "Dimitri . . ."

He held his palms out to her. "Don't start again, Adelaide. Not all fathers are as understanding and loving as yours. Claude Pampalon believes the world revolves around him, and nothing has proven that not to be true. It's the world according to him, whether I like it or not." Dejection hung on his every syllable.

"I'm so sorry, Dimitri. I wish—"

*Ding!*

Adelaide held up a finger to him and lifted the telcom radio from her desk. "Adelaide Fountaine."

"Yes, ma'am. This is Erika. We have a problem here at the front desk, ma'am."

She stood. "I'm on my way, Erika." After replacing the radio, she motioned Dimitri to walk with her.

"I should get back to the kitchen. We're booked up with reservations tonight, and you said your new group would be checking in this afternoon."

"Come on, Dimitri. You know your father will ask employees if you were out and accessible in the hotel while he was gone."

His mouth formed a thin, firm line, and he gave a curt nod.

She didn't like to hurt him with such reminders, but if he wasn't going to talk with his father, then she would do what she could to keep the peace between father and son.

There was a short line at the check-in counter when they reached the front foyer area. Adelaide took a moment to see that the complimentary lemon water coolers on the waiting desk were filled. They were, so she turned to Erika, who stood off to the side of the front desk, Geoff beside her.

"What's wrong?" Adelaide had kept herself busy all last night and this morning with meeting preparations and ideas so she wouldn't think about— Well, she wouldn't have any distractions or detours down memory lane. Now the insomnia pulled at her every muscle, and she wasn't much in the mood for any nonsense like the alarm-pullers.

"One of the guests missed checkout. When housekeeping made their rounds, they found the night latch still engaged. They called out multiple times, to no response, so housekeeping reported. We checked the reservation, it's one from the pharmaceutical group, but there's no late checkout indicated."

Adelaide nodded. "Have you called the room?"

"Yes, ma'am. Multiple times. And we called the cell phone number on file for the guest. It went immediately to voice mail. We left five messages, to no response."

"What about a home number?"

"There isn't one, Ms. Fountaine."

This was very uncommon. Yet another head-ache caused by the childishness of the group's attendees. She turned to Geoff. "Any chance this is one of the men arrested?"

He shook his head. "The judge released them this morning with a fine and a warning. They both checked out early and hightailed it out of here."

Adelaide paused, then let her stare drift from Erika to Dimitri. "What do you think, Mr. Pampalon?" Now Erika could report back to Claude that Dimitri had taken an active role in a management decision.

Dimitri all but rolled his eyes. "What's company policy, Ms. Fountaine?"

She didn't miss the sarcasm and refrained from smiling. "We give the guest until check-in time, then we go in and make them leave. Especially if we need the room readied for another group."

"Like the krewe you introduced us to earlier in the pre-con, correct?"

She nodded.

"Then I would say we should follow policy and go in."

More than likely, another prank of this group. She'd be relieved when every single one of them had checked out. "Geoff, do you have the tool?"

He held up the stainless steel tool.

"What's the room number?"

"Two nineteen." Erika handed her the master electronic key. "Guest's name is Muller. Kevin Muller."

"Send housekeeping back up, please, Erika." They'd have to work quickly to get the room ready for the next guest, and the hotel was nearing 96 percent to full capacity. This little prank had already set them back hours.

"Yes, ma'am."

She sighed. "Let's go." Adelaide walked between Dimitri and Geoff to the elevators, then nodded at the elevator attendant standing by.

"We've got this one," Geoff told the young man as they stepped inside the empty car.

Adelaide shook her head. "I'm so not in the mood for fun and games like this group seems to enjoy playing." They were making extra work on her staff, and she didn't like that.

"Don't schedule them back again," Geoff said but smiled. "I know, I know, boss, we don't turn business away."

"Right. Even if they are a pain in my side."

The elevator dinged and the door slid open. Geoff led the way to the room. He knocked on the door. "Security, Mr. Muller."

No response from inside.

Adelaide used the master electronic key to open the door and pushed it open. It stopped with a bang as the night latch engaged. She put her mouth to the crack. "Mr. Muller, this is Adelaide Fountaine, general manager."

No response.

"We're coming in." Geoff lifted the tool. He slid the opener between the door and the jamb, and the door opened.

Adelaide moved to take a step inside. Geoff gently tugged her arm, moving in front of her and led the way into the entry.

The closet door stood open, several pairs of slacks and a couple of shirts hung haphazardly on the hotel wooden hangers. A pair of Nike tennis shoes lay on their sides on the floor.

The three of them continued into the bedroom. The bed was unmade, the covers tangled as if they'd been caught in two lovers' embrace. A laptop sat on the desk. The chair in the corner of the room hosted a squished throw pillow. An empty glass sat on the side table. A pair of loafers sat off to the side of the chair's ottoman.

As one, Geoff, Adelaide, and Dimitri stopped just in front of the open bathroom.

Adelaide gasped, then immediately covered her eyes. Her heart pounded. She turned against Dimitri's torso. His arms moved around her, and he drew her closer as he turned her away from the bathroom.

"I'll call the police." Geoff's voice broke through the horror.

She took a step back, resting her hands against

41

Dimitri's chest to steady herself. She'd never seen a dead person before. Not that she'd really taken note of anything she'd just seen. All she'd made out was a man's body, wearing boxers and a shirt drenched in blood, sprawled out against the shower, his head tilted back so no one could see his face.

That had been enough.

"Ms. Fountaine? Erika told us to come up."

Dimitri hurried from the bedroom to head off the housekeeping team. He spoke softly to the ladies as Adelaide struggled to wrap her mind around what was happening. And what she should do next.

Geoff slipped his cell into his pocket and joined her. "Why don't you go down and wait for the police?" He cleared his throat until she looked at him. "They're on their way. I'll stay here and make sure nothing is disturbed."

With his words, responsibility snapped back. Adelaide nodded. "Yes, thank you, Geoff." She marched into the foyer to meet Dimitri. "Once the police finish, we'll need to call your father and bring him up to speed on what's happened." She led the way out of the room, closing the door behind her, and strode toward the elevators. She punched the *down* button.

Dimitri's hand on her shoulder made her jump. "Adelaide, are you okay?"

"I'm fine. There's just a lot that needs to be

done." The police would need to know everything about the guest. "I need to let Erika know what's going on." They'd need to move the reservation for that room tonight to another room. If one wasn't available, she'd authorize a complimentary upgrade.

"You just saw a dead man in a bathroom, Adelaide. You can't just be fine."

She wasn't, but she had to appear to be. It was her job. "I'll be okay." Her mind raced. "There's not a set protocol for this, I don't think."

He let out a snort. "I should hope not."

Now she sounded unfeeling. "I don't mean there should be. I just—"

Dimitri gave her a quick hug and kiss on the crown of her head. "It's okay not to know what to do. It's okay to be upset."

The elevator door opened and the attendant waved them inside.

"First floor, please." Adelaide spoke to Dimitri in hushed tones. "I'll be upset later. Right now, I've got to get things handled."

He reached for her elbow and escorted her off the elevator. "*We've* got things to handle. I'm here to help."

Good. She would need all hands on deck. "First things first: we need to have that side of the second floor blocked off from new arrivals, if at all possible."

He nodded. "I'll work with security on it, and

I'll talk to Erika about rerouting new arrivals as much as she can."

The wail of sirens sounded in the distance.

Adelaide took in a deep breath. "Then please pull Mr. Muller's records. I'm sure the police will want them sooner rather than later." She squeezed Dimitri's arm before he rushed away. She couldn't explain what his subtle strength of being with her right now meant.

Two police cruisers, lights flashing in time with the sirens, pulled up and parked right in front of the hotel. She let out a sigh when the two uniformed officers turned them off before brushing aside the poor doorman.

She had a job to do, without borrowing from Dimitri's might.

Adelaide straightened her shoulders and met the officers. "I'm the general manager. My chief of security called you."

"Yes, ma'am. A detective is on his way, but we're here to secure the scene."

"I understand and am happy to escort you to the scene—"

"There's no need for that. We'd prefer to limit possible contaminations to the scene. Just tell us where to go."

She supposed now wasn't the time to tell them she'd already been in the room and possibly contaminated the scene. However, she hadn't realized they'd find a dead body when they'd gone in the room. "Take the elevators to the second floor. It's to your right after you get off the elevator. Room 219."

"Thank you, ma'am."

Several people checking in had stopped and stared. Now they looked to her for some sort of explanation, for reassurance.

She smiled over the group. "New Orleans's finest, ladies and gentlemen. No more pranksters at the Darkwater today." Not pranksters today, that was for sure. She waved toward the front desk. "Ask about our fun foray into the nightlife last night when a couple decided to pull the fire alarm for a prank."

The group of guests chuckled and moved their attention back away from her and the scene of the police making such a grand entrance.

"Erika's taking care of the guests, and I have Kevin Muller's information." Dimitri held up a paper, a print out of the guest's information from the reservation system.

"I guess we should head back up to the room now to deliver the info to the police." Adelaide moved to the elevator without waiting for a response.

Dimitri was unfamiliarly silent.

"I guess the police will tell us what happened," she offered.

He looked at her with wide eyes. "He was covered in blood and slumped into the bathroom. What does that say to you, Adelaide?"

The elevator dinged and opened just as reality barged its way in.

The guest had been murdered!

# FIVE

## BEAU

Detective Savoie stood beside his partner, Marcel Taton, in front of the Darkwater Inn, his heart pounding in his chest. Murder wasn't much of a shock in New Orleans, but this one was a little too close for comfort. This was Addy's hotel. He drew in a deep breath as he began to do the job he was here to do.

Aside from the police cruisers littering the front of the hotel, nothing amiss caught his well-trained eye. He already knew the Crime Scene Unit had responded. Their van was most likely parked in the back of the hotel. It was bad business for any hotel to have such theatrics. Poor Addy.

Beau and Marcel flashed their shields at the uniformed doorman as they made their way inside. The city might be one that hid the secrets of crime and grittiness, but she also had the eccentricities of older, kinder years from decades ago. Like uniformed doormen and elevator attendants. Fresh flowers on hotel entry tables. Real marble floors with genuine mahogany details.

The extra touches that Beau would bet Addy

47

put to making the hotel the luxurious place it was.

An auburn-haired man with years weighing down the corners of his eyes approached Beau and Marcel with uneven steps. "Welcome to the Darkwater, sir. How may I assist you today?"

Beau held up his badge. "Can you please take us to the crime scene?"

The smile slipped off the older man's face. "Of course, sirs. Right this way." He pointed the way to the elevators.

"Thank you." Beau met an elevator attendant just as one of the elevator doors slid open. He stepped inside before he flashed his badge. "If you'll just direct us to the crime scene?"

The young man reached around and pushed the *two* button inside the elevator. "Second floor, sirs. Take a right off the elevators and it's just down the hall. You won't be able to miss it."

Of course they wouldn't. It was a murder scene, so their colleagues would swarm the hotel room. The CSU would have a variety of experts: fingerprint technician, forensics photographer, and evidence collector.

"Thank you." Beau pulled out his trusty notebook and pen. Some detectives preferred a pencil so they could erase, but he preferred ink because the writing didn't fade and sometimes, just sometimes, he needed to see what he'd crossed out.

Marcel didn't take notes. The man had almost

a total recall memory. He was an asset but could also be an annoyance when Beau acted on instinct. There were some things the police academy just couldn't teach—gut feelings. Only experience could do that. Marcel was gradually learning how important a hunch could be in solving homicides. Beau liked to think that was all his doing, despite Marcel's protests to the contrary.

Beau took a moment to quickly process what he'd seen, not bothering to even think about what dispatch had told him, aside from the victim's name—Kevin Muller from Natchitoches, Louisiana. Beau never retained anything more than the address, how many victims, and their names. He didn't want to be jaded by what he'd been told, but would rather rely on his own observations at the scene. Evidence and facts convinced juries.

Marcel, a few years Beau's junior, knew Beau's method from the two years they'd been partners. He stood silently in the elevator, letting Beau process in his customary manner.

The moment they stepped out of the elevator and onto the floor, Beau started taking notes. How many steps it took from the elevator to room 219—twenty-six steps—how many security cameras he detected and how they were positioned in relation to the hotel door and elevators—two facing the elevators and one in the corner just around the curve by the room—and jotted a reminder to find out who had been the elevator attendant on duty during the time of the murder.

One of the department's uniformed officers stood outside the door of room 219, along with a tall African American whose suit defined the cut of his arm muscles. Judging by his stance, he could only be the hotel's security.

As if he'd heard Beau's thoughts, the man blocked the door.

Suddenly, the hallway seemed much smaller with the man filling the space.

"Detectives." The officer straightened. "Dispatch just updated that the coroner should be here any minute, sirs."

As if he didn't have his radio plugged into his ear bud? Beau shook it off. Young uniformed officers didn't know. "Should be right behind me."

The hulk of a man offered his hand to Beau. "Geoff Aubois, Darkwater's chief of security. I discovered the body, called it in."

Firm grip, but not crushing. "Detective Beauregard Savoie. I'm the detective handling this case. This is my partner, Detective Marcel Taton."

Marcel shook the man's hand.

The security man nodded at Marcel. "Anybody ever tell you that you bear an uncanny resemblance to Taye Diggs?"

"Yep. A time or two." Marcel shrugged off the remark he got all the time. "Can you walk us through the details?"

Beau took detailed notes as Geoff explained in short but thorough facts how the hotel came to discover the body.

Beau paused in taking notes, pen poised over the notepad. "You mean Ad—Miss Fountaine was present when the body was found?"

The security officer nodded.

This was awful. Addy shouldn't have been exposed to a dead body. He'd literally been sick the first time he'd been exposed to a murder victim back at the academy. He could only imagine how Addy had to be feeling.

"If you'd like me to walk the scene with you, detectives . . ."

He would have to worry about Addy later. Beau nodded and reached for the two boxes at the uniformed officer's feet. "Yes, thank you." He and Marcel automatically slipped on a pair of latex gloves and disposable shoe covers, and Beau handed the same to Geoff. He was determined not to have one of his crime scenes contaminated. Not if he could help it.

"No one enters without gloves and covers, got that?" Beau asked the officer.

"Yes, sir. They won't."

Beau took note of the CSU personnel already working in the bedroom: Nolan, Robert, and

Erik—all very good at their jobs. They were detail-driven and very thorough. Beau respected all three of them.

Just what this scene needed.

Clicks of the camera were backdrop noises to the flash as Erik moved around the bedroom taking a multitude of photos. Nothing would be missed. Nolan and Robert talked among themselves as they inspected the bed linens.

Beau ignored them and the men beside him, his concentration on the scene. He continued to make meticulous notes of his impressions.

"You said the night latch was engaged?" Marcel asked Geoff, standing just inside the doorway.

This was the second floor. Beau made a note to be sure and check the balcony.

"Yes. We had to use the tool to open the door after Ms. Fountaine used the master electronic key."

Beau inspected the doorjamb. No scratches or dings. "Are the tools only sold to hotels, or can any Joe off the street buy one?"

Geoff shrugged. "I don't know."

Beau pointed his pen at the door's key reader. "I'm sure you have a lock interrogation system. Has that been checked?"

"No, sir. I figured you'd want to be here for that." Geoff lifted his radio from his utility belt. "Hixson, bring the audit trail reader to room 219."

While they waited, Beau flipped through his

notes. "Mr. Aubois, I noticed the security cameras outside the elevators and there." He pointed to the one visible from the hotel room door. "What is your recording policy?"

Geoff glanced at the camera. "They're digital, of course. They record an hour, then download it to our system. After twenty-four hours, the system compiles the footage and archives it into our storage. We hold a week's worth of recordings for every camera on-site. The older weeks are archived in the hotel's private cloud."

Beau nodded. "After I finish here, I'll need to see the video of that camera and the ones by the elevator for the last twenty-four hours."

Another security officer joined them. He handed Geoff an electronic gadget.

"How much data is stored on the lock?" Marcel asked.

"The audit trail will keep the most recent two hundred and fifty-ish transactions and will store them for about ten years." Geoff pushed a button. "Housekeeping department's key opened the door yesterday at 9:42 a.m. Guest's key opened the door yesterday at 4:59 p.m. Guest's key opened the door yesterday at 10:14 p.m. Housekeeping department's key opened the electronic lock at 11:19 a.m. this morning."

He glanced up at the detectives. "That's when they discovered the night latch was engaged. The next electronic transaction was management's key opening at 3:18 p.m. today, which is when we came back and I opened the night latch."

"Do you happen to know if the vacuums are bagged or canister?" Marcel asked.

Geoff shook his head. "You'll need to ask housekeeping."

Beau kept writing. "We'll need to speak to the housekeepers from yesterday and today, as well as"—he exhaled slowly—"management."

"Of course." Geoff punched more on the gadget, then unplugged it and handed it back to the other hotel security guard. "Print out the report I just created and have it ready for the detective before he leaves. Also, pull the video recordings from cameras 200, 201, and 211 from 0800 yesterday through 1700 today, and have them set up in the viewing room. Go ahead and make copies for the detective to take with him."

"Yes, sir." The younger security officer rushed off to do Geoff's bidding.

"Thanks for getting me everything so quickly." It was nice to not have to get warrants and demand to get what he needed to solve a case.

"No problem. It's my job."

Beau moved into room 219, recording a detailed inventory of the closet's contents, complete with brand, sizes, and condition. He checked the carpet leading into the bedroom: no visible stains or issues. In the bedroom, he nodded at the curtains covering the windows and balcony door. "Were those closed when you entered the room?"

Geoff stared at the windows and nodded. "I guess so. We didn't touch them."

Beau eased the curtains back, revealing the balcony door. The door was shut but wasn't locked. He motioned to Robert, the latent prints CSU expert. "Please dust the inside and outside of this door for prints."

"You got it, Detective." Robert reached for his case.

Pulling back the curtain all the way, Beau peered out the window down into the hotel's private courtyard. Little lights draped from the trees and wound around the poles in the center of the wrought-iron tables. No guests seemed to be in the area. Pity, because it was quite nice. Beau looked at Geoff. "Not much of a balcony."

The hotel's security chief flashed a smile, revealing a row of very white, if not perfectly straight, teeth. "It's meant more for ambiance than functionality."

"Fire escape?" Marcel asked.

"A pole." Geoff shrugged. "Mr. Pampalon said if there was really a fire, people would get out faster using a pole rather than stairs."

"I guess he has a point." No rushing out of the room and into a hall of chaos that fires usually brought to a public place. Actually, it was rather clever of the man.

"Hey, Beau."

He turned and smiled as he recognized the voice. "Hey, Walt. How's it going?"

The old coroner with bushy eyebrows and in a perpetual hunch let out a groan. "I'm not retired to some beachfront cottage, so that tells you something." Two younger men wearing jackets with the coroner's office logo emblazed on the back followed him.

Beau laughed. "Me, too, my friend. Me too."

Walter Kelly lifted his case. "Body in the bathroom, I hear."

Beau nodded. "We haven't gotten that far yet."

"Then I'll try to get some preliminary details for you." Walt wove around the techs to the bathroom, his two employees following him.

Beau continued his initial examination of the room. He spied the empty drinking glass at the chair's side table. He turned to Robert. "Has this glass already been dusted for prints?"

"Yes, sir."

He lifted it and sniffed. Whew. "Does this room have a wet bar?" he asked Geoff. It looked like one of the standard rooms, definitely not one of the suites.

"Not in here."

Beau held up the glass.

"Looks like one from the hotel bar."

He set the glass back down and made a note to talk to the bar's crew from last night to see if anyone remembered the vic.

"We're ready to bag the laptop, Detective." Nolan was in charge of collecting evidence. His team wouldn't miss much.

Marcel moved around the bed. "Find anything in the bed?"

One of Nolan's team nodded. "We took some samples of what looks like might produce some DNA and trace evidence results."

"I'm assuming the victim's reservation was for one?" he asked Geoff.

"According to what I know, yes. Kevin Muller was the only name on the reservation. His home address is listed in Natchitoches, Louisiana. Ms. Fountaine will get the full information for you, I'm sure."

Poor Addy. She'd looked beyond stressed last night, and now this.

Beau made a note to check on the vic being seen with someone he might have brought back to his room.

After noting the contents of all the drawers in the armoire and bedside table, Beau made a final turn in the bedroom to make sure he didn't miss anything, then headed into the bathroom.

Time to meet the dead man.

## ADELAIDE

"Ms. Fountaine, this is Allison Williams from WDSU. I'm following up on a report of a murder in the Darkwater Inn. Would you care to comment?"

How did she know already?

"We have no comment at this time." Adelaide pinched the bridge of her nose and rested her elbows on her desk.

"So you can only verify there has been a murder?"

Sneaky woman. "No comment."

"Come on, Ms. Fountaine, we know that homicide detectives have been dispatched to the hotel, as well as the coroner."

"I'm sorry, Ms. Williams. The Darkwater Inn has no comment at this time." Adelaide ended the call and pinched the pressure point harder.

The intercom buzzed again, then her assistant spoke. "Fox 8 on the line for you this time, Ms. Fountaine."

"Vicky, please tell them, and whatever other news outlet or reporter calls, that the Darkwater Inn has no comment at this time."

"Yes, ma'am."

Just what she needed—the news to report a murder at the Darkwater before Mr. Pampalon was informed. She'd be out of a job so fast it'd make her head spin.

She lifted the intercom and buzzed the kitchen. She needed to speak with Dimitri. Now.

# SIX

## ADELAIDE

"I still think you should be the one calling." Adelaide tossed a hard stare across her desk to Dimitri. She pressed the buttons on the phone sitting between them.

"You're the general manager, so by all rights, you should be calling." Dimitri leaned back in his chair.

"And you're an owner, lest you keep forgetting that." She punched the last two buttons with more force than necessary.

"I try."

She ignored his smirk and set the call to speaker. Dimitri might not take his position at the Darkwater seriously, but his father sure did.

"Yes?" Claude Pampalon's voice was as smooth as Dimitri's roux but had just as much bite as the Cajun spiced sauce thickener.

"Mr. Pampalon, it's Adelaide Fountaine." She drew in a breath. The hotel's owner wasn't one to mince words. "We've had an incident here at the Darkwater."

"What kind of incident?"

She swallowed. "A guest has been murdered in one of the rooms. The police are here now."

"Murdered?"

"Yes, sir. The guest missed checkout, so I authorized security to—"

"Where is my son, Ms. Fountaine?"

Dimitri moved the edge of his chair and leaned closer to the phone's speaker. "I'm right here, Father."

"Explain to me how this happened." Claude's voice lost all its smoothness.

"As Adelaide was trying to explain, Adelaide, Geoff, and I entered the guest's room after numerous attempts to reach him with no response. We found his body in the bathroom. We immediately called the police and are assisting with their investigation as they request."

Adelaide bit her bottom lip as a litany of profanity came over the line.

"Father, no one, not even you, could prevent this. Adelaide is handling the situation with professionalism while keeping the other guests as unaware as possible."

"What are *you* doing, Dimitri?"

"My job, Father. Learning the inner workings of the hotel business and assisting Adelaide where needed." Dimitri's face streaked deep red patches.

"You are a Pampalon. You are my son. I expect

you to take charge in my absence." Claude's roar rattled the phone's speaker.

"I am acting as I should. Assisting the hotel's general manager and complying with police requests." Dimitri stood and paced the short span of Adelaide's desk. "Things are as under control now as they would be if you were here."

"I doubt that. While Ms. Fountaine is very qualified, which is why she has the position in the first place, she is not a Pampalon. You are."

Dimitri snatched up the receiver. "We are doing everything you would, Father. This call was merely a courtesy to keep you informed."

Adelaide sat straight in her chair, her stomach churning. She hated being caught in the middle of this never-ending disagreement between father and son. If only Claude could see how much Dimitri loved cooking and creating sublime dishes. He had no desire to take over as the hotel CEO from his father. He wanted to stay here, yes, as chef, but not as owner. Claude wouldn't understand that. Probably wouldn't even try, which was why Dimitri was so hesitant to even broach the subject with his father. Claude never asked Dimitri what he wanted—he assigned his son the task of learning the hotel from the bottom up. Housekeeping, maintenance, front desk, bellboy, attendant, sales, and kitchen staff.

"Yes, sir. But that's really not necessary—" The heat from Dimitri's face traveled down his neck.

"Yes, sir." He hung up the phone and plopped down into a chair.

"What did he say?" Adelaide was almost afraid to ask.

He shook his head. "My father is one of the most frustrating men I have ever met in my entire life."

Her stomach knotted again. "What did he say?"

He looked at the floor, not meeting her stare.

"Dimitri?"

Slowly, his gaze met hers. "He said he'd be back Monday or Tuesday. He said if the case isn't wrapped up by then, we could both find new jobs."

Oh, mercy. This was worse than she imagined. "H-He'll fire us?"

Dimitri shook his head and reached across her desk to grab her hand. "Hey, I'm his son. He isn't going to fire us. He's just doing what he does, roaring and snarling and making threats. He doesn't mean it."

"You're his son. I'm not. He made that perfectly clear." She was going to lose her job! She loved the Darkwater. Loved being general manager. This is what she went to Northwestern State University to become. Even though she'd almost lost herself there.

Dimitri moved around the desk and pulled her to standing. With a finger under her chin, he lifted her head until she met his stare through her pooling eyes. "You aren't going to be fired, Adelaide. I won't allow it."

"But your father—" Claude Pampalon got his way. Always.

"Shh." He planted a kiss on the tip of her nose. "It will all be fine, don't worry. Just do your job." He let her go. "Besides, I bet the police will have everything wrapped up well before Father returns."

She could only hope.

## DIMITRI

His father could be the most arrogant, narcissistic, royal pain that ever walked the face of the earth. That was a fact.

That truth caused all the color to drain from Adelaide's face.

He couldn't stand it. Dimitri squeezed her hand. "It won't come to that. He just hadn't expected this. It was a knee-jerk reaction." *Jerk* being the key word.

"How can you be so sure? Your father doesn't make idle threats." She let go of his hand and sank back into her chair, but the tinges of color started to return to her face.

"He was just taken aback. He'll cool off and then accept that it couldn't be helped. His wrath is highly overrated."

"Really? Then why don't you tell him you

don't want to take over the hotel?" She crossed her arms over her chest.

Dimitri forced himself not to take her jab personally. She had to be caught in a tornado of emotions. "That's not the issue here, Adelaide."

She frowned. "I'm sorry. I didn't mean to snap at you. Everything seems to be exploding at the same time."

"I understand." Dimitri sat on the edge of her desk beside her. "I have faith that everything will work out. That the police will solve the murder and arrest the person responsible. That everything will be resolved well before Father gets home."

"Faith?" She shook her head. "Okay. You go ahead and believe that."

There it was again—that animosity whenever he mentioned God, Jesus, or faith. "What is it with you and religion?"

"Let's just be clear that I don't believe all the Bible stories I was taught in Sunday school. I've grown up and know better."

He needed to tread very carefully. "Adelaide, what happened to you?" It had to be something horrible. He knew her mother died when she was very young. He lowered his voice. "Did you lose someone?"

"Of course I've lost someone. You don't survive nearly three decades in this life without losing someone along the way. That's expected. That's life."

So it wasn't losing her mom. "So, what was so unexpected that turned you away from your faith?" He held his breath and waited on her reaction. He'd gotten bits and pieces out of her over the last four to five months as they worked closer together. Sometimes she would tell him just enough to let him know that she believed in God but had chosen not to follow Him. She'd lowered her wall enough for him to know she was angry with God, or herself, or a mix of faith and reality. Other times, she'd rattle off a flippant remark and change the subject or leave. Today she seemed different.

It'd definitely been a rough day already, and her defenses were down. After seeing a dead man, whose wouldn't be?

"Adelaide?" he all but whispered, afraid to spook her into one of her usual responses.

Tears had welled in those dark-as-night eyes of hers as she stared at him. "There was a time in my life that I believed everything the Bible says. About faith. About His good plans for me. About His never forsaking me."

Dimitri didn't move, didn't speak. He did nothing but listen.

"One day, when I needed His presence and protection more than ever before, He wasn't there. He left me at the lowest part of my life." She swiped at the tears that had escaped her eyes. "A kind and loving God doesn't do that to

66

His children." She let out a breath and stood.

Dimitri eased off the desk. "Adelaide, I don't know what happened, but God never leaves us. It might feel like it, but He doesn't."

"Oh, He did. I called out to Him and He refused to help, refused to answer." She scooped up the index card with the dead man's information and walked around the desk. "I need to take this to the police. I'm sure they need it."

He matched her steps. "I can do that for you."

"No, it's my job. Besides, I'd like to get an idea of how long the police will be here. Erika's been great about keeping the new check-ins to the other floors and other side of the hall, but we'll need those rooms down the right side of the hall soon enough."

"I can go with you." He reached for her office door.

She put her hand on his forearm. "I appreciate that, but I really need to do this myself."

His expression must have revealed he didn't care for that idea, for she continued with, "And I really need you to cook up something amazing to wow all the guests tonight. Great food is always a good distraction."

Dimitri reminded himself this is what he'd wanted, to just be a chef and not an owner. "I'll come up with something so spectacular the guests will go into a food coma."

She flashed him the first real smile he'd seen

from her in hours. "Thank you, Dimitri." She pushed open the door and stepped into the hall of offices.

"But remember, if you need me, just call me and I'll be there." He took hold of her hand. "I mean that."

"I know you do." She leaned in and gave him a sideways hug. The spicy scent of exoticness and sweetness wafted up from her dark hair, teasing his senses more than any spice he used in the kitchen. "And I appreciate you very much." She stepped out of his embrace before he could return the hug.

Dimitri watched her walk down the corridor with purpose, her dark curls swaying against her back. He wasn't sure how much longer he could keep his feelings for her to himself.

Wasn't sure if he wanted to any more.

# SEVEN

## BEAU

Stabbings were always brutal.

"What do we have?" Beau asked Walt, flipping to a new page in his notebook.

The old coroner stood and took a clipboard from one of the men from his office. "White male, approximately thirty to thirty-five years old, with multiple stab wounds to the chest." He pushed his glasses up the bridge of his beaked nose. "Based upon body temp and rigor, I'd set the time of death to be between 11:30 last night and 12:30 this morning."

Beau took in the scene before him. Blood coated the front of the man's shirt, as well as the sleeves.

Marcel beat him to the question. "Defensive wounds?"

Walt nodded. "On both hands, but superficial. I can't say if that's because our boy here knew his assailant and was surprised and shocked. Clearly an initial stab hit his jugular, so he only had a minute to live, at most." He shook his head. "He was stabbed eight more times, none of them needed to do the job."

"You think the assailant knew the victim?" Marcel asked.

"That's your job to say for certain, my boy, but I know stabbings are usually very personal. Multiple stab wounds, an overkill so to speak, are usually proven to be either a crime of passion—love, hatred, or revenge."

"What kind of weapon are we looking for?" Beau asked Walt.

"Best guess is a knife. Serrated. Probably about six to eight inches, although none of the stab wounds look to be deeper than four inches or so. I'll know more when I get him on my table."

Marcel motioned Nolan over to join them. "Did you find a knife?"

"No, sir. Nothing here at the scene, and we've gone over most every inch of this room."

"Keep your eyes open." Beau pocketed his notebook. "Looks like the murder happened here."

Walt agreed. "That's how I see it. There's too much blood present for his jugular not to have been severed here."

Beau walked the paces from the bathroom door to the victim. As was his custom, he started working out the scenario by talking low and to himself. "So the victim is already in the bathroom when the killer comes in. He turns . . ." He took in the direction the bathroom door swung.

"No, he wouldn't have seen anybody if he was already in the bathroom." He walked around the space again, careful not to disturb any of the blood on the floor and streaked down the wall by the shower stall. "The assailant was in the bathroom, waiting on the victim."

He stood still and let that imaginary movie play out in his head. Yes, that worked. He pulled out his notebook and jotted down his thoughts.

If the killer was in the bathroom waiting on the victim, then the victim either let the killer in, or the killer had been inside the room before the victim came back inside.

Definitely needed to find out if the deceased had entertained anyone in his room last night.

"Anything else for us?" Beau asked the group in general.

"I'll perform the autopsy in the morning and get you my report by afternoon," Walt said, pulling a body bag from his case and passing it to his assistants.

"Thanks, Walt, I appreciate it." He looked at the CSU lead techs. "Update?"

Erik still had the digital camera hanging around his neck. "I'll have the digital proofs e-mailed to you as soon as I get back to the office and upload them."

"Nolan's finishing up labeling the samples. I've got a couple of good prints. Let's just hope we get some hits," said Robert.

"We look forward to the reports." Beau pocketed his notebook again.

Marcel moved toward the door. "I'll check with the rooms on either side and across the hall. See if anybody saw or heard anything."

Beau nodded at his partner, then turned back to the security officer. "Geoff, if you'll take me to Ms. Fountaine, please, I have some questions for her."

"No need. I'm right here."

## ADELAIDE

The scent of death permeated room 219.

At least, that's what Adelaide called it. She'd tasted blood before, of course, when she bit her tongue—a coppery, metallic taste. The hotel room smelled that way to her . . . brassy, cold, and unyielding.

In that moment, she realized she lived three floors above in a penthouse suite. That little fact didn't fill her with any warm fuzzies.

She pushed aside her thought train and waited for Beau to join her just inside the entry. "I didn't think you would be working this case."

"It's my jurisdiction."

She didn't know why she was surprised Beau would be working the case. It gave her some semblance of comfort. If anybody could solve the case and save her job, it was Beau. She smiled

72

and handed him an index card. "Here's all the information I have on Mr. Muller."

"Can we go to your office to talk?"

"Of course." Mercifully, yes. She knew the body hadn't been removed yet, and she didn't know if she could take being there for the event, body covered or not.

"I'll make sure the videos are up as you requested, Detective," Geoff said as they passed him as they exited.

"Thank you," Adelaide and Beau replied in unison. They caught each other's stare and smiled, despite the circumstances.

She led the way out of the room and toward the elevators. "Mr. Muller was an attendee of the pharmaceutical convention we've had in-house this week."

"The room reservation was in his name?"

She stepped into the elevator as the door opened. "One, please," she told the attendant before turning her attention back to Beau. "Yes, and the reservation was in the group's block."

"What, exactly, does that mean?"

"It means that the group's planner would know what room he'd been assigned because this group requested a listing of all the rooms in their block."

The elevator door opened and she led the way toward her office.

"Is that common?" Beau had pulled out a

little notebook and pen and was writing as they walked.

"For some groups, yes. Especially if their block was full. The planner might review the list to make sure no one outside the group had gotten into the block. They would want that person moved out of the block to make room for one of their registered attendees." Adelaide opened her office door and motioned Beau in ahead of her.

"Why?" He sat in one of the chairs facing her desk.

She took her seat. "Well, planners negotiate cheaper rates for their block, depending upon how much food and beverage they agree to guarantee, number of meeting rooms . . . stuff like that. So attendees want to be in the group's block because it can save them a significant amount of money." She lifted her pen and reached for paper to doodle on.

"Smart." Beau looked over the index card she'd given him. "Natchitoches, huh?"

"About four hours or so from here."

He snapped his fingers. "That's right, you went to Northwestern there, didn't you?"

"I did." Her breath went stale. She avoided discussing anything about her college days. She could deflect like a master. "We don't have any more information on him. I can contact the group's planner and see about getting Muller's convention itinerary for you."

"If it's not too much trouble. Are they still here?"

Adelaide opened the file she'd already had pulled that sat waiting on her desk. "Shows she should be, since they have a post-convention meeting with Kellie tomorrow morning."

"Make the call. I need to make a couple of calls too." He stood and went to the corner of her office, his back to her.

Adelaide dialed the number, wondering what, exactly, to say. It wasn't as if she'd ever had to make such a call before.

The planner answered on the second ring.

"This is Adelaide Fountaine, general manager of the Darkwater Inn. Do you have a moment for us to speak in person?"

"Is something wrong?"

Wrong? One of your attendees was murdered in his hotel room. Yeah, she'd call that something wrong. Adelaide didn't even know if she was allowed to tell her one of her attendees had died. Beau hadn't said, and his back was still to her, phone pressed against his ear. Adelaide cleared her throat. "If you could please gather your attendees' itineraries, I would appreciate you coming to my office now."

"What have they done now?"

"Please, just come to my office."

"Okay. Where is that?"

"Go to the front desk and someone will bring

you. See you momentarily." Adelaide hung up the phone and stared at Beau, who returned to sit in front of her desk. "Now what?"

"The Natchitoches police are on their way to Muller's home to notify his family. They'll also do some questioning of Muller's friends and coworkers there."

Adelaide's heart clenched. How horrible. To expect your husband to be coming home today, only to have the police show up and tell you he's dead. Murdered. She shuddered.

"Addy, are you okay?" Beau's soft voice was soothing.

She hoped the Natchitoches police sent someone like Beau—kind, gentle, and caring—to tell Kevin Muller's wife. She exhaled slowly. "I will be." She rubbed her shoulder. "It's been a long week."

"I'm so sorry you're having to deal with this." Beau stood and moved behind her. His hands were firm, yet tender as he worked kinks from her neck.

She closed her eyes and let his fingers dig into the knotted muscles.

The intercom buzzed.

Adelaide jumped. Beau gave a final squeeze before moving to the front of her desk and leaning on the corner. She lifted the receiver. "Adelaide."

"A Ms. Sidney Parsons is at the front desk

asking for directions to your office, Ms. Fountaine."

"Yes. Please bring her back." She hung up and nodded at Beau. "The planner is here. Her name is Sidney Parsons." She stood as her office door opened.

The woman who entered had to be close to thirty, but with her pixie haircut could be easily mistaken for much younger. She carried a tablet and rushed right up to the desk. "I'm Sidney Parsons." She cut her eyes to Beau, then back to Adelaide. "What's going on?"

Adelaide waved to the chair in front of her desk opposite the corner Beau perched on. "Please sit down."

Sidney slumped into the chair and waggled the electronic tablet. "I have everything about the group here. Now, if you'll just tell me what's going on."

"Ms. Parsons, I'm Detective Beauregard Savoie with the New Orleans Police Department. I asked Ms. Fountaine to have you join us."

Sidney let out an exasperated breath and leaned against the back of the chair. "Who in the group has done what now?" She shook her head. "I swear, you let these sales reps get together and they act like silly frat boys."

Adelaide's stomach tightened, then turned.

"If they've damaged anything—"

Beau interrupted. "What can you tell me about Kevin Muller?"

"Kevin?" The planner gave a quick shake of her head. "Kevin's one of our best reps in the southern region."

"As a planner you know this?" Beau asked, his little notebook already open.

She shrugged. "I'm the planner for the group. I work for Arg's Drugs. I plan all the regional conventions, corporate events, every meeting the company holds."

"So Kevin is your coworker?" Beau asked.

"In a way. I mean, I work at the company's home office in Dallas, but I know most all of the movers and shakers."

"And Kevin is a mover and shaker?"

Sidney glanced at Adelaide, then back to Beau again. "I'm not quite sure I should be giving out personal information. What's this about?"

"Ms. Parsons, Kevin Muller was found dead in his hotel room this afternoon. This is a police investigation, so I can assure you that you'll need to answer my questions." Beau sounded so assertive. Adelaide had never seen him so . . . so in charge. In control.

It was a new side to him that Adelaide suddenly appreciated.

A lot.

"Kevin's d-d-dead?" Sidney shook her head. "No, that can't be. I just saw him last night."

Beau leaned forward. "What time did you see him? Where?"

The woman stood, clutching the tablet to her chest. "I think I'd better check in with my boss before I say anything more."

Beau stood. "You do that. I'm going to have an officer escort you to the station so we can talk."

"I'm arrested?" The horror was evident on Sidney's face.

"For questioning, of course." He pulled his phone from his hip and spoke briefly, then spoke to Sidney again. "My partner will be here shortly to take you to the station. You can call your boss from there."

Sidney looked at Adelaide. "Do I need to call a lawyer?"

Beau answered, "Have you done something to need a lawyer?"

"No, of course not."

A knock sounded at the door.

Beau motioned for Sidney to precede him to the door. "Detective Taton will take you to the station and get you settled. You can go ahead and call your boss and/or your attorney. I'll be along shortly." Beau said the last sentence more for his partner's benefit than Sidney's.

Adelaide waited until they were gone. "Why are you taking her to the station?"

"It's my job to question everyone. I picked up on several microexpressions with her. The slight flush to her cheeks when she talked about knowing the victim. The widening of her eyes. Not holding eye contact as I asked when she'd last seen him. She knows him but won't quite reveal how well she knows him. She admitted seeing him on the night he was murdered, but clammed up when I asked when and where. And she didn't ask what he died from."

Adelaide dropped back to her chair. "Wow. You're good, Beau."

"It's my job." But his smile widened.

Her phone rang. It was her father's number. "I have to take this."

"I'm going to check out the security footage your guy has ready for me, then I'm heading to the station. I'll have officers guarding the room." He leaned over and gave her a quick hug, then rushed away.

She put her phone to her ear but couldn't ignore the warmth his hug gave her. He'd hugged her many times over, but all of a sudden, she took note of how it actually felt.

What was going on with her?

# EIGHT

## BEAU

Not that the guests would ever know it, but the Darkwater Inn housed quite the security setup. Top of the line, high-tech stuff. Beau couldn't help but be impressed. He'd ordered uniformed officers to scour the courtyard, Dumpsters, and surrounding areas—looking for anything that might be useful to the investigation.

It bugged Beau that Muller's guest room had been locked from the inside. When he finished viewing the security footage, he'd inspect that pole up to the balcony himself. Maybe it was possible that it was an easy climb. The balcony door had been, after all, unlocked.

"I'll fast-forward until there's movement by his room, okay?" Geoff asked.

Beau nodded and pulled out his notebook. Addy might not realize what a gem she had in the man as her chief security officer. He was thorough and good.

"Okay, here Muller is, leaving his room at 8:14 yesterday morning. He's wearing the pharmaceutical convention's name badge."

Beau jotted the information down in his notes while Geoff fast-forwarded.

Geoff continued reading out the details. "There's housekeeping, 9:42 yesterday morning, going in to clean the room, just like the data from the door registered." He fast-forwarded, then paused. "And she's leaving at . . ." Geoff leaned closer to the monitor. "Video time stamp shows 10:08 a.m."

Beau hovered his pen over the paper. "Twenty-six minutes. Is that about average time?"

Geoff shrugged. "I'd guess. Sounds about right. Okay to go on?"

Nodding, Beau stared at the monitor.

Geoff fast-forwarded the video of Muller's door. Many people walked by, some even stopping across the hall or next door, but nothing happened at Muller's until 4:59 p.m. "He's going in, by himself."

Beau watched the video as Geoff advanced frame-by-frame.

"He's leaving at," Geoff tapped the time marker on the feed, "5:28 p.m. He's wearing the shirt he was found in."

"Also the loafers kicked off by the chair." Beau scribbled notes.

Geoff fast-forwarded until Muller came back into vision. With a woman leaning against him as he struggled to get his key card into the reader.

"Room opened at 10:14, just like the data recorded," Geoff said.

Muller shoved the woman's back against the door and kissed her, pushing open the door. The two stumbled inside. The door closed.

Beau paused in his note taking. "Any idea who that woman is?"

"She looks kind of familiar. Maybe we'll pick them up on some other security footage." Geoff reversed the video in slow motion. Then moved forward. Then back again, freezing the frame on the woman's face just before Muller kissed her. "That's the clearest image I have of her face."

"Do you recognize her?"

"I think I've seen her in the bar, maybe." He opened another window on the computer, copied and pasted the woman's picture into that program. "We'll see if the system can pick her up anywhere else."

Beau was more than impressed. "You have facial-recognition software?"

"Yes, sir. Mr. Pampalon bought all the bells and whistles when he upgraded the security system here."

"When was that?"

"Three or four years ago." The system flashed on the woman's face. "Hang on, let me stream these together so you can get one long chronological trail. Give me a second." Geoff's fingers flew over the keyboard. For such a big guy, he seemed quite adept at the technical side of security.

"Okay, here we go." Geoff pushed *play*.

The woman held a drink and smiled at a man. "Where is she?" Beau asked.

"The hotel bar." Geoff tapped the time on the video. "About 9:30 last night."

The woman set down her drink and ran her fingers over the man's hand and up his arm, under the loose sleeve of the shirt he wore.

"That's Muller. I can tell by the loafers." Beau jotted down the details.

Muller shifted on the barstool and pulled the woman to him, his thighs on either side of her legs. He tilted the woman's head back with both hands on her head. He hesitated a moment, then straightened.

Beau had been sure he would kiss the woman. By the look on her face in the video, that's what she'd been expecting as well.

Another woman barged onto the screen. Her face scrunched as she glared at Muller.

"That's Sidney Parsons, the group planner." That familiar tingle tiptoed up Beau's spine. He had been right in his gut feeling there was more Parsons knew than she was telling.

On the video, Parsons slammed her cocktail glass on the bar right in front of Muller. She said something to him, glanced at the woman over her shoulder, then shoved Muller's shoulder hard enough for his movement to show up on the video, before she stormed off.

Beau made detailed notes.

Muller stared after her, then the woman on the screen cozied back up to Muller, leaned in, and kissed his neck. The angle of the camera didn't allow them to see Muller's facial reaction, but minutes later, he pushed the woman back, stood, and handed the bartender a credit card.

"Do you recognize that bartender?" Beau asked.

"That's Corey Devereaux. Good guy."

Beau wrote the name as the video paused.

"We lose them on feed until . . ." Geoff pushed buttons. "Here."

Muller and the woman stepped off the elevator, the woman's dress askew, her bare rump showing as she let Muller lead her down the hall to his room. The elevator attendant stepped in the hall to watch them until they disappeared into Muller's room.

"And do you know that attendant?" Beau asked.

Geoff nodded. "Richard Norris. He's just a college kid we hired on during break to help with the overflow of guests for the holidays and the upcoming festival."

Beau made a note as the video replayed them getting off the elevator and making their way down the hall to his room. Their weaving wasn't due to inebriation as Beau had first suspected. No, this looked more like they were having difficulty containing themselves. The video concluded as the hotel room door shut behind them.

"Doesn't look like Muller is missing his wife too much." Beau shook his head. That so numerous men, many of them on the force, didn't believe in being faithful to their wives, bugged Beau. He believed wedding vows were sacred.

Geoff tapped the screen's time stamp. "Yet she leaves at 10:58. Only there for forty-four minutes."

Beau made a note, then flipped back a couple of pages. "Coroner puts his time of death between eleven-thirty and midnight thirty."

"At least thirty minutes after she left." Geoff pushed *play* on the video. "Well, lookie here." He paused the playback.

"That's Parsons banging on his door." Beau noted the time: 11:09 p.m. "She had to have passed the other woman in the hallway."

"Bet that made her mad." Geoff let the video play.

Sidney Parsons banged on the door again. Muller jerked it open. He glanced around the hallway before grabbing her by the arm and jerking her inside. The door shut on the camera.

Good thing Beau had sent Parsons to the station. She had a lot to tell him. A lot to explain. A lot to answer for.

"And now she's gone. That was quick. She leaves nine minutes later," Geoff said.

Beau made notes as Geoff fast-forwarded, then went double, then triple time. "And here it is, 11:19 this morning when housekeeping opened the door, but realized the night latch was on." He paused the video.

"Keep going. Let's see if anyone leaves between then and when you entered." It could be possible that someone could've climbed up the fire escape pole, entered the balcony, killed Muller, then left through his room. Unlikely, but he had to rule out every possibility.

Geoff forwarded until the screen showed Geoff, Addy, and Dimitri Pampalon at the door. "This is at 3:18 this afternoon when we entered. See, Ms. Fountaine is using the security card to unlock the door, and I use the tool to unlock the night latch."

Beau tapped his pen against his notebook. "Can you back it up to when Parsons is banging on the door?"

"Sure." Geoff did so. "You think she's a possible suspect?"

Beau shrugged, refusing to divulge his ideas and considerations at this point. "Coroner set the earliest time of death at eleven-thirty, but that was in the field. That could fluctuate once he does the autopsy."

"It's only a twenty-minute window or so at most as it is now." Geoff hit *play* on the replay. "She sure looked upset in the footage from the bar."

"And she looks furious now." The video replayed of her banging on the door. Muller jerked it open. Looked around. Grabbed her arm—

The door to the security room opened. Geoff paused the video and turned.

Beau stood as Addy joined them.

"I just wanted to make sure you had everything you need from us." Her eyes were locked on Beau's.

"Yes. Geoff here is quite the security supervisor. You've got a good one here, Addy."

She smiled and moved her gaze. "He is. I think we're—" She tapped the image of Muller and Parsons on the screen. "Who is that with Sidney Parsons?"

She didn't recognize him? Beau furrowed his brows and cocked his head, studying her.

All color had drained from her face. She gave a new meaning to the word pale. Was the stress really messing with her? She wobbled.

Beau reached up and steadied her, his concern growing by the minute. "That's Kevin Muller. That's the murder victim."

## ADELAIDE

*Victim?* That man was anything but a victim. But his name wasn't Kevin Muller.

"Addy, are you okay?" Beau's voice broke through her internal emotional rampage.

"What? Yes." She tapped the screen with a trembling finger. "You're sure that's Kevin Muller?"

"Positive." Beau gently turned her to face him, away from the monitor. "What's going on?"

"I just didn't know." Boy, was that the truth.

"But you saw the body."

"She couldn't see his face," Geoff offered. "The position of the body."

"I'm so sorry." He gave her arm a quick squeeze.

Her muscles tensed. This didn't make sense. None of it. But she'd find out what was going on. "It's fine." She let out a breath, her mind tripping over itself. Past memories bursting against current events. "I just wanted to make sure you didn't need anything else."

"Not at the moment. I'm going to finish watching the video surveillance with Geoff, then I'll need to speak to a couple of your employees."

"Of course, anything you need. You know where my office is." She opened the door and managed to get out of there before making an even bigger idiot of herself.

Her mind churned as she rushed to her office. There had to be a logical explanation. Something that would demand everything make sense.

Hidden behind her closed office door, she opened her laptop. She'd pushed everything away for so long that she hoped she'd forgotten the details. But she hadn't. She cracked open the door on her past and the memories blasted past her carefully built-up wall.

She typed in his name in the search bar. The name she knew him as back then: Brayden Colton.

None of the images loaded were *him*.

Cold sweats shook her body. She typed in Kevin Muller.

Several images loaded, all of the man she remembered. The man who'd shattered her trust in men. The man who'd stolen her innocence.

Adelaide pressed her lips together and closed her eyes, as if that would change how she felt, but the shame and fear and . . . *dirtiness* remained, just as it had those many years ago.

"Adelaide?"

She slowly opened her eyes to see Dimitri standing in her office doorway. She waved him inside and shut her laptop.

"What's wrong?" He ignored the chairs in front of her desk, moving around her desk and leaned against it, staring down at her.

"I just . . ." She couldn't tell him. She'd never told anyone outside of university police and her best friend, Tracey, and look how that'd turned out. "I'm fine."

"No, *mon chaton*, you are not fine." He took her hand. "I see the pain in your eyes. Tell me."

Maybe it was his thumb rubbing on her hand

that felt so reassuring, or maybe it was just time to unburden. "The man who was murdered?"

He nodded. "Yes?"

"I met him years ago when I was in college. He gave me another name, which is why I didn't immediately know it was him until I saw him on the security video."

Dimitri's thumb spread warmth throughout her, building her confidence.

"He used to come to one of the coffeehouses where some of us shared our poetry in an open mic kind of way."

He smiled. "You write and perform your poetry?"

Heat fanned her face. "I used to." But she hadn't been able to recite a single poem in front of a mirror, much less in front of a group since that night. She gave her head a quick shake. "Anyway, he came in a couple of times. Seemed nice. Flirted a little."

Oh, did he flirt. She could still recall how her heart had quickened when he smiled at her, the traitorous organ living in her chest. Why hadn't it warned her of the impending danger? Of the coming pain? It was part of her, did it have no sense of self-preservation?

"Flirted with you?" Dimitri's question brought her back to the present.

"Yes. He flirted, and I bought into it. I was a dumb college sophomore, thinking I was so much smarter than the incoming freshmen. I had survived the first year, so naturally, that had to make me smarter, right?" Her throat felt as if it were closing. Slowly. Slowly.

Dimitri's grasp tightened. "What happened, Adelaide? What did he do to you?"

She couldn't stop the tears—wasn't sure she wanted to even if she could. "One night, he asked me to go for a ride with him. I thought he was nice. I thought he liked me."

Her lungs tightened, her breath barely escaping through their clenched grip. "We got into the car, he started driving. He took me just off campus, to a place he said we could see the beautiful sky and a clear view of the stars. And I believed him." The tears streamed down her face.

Dimitri stood, pulling her up and to him. He held her tight in his arms. His lips brushed her forehead as he whispered into her hair, "Oh, no, *mon chaton*."

"I shouldn't have gotten in the car with him. I shouldn't have left campus, at least, that's what university police told me when they said there was nothing they could do about it unless I wanted to call in the police."

She'd kept it inside for so long. Adelaide pushed out of Dimitri's embrace and met his pity-filled stare. That's what she'd never wanted to see. That's why she'd kept her secret. "I couldn't fight him off. He laughed at me as I was so groggy. I think he put something in my coffee before we left. But it doesn't matter, I knew better. I knew not to get in a car with anyone I barely knew." She sniffed and grabbed a tissue from the box on her desk.

"It wasn't your fault, Adelaide."

"I'm the daughter of a crime novelist, for pity's sake. I've grown up with learning what can happen to people. My father drilled into my head the most vile of things, and yet, when it came down to it, I totally disregarded everything he'd ever taught me." She dabbed her eyes before gently blowing her nose.

"He loves you. I bet he wanted to kill this man."

Oh, that would be putting it mildly. Her father would've gone after Brayden/Kevin/whatever his name was in a flash, giving no thought to repercussions or consequences. At least she'd managed to stay ahead of that complication. "He would've, but I never told him. I never told anyone besides my best friend."

At least she'd done something right in the whole situation.

# NINE

## DIMITRI

How had she gone through such horror, such an atrocity, alone?

Dimitri wanted to hold her again, to pull her tight into his embrace and comfort her, but the way she stood—spine straight, shoulders squared, and stance secure, he knew she couldn't be. He eased back down to sit on her desk. "What did you do?"

"Afterward, he dropped me off at my dorm. I could barely walk. One of my friends helped me into my room." She shook her head. "I guess my roommate got me into bed because when I woke up, it was ten the next morning and I was alone in my bed." Adelaide tossed the tissue she'd balled into a tight wad, then grabbed another before sitting down in her chair.

Dimitri laced his fingers together in his lap to stop them from smoothing back that one long dark curl that fell over her face as she spoke.

"I went to the university police that morning and they took my statement before they told me since the assault had actually occurred off campus, I'd need to go to the Natchitoches Police Department. I was prepared to do just that, then the campus police officer told me I'd have to go to the hospital and have a rape kit, then I'd have to give my statement again and again to the police, then there would be a trial. I realized it wasn't worth it."

Dimitri's heart nearly broke. Of course it was worth it. *She* was worth it. "The campus police discouraged you from reporting it?"

She lifted a single shoulder. "Not directly, but the implication was definitely there. He made quite sure I knew what I'd be up against if I opted to push it further." She licked her lips. "Later, I thought maybe the university police officer knew who I was talking about. When I'd mentioned how groggy I'd felt, he actually accused me of lacing my coffee and that perhaps my memory of the details were a little muddied."

Dimitri kept his mouth shut as she continued, her words speeding up as she unburdened.

"I can assure you, I've never drunk. My mother was an alcoholic and that's what killed her. I would never take a drink. That's why I was pretty certain I'd been drugged."

"Did you tell this officer that?"

She nodded. "I did, but he gave me a look that let me know he didn't believe me. I explained that this guy had been in our campus coffee-house many times, but the officer said it was out of his hands because the alleged assault—yes, he actually added in the word *alleged* when taking my statement—took place off campus."

"The officer clearly was negligent and mis-informed." Idiot.

Adelaide continued, her words tumbling over one another. "I tried to go back to classes as if nothing had happened, but I just couldn't. I felt like everyone knew. They all stared at me like I was a leper. At least, I imagined they did."

Dimitri couldn't imagine how she had to have felt. "But you overcame." She was a strong woman. He'd always known that, but now he was more impressed with her than he'd ever been before.

She ripped small pieces off the tissue, letting them fall against the soft fabric of her slacks. "I took off a semester and went into therapy, only because my best friend threatened to tell my father if I didn't. I told my dad I was just taking a break to prepare for the next semester that would be really intense. He was okay with that, happy I was back home. It worked too. I got past it. Started college the next semester and graduated only a little late."

Adelaide kept shredding the tissue. "I came back home to spend the summer with Daddy before I started a job search, but then your father posted an ad for a manager trainee, and I've always loved the Darkwater. Ever since I was a little girl. Staying here would keep me close to my father and my best friend. My safe zone." She smiled, taking all the shredded tissue and tossing it in the trash. "So that's my sad story."

Now he knew he couldn't ever let his father fire Adelaide. It would break her, which he could not allow to happen. "It's a story of strength and determination and grace, Adelaide. As beautiful and exquisite as you are. I'm very sorry for what happened to you, and I don't know God's purpose in your going through that horrible time, but I'm grateful He brought you here."

The emotions on her face changed in that split second.

"Do you know, Dimitri, that during my assault, when that . . . that . . . that pig was hurting me, I cried out to God to make him stop. I begged God to intervene, but guess what? He was silent. I'd been taught that God would never leave me, but he did. That night in Brayden/Kevin's car, God left me alone."

He reached for her hand, but she pulled it back. "He didn't leave you alone, *mon chaton*. He would never leave you."

She stood, and he stood as well. "But He did, Dimitri. I was there. You weren't. It was just me and Brayden. Kevin. Whatever. It was just us two. No one came to save me. No one intervened. Not a person, and not God, who could have. He chose not to."

"You can't believe that. God—"

She held up her hand. "No, I'm not going to discuss this any further, Dimitri. I respect your faith and I'm glad you have it, but me? I know where God and I stand. Just drop it, okay?"

One look at her face and Dimitri knew he couldn't push any further. "Okay." He eased back down to sit on the edge of the desk.

She sat back down at her desk. "Thank you."

Dimitri needed to say what he'd realized, because she might not have thought of it. "Adelaide, you realize what you've told me opens a door you might not want to go through, but you should probably prepare for."

"What?"

"Because of your past, um, association with Kevin Muller, you will be a suspect in his murder."

## BEAU

"Just to be thorough, fast-forward it one more time to when you three entered, and then until the uniformed officers showed up." Beau needed to make sure that no one entered or snuck out after the door was opened. He tapped his pen against his notebook as Geoff did as requested.

Poor Addy, she'd had a rough day, all right. He glanced at his watch: 5:30 p.m. He hoped she was eating something in her office. She'd never been one to take the best care of herself when things were crazy. Her dad stayed on her all the time about it.

Speaking of Vincent, he was more than a little surprised his phone hadn't rung off his hip with—

"Wait. Let it play now."

The video showed the three going in, just as before. Beau verified his notes of the time stamp: 3:18. On the video, at 3:38, Addy exited with Dimitri Pampalon on her heels. She wobbled a little as she marched down the hall and punched the button on the elevator.

The meshing of the multiple camera feeds cut to a different angle, so Beau could see all the way down the hall to the room, but also could see both of their faces. Both were drawn. Pampalon put his hand on Addy's shoulder. She jumped and turned to face him, her back to the camera.

Beau leaned a little closer to the monitor. What was this?

Addy and Pampalon spoke to one another. By Addy's gestures, it seemed as if she was agitated. Then Pampalon pulled her to him into a hug, closed his eyes, and kissed the top of her head.

Beau's breath stuck in his lungs for a moment before rushing out.

The two separated and stepped onto the elevator. The video showed the hall. Some people moved in other rooms, but no one near 219.

Time stamp at 3:53 p.m., Geoff filled the video

screen as he led the two uniformed officers to the room. At 4:10, the CSU team showed up, and at 4:18, Beau entered.

The door to the security room opened and a uniformed officer stood in the doorway. "Sir, we've found something in the alley behind the hotel we think you'll want to see."

"Thanks, Geoff." Beau stood and followed his officer. "What did you find?"

"We think it might be the murder weapon, sir."

This would be excellent if so. "Where?"

"Dumpster in the alley behind the hotel. It was in with all the rotting produce, sir." He led the way outside.

The early evening breeze danced through the Quarter, causing the familiar wind-tunnel effect. The sun would set soon and the temps would drop over the city. The city burst with tourists and visitors, all ready for tomorrow's Twelfth Night festivities. There'd be more thefts, more assaults, and more murders to come across his desk. If he could wrap this murder up quickly . . .

"Here, sir." Another uniformed officer, properly gloved, held the knife with his fingertips. It was a brown-handled serrated knife, with approximately a four- to five-inch blade. There was a substance that looked like blood on the blade, but hard to tell with wilted lettuce stuck to it.

"Don't remove anything. You could destroy critical evidence." Beau reached for his phone and called the CSU team, requesting they come into the alley as soon as they could. While he waited, he inspected the Dumpster without touching it.

It was just like all the others in downtown—smelly and green and almost full. The lid had been propped open, explaining the stench barreling down the alleyway. Beau turned and drew in clean air from the opposite direction.

"Yes, sir?" The CSU team stood at the ready.

"All done in the room?" Beau asked.

Nolan nodded. "Body was removed and we gathered the last pieces of what might hold any evidence. Ready to get it back to the lab and start processing."

Beau waved over the uniformed officer holding the knife. "Possible murder weapon."

"Nice," Nolan whispered under his breath as he pulled out an evidence tag. "By the looks of it, I'm guessing it was found in the Dumpster?"

"Yep."

Erik snapped photos of the Dumpster, the alley, even the cars parked in the back lot. Beau knew he could count on this team.

"All done. We'll get started as soon as we get back to the unit."

"Thanks. Hey, one more thing, please." Beau led the way into the courtyard. He stopped below the balcony of room 219. "Could you please check that pole for prints?"

Robert nodded. "I dusted the rails up there and the top of the pole—didn't find anything, but maybe we'll have better luck here." He pulled out his kit and got to work.

Beau stared up at the balcony.

"You think that was the point of entry?" Nolan asked.

"Maybe. It was the only door unlocked, and we saw who went in and out through the hall." Coming down the pole wouldn't have been a problem for the murderer, but climbing up?

"Seems a complicated way to get in."

Beau nodded. "It sure does." But how else would the murderer have gained entry? He headed toward his vehicle, lifting the yellow crime scene tape.

"Detective, can you comment on the murder at the Darkwater Inn?"

He turned to face the four or five reporters with cameras and microphones. "No comment."

"Can you release the name of the victim?"

"What was found in the Dumpster?"

Vultures, all of them. He ignored them and made his way to the car. He took a moment to call Geoff Aubois and mention the reporters. The hotel would probably need to beef up security to stop the leeches and seekers.

As Beau drove back to the station, he mulled over details of the case. The security footage was clear, the only person who entered and exited close to the estimated time of death was Sidney Parsons. Was she a killer?

Good thing he knew exactly where she was at the moment, and he was about to get some answers from her.

One way or another.

# TEN

## ADELAIDE

He deserved to be dead.

That's what Adelaide kept mentally repeating as she read the file Geoff had brought her on Kevin Muller. He wasn't really a person, not with what he'd done to her. Yet there were these pesky facts she had to face.

Kevin Muller had been thirty-three years old, lived in Natchitoches, Louisiana, and was a pharmaceutical sales rep for Arg's Drugs. He had been married for four years, and his wife was expecting their first child.

And that was the part that made him most human.

Adelaide's eyes burned. She didn't want to see him as a human. Not as a husband or father. He was scum. An attacker. A rapist.

She slammed the folder shut just as Geoff knocked on her doorframe. She waved him inside. "Please, no more bad news."

He sat in the chair in front of her desk. "No, nothing new. I did put in a call to a friend of mine in the police department and asked him to give me a heads-up if he heard anything."

"Good thinking. I don't think I could take anything more today." She let out a long breath.

"Have you heard anything from *your* friend about the case?" Geoff crossed his ankles as he spread his long legs out in front of him.

"My friend?"

"Detective Beauregard Savoie."

Her face heated.

Geoff snapped his fingers and sat up straight in the chair. "Ah, see, I knew you two knew each other more than y'all were letting on."

She leaned back in her chair and tried to stop the little smile. "Beau and I have known each other since we were children. He lives close to where my father does."

"Mmmm-hmmm." If Geoff was even trying to hide his smile, he was failing miserably.

His grin was contagious, and the corners of her lips turned up of their own accord. "Stop. We're just friends. He's actually a friend of our family. He spends a lot of time with my dad."

"If you say so, but I think it's nice."

"Really? How so?" She crossed her arms over her chest.

"Don't go getting all defensive, Adelaide." Geoff's smile could disarm just about anyone. Add in his Southern charm, and most women would be done for. "I'm just saying that you work hard. You always have."

"That's not a bad thing."

"No, it isn't, necessarily. But you also need to have a life. You came here straight from college. I've never seen you go out with anyone more than once, and you're an attractive woman." He held up his hand. "Don't get me wrong, you remind me a lot of my little sister, so I notice. And I care."

She uncrossed her arms and let the tension roll from her shoulders. "I'm not sure I knew you had a little sister." She leaned forward and propped her elbows on her desk. "Tell me about her." Anything to distract her from the file on her desk.

"Jada was energy in life form. Vivid. An artist. Full of ideas and laughter. Yet she could also be caught up in herself, even to the point of missing a class or two. She was beautiful, honest, and had the biggest heart."

Adelaide straightened as her chest tightened. "Was?"

With tears in his eyes, Geoff nodded. "She passed away a few years ago."

"I'm so sorry, Geoff." She couldn't imagine having a sibling who died. She'd wanted a sibling all her life. To have one, then have them die . . . what kind of God would allow that?

The same one who would leave a girl alone in a car on a dark night with a man whose evil heart was void of humanity. Even if he did find someone to trick into marrying him and carrying his child.

"It's okay." Geoff's soft words pierced her thoughts.

"It's a tragedy to lose someone we love." A brief image of her mother near the end of her life flashed through Adelaide's mind. "Even if it's not a surprise, the grief can still be overpowering."

"Very true. It's harder still when they take their own life."

Oh, gracious! "Geoff, I am truly so sorry." Mere words didn't seem like enough.

He shrugged. "I don't know why she didn't come to me with her issues. I would've helped her. I would have handled everything. I'm her big brother." His eyes shone with tears, breaking Adelaide's heart. "It was my job to protect her and I failed."

She moved around her desk and sat in the chair beside him, then leaned over and gave him a hug. "I'm sure you didn't fail her."

"I wasn't there when she needed help the most."

Still at a loss for anything to say that could bring him comfort, she just hugged him tighter.

A quick knock sounded on her door, then Dimitri barged in with a tray. He froze as his gaze locked onto Adelaide and Geoff.

Adelaide stood and dabbed her eyes. "Yes?"

"I thought you might be hungry." Dimitri still stood rooted to the spot in her office, holding the tray.

"That's thoughtful. Thank you." She went to the little settee in the nook of the office and cleared off the table. "I think the tray will fit here."

As Dimitri set down the tray, Geoff stood, having composed himself. "I'll let you know if I hear anything back from your friend." He winked, then headed to the door.

Adelaide smiled back. "Thank you, Geoff."

The door shut behind him, and she turned to Dimitri.

"I hope I didn't interrupt anything." His voice cracked.

"You didn't." She ignored the questions in his eyes and sat on the little loveseat. "It smells wonderful."

Dimitri lifted the plate cover. "Nothing too elaborate tonight. Just regular gumbo and brioche."

"Well, it was very thoughtful, and I appreciate it very much." She motioned to the seat beside her. "Please, join me."

"I've already eaten."

"Then sit with me?" She lifted the spoon to her mouth as he sat beside her. Spicy warmth tingled her taste buds. "Oh, my, Dimitri, this is wonderful."

"Thank you. I thought you might like something familiar and comforting."

"It's perfect." She broke off some of the bread and dipped it into the steaming bowl.

"How are you doing?" Dimitri's eyes were filled with concern. It warmed her as much as the gumbo.

"I'm going to be okay."

"Have you decided what to do with the information of knowing Kevin Muller?"

She swallowed, the spices tasting a little flatter than a moment before. "I'm not going to say anything just yet."

"Adelaide. You know how that will look when the police find out later."

"They might not find out." She set down her spoon and lifted a finger as he opened his mouth. "Hear me out for a minute." She swiped a napkin over her lips, then took a sip of the bottled water from the tray.

She'd thought about this as she had reviewed Kevin Muller's file. "The police took samples of everything—they still haven't cleared the room. They fingerprinted everything, took the sheets and goodness knows what else, so if there is any physical evidence of the killer, they recovered it, right?"

"I suppose."

"Well, I know for a fact I didn't kill him." Maybe she would have, if given the chance? She couldn't go down that rabbit hole at the moment. "So I know none of the evidence will point to me, but it *will* point to the killer."

She took another sip of water. The coolness

dulled the tightening of her throat. "Why would I tell the police and give them what they would have to follow up as a suspect, which we know would be a waste of their time and resources?"

"Because when they find out and you didn't tell them, it'll look suspicious, even if you are innocent." Something about his tone . . .

"Dimitri, you know I had nothing to do with his murder, right? Surely you can't think I was involved in any way." Her pulse pounded in her head.

"Of course I don't think that. I'm just saying how it'll *look*. To the police."

"I don't think it will come to that. I think the police will get a lead from the evidence found here at the hotel, which will put them on the trail of the killer. I have confidence the police will arrest someone within a week." Which she desperately needed to happen before Mr. Pampalon returned and fired her.

Dimitri didn't look convinced.

She set the tray over the barely touched bowl of gumbo. "Look, I know it's asking a lot, but if you could just not say anything about my past. My . . . connection to Kevin Muller, I'd really appreciate it. At least for right now."

She hated how her voice sounded whiny and begging, but she was doing just that, and it couldn't be helped. "I don't want what happened to me to be a topic of conversation. I never did, which is why I never went to the police." She swallowed. "Please, Dimitri." She took his hand and held it tightly.

"Of course, I won't say anything."

Adelaide felt like she could breathe again. "Thank you." She leaned into him and gave him a hug.

His warmth seeped from him and into her. She relaxed against him. Just for a minute, she'd let herself feel what could never be.

He pulled back from her, but only a few inches. His gaze locked on hers. His breath, a whisper against her skin. "*Mon chaton.*"

Buzz!

They both jumped, then she gave a little giggle before heading to her desk. Her heart raced, pounding against her chest.

She lifted the in-house phone receiver to her ear. "Adelaide Fountaine."

"It's Geoff. I heard from my friend at the station. It's not great news."

## BEAU

The warmth of the police department's interrogation room was deliberate. Not exactly hot to make the phrase *sweating the witness* legitimate, but it was rather close in comparison to the cool January evening. Marcel had given her a bottle

111

of room temperature water, enough to keep her hydrated so her lawyer couldn't complain but not enough to be refreshment.

"Now that your attorney is present and accounted for, I'll ask again. Ms. Parsons, what was the nature of your relationship with Kevin Muller?" Beau had waited long enough, flipped his notebook to a new page.

By the time he'd gotten to the station, the lawyer Arg's Drugs had called in had already had time to speak to Sidney Parsons alone. Now was the time for getting some answers. Marcel hovered in the corner like a massive shadow. Not enough to cause an intimidation complaint, but enough to be persuasive to tell the truth.

She glanced at the attorney sitting beside her, who nodded. Sidney took a breath. "We were coworkers, friends." She paused. "Then a couple of months ago, we began having an affair."

As if that was a surprise. Beau took notes as she continued.

"I'm not in the habit of getting involved with married men, just so you know, but there was something about Kev. I believed him when he said he and his wife were separated. Until I found out she was pregnant."

"So you two were involved for a couple of months before you found out she was pregnant?" Beau tapped his pen against the notebook sitting in front of him on the table and glanced up at his partner.

Sidney looked at the attorney for permission before she nodded. "He finally broke down and told me a couple of weeks ago. Guess he thought he should tell me since she'd begun to show."

"Were you angry?" Marcel asked, pushing off the wall he'd been leaning on.

"That's not really relevant," the lawyer interjected.

"I have a murder victim who might disagree, counselor." Beau wasn't a big fan of defense attorneys.

The attorney whispered in Sidney's ear before she continued. "I was very disappointed, of course. He'd lied to me about being separated, obviously."

Disappointed, huh? Beau stared at her from across the table. "When was the last time you saw Mr. Muller?" Would she lie?

She looked at the lawyer who tilted his head. "I saw him in the bar last night. Flirting and being obnoxious."

"Did you have words? An argument?" Marcel asked. He already knew Beau had brought a copy of the hotel's security video back to the station. They could easily catch her in any lie she told about last night.

She hesitated. "I told him he should go to his room and call his pregnant wife."

Marcel leaned back against the wall, crossing his arms over his chest. "You told him this when you two were alone?"

"No. He had a woman hanging onto his every word. I called him out in front of her."

"Did that make him angry?" Beau looked up from his note taking.

The attorney put his hand on Sidney's arm. "Ms. Parsons has no way of knowing how Mr. Muller felt or what he thought, Detective."

Legalese runaround. Fair enough. "How did Mr. Muller respond to your *calling him out* in front of someone?"

Again, she looked at the lawyer before speaking. "He told me to shut up and leave him alone. I left."

Beau recalled the video from the hotel bar. She had shoved Muller's shoulder after slamming down a glass on the bar. "You just left?"

"Pretty much."

"No, we need you to be specific." Marcel leaned over, resting his palm on the table. Tall and very present in the small interrogation room. "What did you do? What did you say?"

She whispered to the attorney, who whispered back.

Beau had endured about as much as he could. Maybe he should step out for a while. Cool off a little.

"I don't remember exactly what I said, but it

114

wasn't nice. I shoved him, then moved away. The woman stayed with him, and shortly after they left the bar together."

Good deflection, but Beau knew the score. "And that's the last time you saw Mr. Muller alive."

She bit her bottom lip. "I think so, but I'm not sure."

The lawyer leaned over and whispered in her ear. It was very clear he wasn't too pleased with her response.

They were in a discussion, while Beau's upper lip heated.

Marcel moved to hover behind her. "It's a yes or no question."

The attorney nodded, but he looked like someone had just grabbed the designer beads out of his hand during a Mardi Gras parade.

"I went to his room, but only stayed a minute or two."

Nine minutes to be exact. "Why?"

"Because I was ma—disappointed Kev was being such a jerk."

"To his wife? The woman at the bar? You?" The more Marcel agitated and intimidated her, the more likely she was to let something spill out before the lawyer could stop her.

"His wife. Me. I don't know." Her eyes filled as she ignored the troubled gaze of the man beside her. "He'd told me that he loved me.

That he was going to make the separation permanent and divorce his wife to be with me. But then he told me she was pregnant, so he couldn't leave her right yet. He asked me—begged me, actually—to not leave him. To give him time to figure something out. To let the baby be born so he could file for joint custody when he divorced her." Sidney met Beau's stare. "I believed him until last night when I realized it was all lies."

"How did you figure that out?" Beau asked.

"When he'd asked me to not leave him, I told him that I'd wait for him, but our relationship would be put on hold until he'd filed for divorce. He didn't like it, and we'd argued about it, but that was the best I could do. I thought he'd accepted that. Until I saw him kissing that woman in the bar. That's when I knew he'd never loved me. Never planned to divorce his wife for me." The tears streaked down her face.

"So I went to his room to tell him I never wanted to see him again." She shook her head and wiped her nose on her shirtsleeve. "I told him that he disgusted me and maybe his wife should know about his extramarital activities."

Ah, now they were getting somewhere. "Bet he didn't like that."

The lawyer touched her arm. "Again, Ms. Parsons can't know what Mr. Muller thought or felt, Detective."

Marcel stared directly at her. "No, but Sidney,

you know what he said in response. What he did."

She sniffed. "He laughed at me. Told me she'd never believe me because she knew he only went after sexy women, and I definitely wasn't. Said she knew he only liked curvy women, and I was more fat than curvy."

Wow, what a prince. Beau couldn't believe chauvinists like Muller ever conned any woman to settle down with them. "What did you say?"

Sidney wiped her tears. "I told him he was a sorry excuse for a human being."

Beau didn't disagree. "Then what happened?"

"I slapped his face and left." She wiped her face on her sleeve again. "It sounds like it was a long time, but I promise, it was only a few minutes."

Nine. Was that enough time for her to stab him?

Stabbed nine times. Beau didn't miss the irony. But could this woman have gotten into the room, had an altercation with Muller who definitely could defend himself against her, gotten him into the bathroom, then stabbed him nine times? In nine minutes?

As much as Beau liked her motive for being the murderer, he didn't see how it added up. On the video, when she'd left his room nine minutes later, she had no visible bloodstains on her shirt. To have been close enough to stab the man so violently, she'd most likely either have had blood all over her or would've had to have changed clothes, but the video showed her leaving in the same shirt.

Still, she had motive and means and opportunity.

"Do you have what you need, Detective? I think Ms. Parsons has been more than cooperative."

"Yes. You may leave the station, Sidney, but please don't leave town," Marcel said.

"But I live in Dallas."

"I understand. We'll wrap up what we need from you as quickly as possible, I assure you." Beau stood and opened the door to the interrogation room. Cool air blew against his face. "We'll most likely need to ask you more questions in the next day or so."

"I guess I'll see if I can extend my stay at the Darkwater Inn." She gave a slight shiver. "Not that I want to stay there now, knowing what happened."

"If you move elsewhere, please just let us know." Beau handed her one of his cards.

She thanked him, then followed the lawyer down the hall.

"Detectives, I'm glad I caught you." Nolan rushed toward them.

"What's up?" Beau leaned against the wall, enjoying the coolness from the brick wall.

"The knife. It was the murder weapon. Blood on the blade matches the victim's DNA."

Finally! Something going right with the case. "What else?"

"Robert dusted the handle for prints and got three different sets, even though there was quite a bit of smudging."

"Smudging like someone tried to wipe it down but didn't do a thorough job?" Marcel asked.

Nolan shook his head. "Smudging like someone wearing gloves handled the knife."

Marcel shifted his weight from one foot to the other. "Handled the knife before or after?"

"I'd guess after, but no way to prove it one way or another."

"So, three sets of prints?" Marcel asked.

"We just got matches back on all three." Nolan handed a folder to Beau.

Beau's gut tightened. "This first set belongs to Ethan Morrison, who has a record for petty theft?"

"And his last known place of employment was the Darkwater Inn, as a part of the kitchen crew." Nolan smiled. "Thought you'd want this immediately."

"Thanks." Beau nodded as Nolan rushed off with a, "I'll let you know what else we find."

Beau scanned the rest of the information, flipping the page. The second set of prints belonged to Dimitri Pampalon. Why would owner junior's prints be on a kitchen knife that was used to stab someone? A question worth asking.

He flipped to the last page and clenched his jaw.

The last set of fingerprints belonged to Addy.

# ELEVEN

## DIMITRI

Adelaide's knuckles turned ghost white as she gripped the hotel's receiver. "What?"

Dimitri rose from the settee and stood in front of her desk.

"So quickly? I mean, I thought it would take days." She paused, wrapping the cord around her finger. "Really? I guess that's good."

She chewed her bottom lip as she listened to whatever the person on the other end of the phone said.

Dimitri ran his hands along the top of the high-back chair. The fabric smooth and cool to his touch.

"So what does that mean?" Her eyes were wide as she stared at him. "I see." She leaned her hip against her desk, propping herself up.

The pause between her few words grew longer. With every second that ticked off the clock, Dimitri grew more concerned as her face paled.

"M-mine?" Her slight stammer sent shivers over Dimitri, although he wasn't quite sure why. "I see."

121

What did she see? Dimitri gripped the back of the chair.

"I appreciate you letting me know. Please call again if you hear anything else."

Another pause.

"Yes, of course. Thanks." She set the receiver back on its cradle and sank into her chair.

"What is it?" He hated seeing her like this.

"That was Geoff. He has a friend on the police force who called him about the case. Nothing official yet, of course, but just giving him a heads-up, per se."

Now what? The police had been gone only three or four hours. Dimitri wouldn't push her, even though curiosity surged through him.

"It seems that they found a bloody knife in the Dumpster in the alley behind the courtyard. They've verified the blood on the knife is Kevin Muller's, so they have the murder weapon. Apparently they can get DNA matching results within two hours."

Why wasn't she smiling over the news? "That's good, isn't it? Because finding the murder weapon will help the investigation?" At least, that's what those forensic shows that he sometimes had on the television while he played in the kitchen in the evening said.

"It usually is." Yet her voice sounded rough and gravely. Emotional. "But they've found some fingerprints on the handle."

"That's good news, right? It should help them track down the killer." Why wasn't she more excited about this? It could be the answer that she'd just told him would be best: she wouldn't have to tell anyone about her connection to Kevin Muller if they could find the killer.

"I guess that depends."

"On what?"

"On how innocent people's fingerprints got on the murder weapon. They found three sets of prints they were able to run through whatever system they use to get identities."

"Did Geoff's friend tell him who the prints belong to?" This could really be great. Dimitri couldn't understand why Adelaide was still so pale and drawn— "Oh. Your prints are on the knife, aren't they?"

She slowly nodded. "They verified my thumb print against my insurance and bonding records."

He plopped down into the chair facing her desk. "How?"

"It's a knife of the hotel's. One of the kitchen ones, Geoff figures by the description. I guess it's one I used recently. I don't really know."

How was this possible? Her prints on the murder weapon, one of the knives from the kitchen. While she certainly had motive to kill the man, there was no way she had. "Who else's prints were found?"

"Ethan Morrison's."

What? "My dishwasher?" No way. "Ethan's a good enough kid. A little mouthy sometimes, but he gets the job done." At least it was logical why his prints would be on any and all of the silverware in the kitchen. After washing, he would've dried them, wiped them down to make sure there were no water spots, then put them in the tray for the staff to roll into the napkins before putting them on the restaurant tables.

"Ethan apparently has a record for petty theft too."

The tangle kept tightening around them. "How'd he get hired? Father is very adamant about the hiring policies here. This will put him into a major tailspin." That was putting it mildly. His father didn't have any qualms about the caliber of people who worked at the Darkwater Inn. Someone with a record of petty theft would never get hired, in any position.

"I know." She shook her head. "I'll pull his records from human resources and find out who hired him and if they knew about his record. It just keeps going from bad to worse."

True. His father would fire people over this. If he didn't fire Adelaide, he'd give her a good tongue-lashing, as he would hold her accountable as general manager. Dimitri couldn't have that. Not now. "We'll figure this out."

"Oh, it gets better."

"What?"

"The third set of fingerprints?"

He nodded, a chill settling unexpected and unexplained over him.

"They're yours."

"Mine? Are they sure?"

Adelaide nodded. "They're sure."

"Well, I guess that makes sense. I've been in the kitchen most of the last couple of days, at least since Father left."

"But how did our prints get on the same knife that killed Kevin?"

"I don't know." He ran his fingers over the chair's armrests. "But this means you'll need to tell the police immediately about your connection to him."

"I can't." She shook her head.

"You have to, Adelaide." He inched to the edge of the chair. "Don't you see? If you don't, when they find out, you'll look even more like the prime suspect." How could she not immediately see the obvious? She was a smart woman, but in this instance, she acted as if her senses had taken leave.

"They won't find out."

"Oh, Adelaide." Her emotions had totally blocked out logic and reasoning. "They'll find out. The police always do. Then it will look like you were hiding the truth because you killed him." Pain shot across her face, but he couldn't help it. He had to make her understand. "Like you planned everything."

She shook her head. "I can't, don't you see? No one knows what happened besides Tracey. No one. After all this time, if I told now, no one would believe me, and they'd think my best friend was lying for me."

"At this point, who cares? You've moved on. You're stronger." He held up his hands in mock surrender as her look turned into a glare. "Look, what happened to you was horrible. The man deserved to have been punished back then, but what happened can't be undone at this time. There is no do-over. You need to tell the police because, despite the horror you went through that no woman should ever go through, you survived. You thrived. You succeeded in spite of his assault."

"It's not that simple."

"Nothing about this is simple, Adelaide, but the truth will come out. You should be the one to tell it to make sure it is the truth and not some glossed-over version. Only you can tell what really happened."

She shook her head slowly. "They didn't believe me then. I doubt I'd be believed now. Especially with him dead. Stabbed. In my hotel. With a knife my fingerprints are on."

He reached across her desk and took her hand. "Which is why you need to talk to the police immediately. Tell them the truth of what happened."

She snorted and pulled her hand from his. "I can't. Even if I wanted to, I can't."

"Why not?" The woman was going to make him pull all of his hair out.

"Because no matter what they believe, what happened to me would get out. To your father, which to him would just be a show of weakness in me."

Dimitri wished he could argue that, but she was most likely 100 percent right on target.

"To everyone here, which would make me lose the respect I've fought so hard to acquire because of the cards stacked against me: young, no experience—hired straight out of college, and a woman."

"I don't think so. People respect you because of your work ethic."

"It's nice that you think so, Dimitri, but that's unrealistic. You've never had to fight and claw for employees' respect. It's a hard-won battle that I don't want to go through again."

"I think you're selling yourself short."

"I'm not. But most of all, it would get out to my father. This would kill him."

Dimitri could only imagine. Right now, he was glad Kevin Muller was dead. He couldn't fathom how Adelaide's father would react. "But he loves you."

"Yes, he does, and that's why he can't know. It would kill him. He didn't want me to go off to college in the first place. Finding out would prove that he was right."

"Adelaide, you can't help what happened to you. That was all Kevin Muller."

She sighed and leaned back in her chair. "Don't you see? He would be furious that it happened, then guilty because he wasn't there to stop it or protect me, even though there was nothing he could have done. He'd be disappointed I hadn't stood up for myself and gone to the police. And he'd be disappointed I hadn't told him."

Ah. There it was.

"I'm not trying to judge you in the least, Adelaide, but I have to ask. Why didn't you tell him?"

"I couldn't." She gave him a weak smile that nearly broke his heart. "You don't know who my father is, do you?"

He slowly shook his head, replaying every conversation they'd had about fathers for the last few years. "You talk about him a lot, and your loving relationship is obvious, but you've only really referred to him as *Dad*."

"Because he's a hermit, but he's had to be. He was stalked, hassled, and harassed because of his name alone. He does very little in the public eye. He has to vigilantly guard his privacy, and his identity."

Dimitri tried to recall anything about a Fountaine, but came up empty.

Her smile was warmer now. "My dad is Vincent Fountaine, but that's a hard-earned secret. He's an author and writes under the pen name of R. C. Steele."

Dimitri tried not to let his jaw drop, but he couldn't. "He's like the best-seller of all time! I've read all his books, seen all the movies." Excitement sped up his speech, but he didn't care. This was R. C. Steele!

She nodded. "Exactly. When I was attacked, he'd just finished promoting his movie, *Cries for Help*. He'd made one of his few personal appearances. He was in the news everywhere. I couldn't pick up a paper or turn on an entertainment show or cruise the internet without seeing Dad." She lifted a pen and began to doodle on her desk pad. "If I had told him what happened, he would have dropped everything and come to Natchitoches to strangle the guy and then bring me home. Can you imagine the media circus that would have caused?"

Now the picture started to come into focus. Dimitri slowly nodded and scooted back in the chair.

"It would have been splashed everywhere for everyone to know. I would have been humiliated and my dad would've as well. With all the exposure he'd been getting, my assault would've been front-page coverage. I don't know if he could've handled it. I don't think I could have."

"But when you came home, why didn't you tell him then?"

She shook her head, not looking at him but concentrating on her sketching. "I couldn't. He was so proud of me and happy to have me home. I couldn't break his heart and tell him how broken I felt."

Dimitri ached for her. "But, Adelaide, now . . . you should go ahead and prepare your dad, because this is going to get out. You know it will."

"I know no such thing. I managed to keep it a secret when it happened, I'm pretty sure I can keep it a secret now."

Oh, she wanted to believe that, but he had to make sure she understood the risk she was taking by not coming forward. "There wasn't a murder then. A murder where your fingerprints are on the murder weapon, and you have a valid reason for murder. The police *are* going to ask you about your fingerprints. They *will* ask if you knew Kevin Muller. Do you plan on lying to them?"

She tossed the pen onto the desk. "No. I didn't know Kevin Muller."

"Adelaide!" She was going to get herself in such deep trouble, Dimitri didn't know if he'd be able to help her. "You did know him."

She crossed her arms over her chest. "No,

you're mistaken. I knew a Brayden Colton briefly when I was a student at Northwestern University. That's it."

He could tell by the stubborn set of her jaw that she wasn't going to budge on this. No matter what she said, if she didn't tell the police about what had happened back in college, she would be lying.

Which would make her the prime—maybe only—suspect in the murder.

# TWELVE

## ADELAIDE

The January wind gusted outside St. Louis Cemetery No. 1, rustling the leaves and adding to the creepiness of the location, but it didn't bother Adelaide. She tightened her windbreaker around her and leaned against her car parked just outside the cemetery's entrance. Not only had she grown up in the area, but she had memories of many nights in her misspent youth climbing the fence to get into the famous cemetery. Now it was just the place her best friend worked at midnight.

Tracey Glapion had been Adelaide's best friend for as long as Addy could remember. Tracey's long black hair, pale skin, and her ever-present bright red lipstick added to the mystique of her last name. Family legend claimed Tracey was a direct descendant of Louis Christophe Dominick Duminy de Glapion, the "left-handed husband" of renowned Voodoo Queen Marie Laveau.

Rumor had it, de Glapion was a man of noble French descent when in the 1830s he was in a *placage* relationship with Laveau. Together, it was said, they had at least seven children, but only two survived: both daughters named Marie, one the look-alike of Marie Laveau, who embraced the darker side of voodoo in Bayou St. John. It was from this line Tracey descended. Supposedly.

Addy didn't believe or disbelieve her friend's heritage, but it sure helped Tracey in her job.

"Some say if you listen carefully outside the cemetery, when it's around midnight, the witching hour, if it's quiet enough, you can hear Marie's mumbled spells against those who wronged her." Tracey finished her spiel, accepted the tips, then sauntered over to Addy.

"When you sit out here so casually, it ruins the ambiance." She hopped up on the hood of Addy's car.

"Sorry." Addy inched up beside her.

Tracey nudged her. "What's up? Gotta be something important to get you out here at midnight on a Friday night. Spill."

Where to start?

"Addy?"

Once she started with seeing *him* again, it was as if the floodgates opened, and everything that had happened in the last twenty-four hours spilled out in a gush until Addy sat still and breathless.

"Okay. I'm trying to follow this. You saw Brayden at your hotel, during the fire alarm, but you didn't try to find him? Did you search for a reservation in his name?"

"It wouldn't have mattered. He used a fake name back then. Because he all along planned what he was going to do to me." She shivered, and it had nothing to do with the wind milling about Basin Street.

Tracey held up her hand, her bright red nails flickering by the almost half-moon's light. "Okay. So you skip out of dinner with your dad, then eat something with the owner's son before you go on a late-night run and then go to bed?"

"Right."

"Next day, it's business as usual until you get the call that someone missed checkout and you need the room. So y'all go busting in and find the body."

"Well, we didn't really bust in, but basically that's it."

"Only you don't realize the dead guy is Brayden?"

Addy ran her hands through her hair and hung her head. "I know it sounds crazy. I never saw his face in the bathroom. I was too horrified by the blood, so Geoff and Dimitri got me out of there as quickly as they could."

Tracey wrapped an arm around Addy and hugged her. "I'm sorry, sweets. I can't imagine how you felt."

"It was awful. It was like I froze."

"Well, what else should you have done? Seriously." Tracey squeezed her tighter. "So

134

you didn't find out the dead guy was Brayden until . . ."

"Until I saw him on the security footage Beau and Geoff watched to generate the murder timeline."

"And you haven't told anyone but Dimitri about it, right?"

"Right."

Tracey shook her head. "You should've told your dad back then, Addy."

"No. And I'm not telling him now."

"You said that they found the murder weapon and your prints are on the knife?"

"Yes." Addy stared into the darkness. She couldn't understand how her prints got on the knife. The knife that killed the man who raped her. "I know how it looks, Trace."

"Do you? Do you really, Addy?" Tracey shifted and stared at her. "A detective will see a girl who saw her rapist who was never punished, had the means and opportunity, took advantage of the fate of having him in her hotel, and decided to settle the score."

"Beau's the detective, Trace. He won't see that."

"That's even worse. You never told your dad or Beau or anyone when you came back. When it comes out now, how do you expect Beau to be able to defend you?"

"I told you."

"And you swore me to secrecy, even when I begged you to tell your dad."

"I know." Addy let out a heavy sigh. "I know I've made a mess of things, but I promise, I didn't kill him."

"How did your fingerprints get on the knife?"

"I don't know. I eat in the kitchen all the time. To have mine and Dimitri's and Ethan's prints, it had to have been taken from the kitchen."

"And used to kill a man who raped you."

"I know, Trace, I know." She let out a long breath.

"Have they determined how the killer entered the room?"

Addy shook her head. "They know he didn't come in through the door because of security footage."

"The balcony?"

"That's not really feasible. I mean, I guess it's *possible,* but most likely not."

"Then how?"

Addy grinned. "I told you the hotel had lots of hidden passageways."

"Does one go into that room?"

Addy nodded. "There's a passage that runs along that side of the building. Every room on that side of the hall can access the passage if they know where it is."

A scream, then a girl's giggle sounded from the other side of St. Louis Street.

Tracey slipped off the hood of Addy's car. "Who all knows about the passageway and how to access it?"

"Inn management. Security. A couple of staff who've been at the hotel for decades. Maybe some previous guests. Why?"

"Because it's limited information, it narrows the list of people who knew how to get into that room without being seen on security footage. And it might make your guests a little unnerved to know their rooms aren't as secure as others."

A couple of teenagers turned the corner onto Basin Street. They kicked a beer bottle, rolling it across the broken cement to land against the curb.

"We usually take those rooms out of service, but when we're at full capacity . . ." Addy sighed. "That still makes me a viable suspect. Motivation. Access. And my prints are on the murder weapon." Addy slipped off the car and buried her face in her hands. "I just don't know what to do."

"You should tell Beau about Brayden being Kevin Muller."

"I just can't. I have to figure out another way."

"Come on, Addy. Give me a ride home." Tracey opened the passenger side of the car and slipped inside. She put her cell phone to her ear.

Addy got behind the wheel and started the car. "What's wrong?"

Tracey held up a finger. "Hey, it's me. Listen, there's a group of kids right outside the entrance of St. Louis No. 1. One of the teens is wearing one of those masks. Thought you might want to check it out."

Addy stared at the kids she hadn't paid much attention to before. There was one wearing a mask, one of the popular "city of the dead" masks selling in just about every gift shop in the Quarter.

"I will." Tracey ended the call, but instead of putting her phone away, snapped a couple of pictures of the group heading toward them. "Drive away."

Not waiting for further direction, Addy put the car in drive and wove around the group. "What's going on?"

"Just these kids. The closer it gets to Twelfth Night, the more they act out. Wearing those silly masks and vandalizing cemeteries and certain areas in the Quarter. Congo Square was desecrated twice last week. Part of Armstrong Park was vandalized earlier this week. Some of us have been keeping our eyes open and working with local security." Tracey shook her head. "Kids messing around in something they know nothing about."

Addy turned onto St. Ann Street. "Speaking of kids, what do you know about kids putting snakes in mailboxes?"

"Snakes in mailboxes?"

Addy eased into Tracey's driveway and turned off the headlights. "Yeah, Dimitri found a small boa constrictor in his mailbox. Thinks some kids did it as a prank." She shivered in the darkness.

"That's not a prank, Addy."

Even by the dashboard light, Addy could see Tracey's face had paled. "Then what would you call it?" But before Tracey answered, the hairs on the back of Addy's neck rose to attention.

"Someone's practicing voodoo on him."

## BEAU

How in the world had Addy's prints ended up on a knife used in a murder?

Sure, she worked there, had easy access to the kitchen utensils, but this particular knife? And Dimitri Pampalon's prints on it too? And Ethan Morrison's?

Beau shook his head as he locked up his files for the end of his shift. He glanced at his notes:

FIND WOMAN FROM BAR
TALK TO ELEVATOR ATTENDANT
QUESTION BARTENDER

He lifted his pen and added: QUESTION ADDY, PAMPALON, & MORRISON. Just writing her name with theirs tightened the knot in his gut.

Something about this case rubbed him the wrong way all over. His detective "spidey sense" was tingly all over, and that was never a good sign.

He finished his duties, said good night to Marcel, then headed to the car. He sat behind the wheel, staring out the windshield.

The sun would soon drag itself up from the horizon and settle dawn over New Orleans. Twelfth Night. Tourists and locals alike would fill the streets with revelry and carnival mind-sets—drinking, smoking, partying. These people would allow themselves to do things they would normally never do in their everyday lives. Something about a Big Easy festival caused defenses, and, sadly, too often common sense, to flee like the rumored witches on All Saints Day.

Beau started the car and turned it toward home. His mind continued to race about the case. Addy and Pampalon's prints on the murder weapon. He'd seen how cozy the two of them appeared, even on the security footage. Were they more than employer and employee? It sure appeared that way. Pampalon had kissed Addy's head in quite a possessive way.

As if he had a right to hold and comfort and kiss her.

Beau tightened his grip on the steering wheel as he turned onto his street. He couldn't allow his feelings for her to get in the way of the investigation, no matter how much it made his stomach turn to think of Addy with the pompous Pampalon.

He passed Vincent's house and slowed, as he always did, to see if there were any lights burning inside. There weren't, which was probably a good thing. He couldn't talk to Vincent about the case, which was very unusual—normally, he and Vincent discussed all his cases. It felt wrong not to be able to talk to the man he thought of as a father. He'd talked to Vincent about girls in high school, his parents' deaths, his desire to follow in his father's footsteps to be a cop, and even now, as a man, he discussed things that bothered him with Vincent. Except things that had to do with Addy, like his feelings and this case.

Only one other time had he deliberately kept something important from Vincent. Now, over a decade later, he still kept his secret. No amount of guilt could change the past anyway.

After parking under his carport, Beau made quick strides into the house and turned off the alarm. Columbo met him at the door, weaving through his legs and meowing insistently.

Beau lifted the large cat into his arms. Weighing in at almost twenty-five pounds, Columbo was categorized as obese, and his vet stayed on Beau to put him on a diet.

Beau couldn't do that to his buddy. The cat turned up his nose to all but one brand of cat food and demanded to eat all day. Who was he to deny the finicky feline? "Did you miss me, buddy?"

He rubbed the cat's head to the response of purring and head-butting his hand. As always, Columbo made a stressful day better. With a final rub, Beau set the cat down, refilled the food and water bowls, then snatched up the mail he'd brought in with him.

Two more invitations to Mardi Gras balls. He knew he was only on the invitation list because of his position in the police department. Still, over the years, he'd tried to work up the courage to ask Addy to attend one of them with him. He'd never been able to muster the courage, and now this year, it looked like it would be an impossibility.

He tossed the invitations and junk mail onto the counter. He should make himself something to eat but found himself with no appetite, unlike Columbo, who crouched his elitist self over the pricey cat food.

Instead, Beau headed to the bathroom and turned the shower on. Maybe the steam would clear his head and let him get some rest. He had a feeling he was going to need it as long as the case remained unsolved and open.

He let the hot water sluice over his head, pounding his scalp.

If only it wasn't Addy's hotel. If only it didn't seem like she and Pampalon were on such a personal level. If only her prints weren't on the murder weapon.

If only he'd been able to tell her how he felt before now. If only he'd been able to tell her and her father the truth so many years ago.

# THIRTEEN

## ADELAIDE

"Voodooing him?" Adelaide sat in Tracey's kitchen, sipping hot tea.

"Come on, Addy. You've lived here all your life. You know what it means when someone's got someone messing with them using voodoo."

"All because of a snake in his mailbox?" She took another sip of tea, not that she liked the bitter stuff, but it gave her a moment of warmth.

"Seriously, Ads?" Tracey shook her head and set her cup on the table. "A boa constrictor just happened to end up in his mailbox?"

"He said it was kids pranking."

"An expensive prank. Boas are rather expensive. Even the cheap ones are seventy-five bucks or higher."

Adelaide didn't want to believe her friend, but she accepted that Tracey knew her stuff in this area. After all, some said Tracey was a witch in her own right. That was a rumor, of course. At least, Adelaide was pretty sure it was just gossip. "Okay, I'll bite. Why a snake?"

"Pun intended?" Tracey grinned as she slipped her earrings off and tossed them in the big wooden bowl on the counter. "Snakes are very honored in voodoo and hoodoo. They are believed to hold intuitive knowledge. The main snake, the Grand Zombi, is the temple snake and contains many powers."

"So putting one in a mailbox does what?" Adelaide took another sip of the tea that suddenly wasn't as bitter as before.

"It can be a number of things—a bonding spell, a hex, a curse, an attraction spell, many different things. Depending upon the witch."

Adelaide snorted, then stared at her friend's face and sobered immediately. "You're serious."

"I am." Tracey topped off both of their cups with more tea from the pot. "You should know this, Ads. Don't you remember when we were kids and we snuck behind old woman Josephine's shed? What did you think they were doing but witchcraft rituals?"

Chills slithered up Adelaide's spine, and she grabbed the cup, wrapping her hands around the hot porcelain. "We were kids. We probably have exaggerated what we saw over time and with each telling, scaring each other silly."

Tracey frowned at her. "You know better. You know what we saw. I know what we saw. I deal with it in and out at work all day. Everybody asks the cemetery ghost tour if I've seen ghosts. Does

Marie Laveau haunt the place?" She shook her head. "If they only knew."

Adelaide took a sip of tea. She would avoid this topic at all costs, if she could. Tracey believed her ancestors had practiced witchcraft, voodoo, and hoodoo—all subjects that gave Adelaide the heebie-jeebies.

While the original Marie Laveau, the Voodoo Queen, was said to have turned from voodoo practices near the end of her life and dedicated herself to the Catholic church, her look-alike daughter had gone deep into the dark side of witchcraft. Although not confirmed anywhere, it was said that the second Marie murdered her own older sister, the only other living descendant of Marie and Louis Christophe, Marie Philomene Glapion.

It was from the murdered sister's line that Tracey had been born, and she was proud of her heritage. Tracey had even inherited the house on St. Ann Street that was rumored to have been on the site of the original Marie Laveau's home back in the 1830s.

Remembering that, Adelaide shivered and took another sip of the quickly cooling tea.

"Look, just tell Dimitri to be careful. Let me know if he has any other strange deliveries."

"I will, but he doesn't believe in all that. He has a strong Christian faith and disregards everything else."

Tracey pulled her curly hair up into a ponytail on the top of her head. "Just because someone doesn't believe something doesn't make it less real."

"I guess so." Adelaide set down the cup and stood. "I better get back to the hotel. I have a feeling tomorrow's going to be a very long day."

"I wish you would stay here tonight."

"It'll be an early start, so I really should get back to my place."

Tracey stood and hugged her. Tight. "Be careful," she whispered before releasing Adelaide.

"Of what?"

"I'm not sure. It's just a feeling I have."

Adelaide forced a laugh, even though little goose bumps jumped up on her arms. "Don't start."

Tracey grabbed her arm. "I'm serious, Ads. Something's going on, and I feel like you're being set up or something."

Now the goose bumps grew goose bumps. "Why do you say that?"

"How else would your prints have gotten on the knife that killed him? If I'm the only one who knew your link to him, how did the killer know you'd have motive? Something doesn't add up, Ads, and either way you look at it, the situation doesn't look good for you."

"Tell me about it."

"Don't shrug this off like you normally do.

This is serious. You need to talk to Beau and tell him about your past. He'll understand. At least it won't catch him unaware. He will know you aren't hiding anything."

"I can't tell him." Adelaide grabbed her purse and headed into the living room.

"Just why not?"

"You know why."

"It happened almost a decade ago, Ads. I know you won't discuss it, but you at least need to come to terms with it again. You aren't a victim, you're a survivor."

"I know that well. The therapist drilled all that into my head." Adelaide slumped against the back of the couch.

Tracey took her hand. "It's going to come out, Ads."

Adelaide opened her mouth to argue, but her friend held up her hand. "Despite your best efforts, it's going to come out. Wouldn't you rather be the one telling Beau than him finding out? It will look really bad for you if you aren't the one who tells him."

"It looks bad now. My fingerprints are on the murder weapon. If I tell Beau what happened, he'll see how badly I wanted that scum taken off the face of the earth. He'll see my anger. My rage. And the wrappings of my motive tighten more."

"What happens when he finds out the truth

anyway, and realizes you didn't tell him? It looks like you're hiding the connection to cover your guilt."

"With my fingerprints on the knife . . ."

Tracey gave her hand a squeeze. "At least if you tell him, you can look him in the eye and tell him you didn't know him by his real name. He'll be able to see that you're telling the truth. That you're innocent."

"Will he, Trace? Because whenever I think of that piece of garbage, I know how I look: angry, murderous even."

"It's *Beau,* Ads. The boy you've known practically your whole life. The guy your dad trusts with his true identity. One of your best friends. He'll believe you."

Adelaide hung her head. "I'm just not as sure, Trace. He's so dedicated to his job. To justice."

"Which is why you need to tell him so he can find the killer and bring him to justice."

If only it were that simple.

## DIMITRI

"There are two detectives here to see you, Mr. Pampalon." Erika from the front desk stood in the kitchen's doorway.

The hotel had just finished serving the early breakfast rush. Knowing that his fingerprints on the murder weapon would garner questioning,

Dimitri washed his hands and pulled off the chef's jacket covering his heavy-starched button down shirt. "Show them to my office, please."

He grabbed his suit jacket hanging in the closet and shrugged it on. The crisp lines of the custom-made suit settled over him. He took a moment to run a comb over his hair and check his appearance in the kitchen workers' washroom mirror. He probably should have shaved this morning, but he rather liked the gruffness of the dark stubble lining his jaw. Especially since Adelaide had once mentioned she thought it added character to a man's face.

It would have to do. Dimitri gave final orders to his sous chef and general kitchen workers as he walked through the kitchen before heading to his office. He let out a long breath before entering and moving behind the desk. "Sorry to have kept you waiting, detectives." He offered his hand.

The African American detective stood and shook his hand. "Detective Taton."

Detective Savoie stood, gave a sharp hand-shake, then returned to his seat in front of the desk. "We have a few questions for you, Mr. Pampalon."

Dimitri eased into his executive chair, tenting his fingers over the polished mahogany. "Call me Dimitri, please. Mr. Pampalon is my father." He flashed a smile.

Adelaide's detective friend didn't smile back.

"Dimitri, your family has owned this hotel for generations."

"Is that a question, Detective? If so, you are correct. My great—however many generations back—grandfather built this hotel in the 1840s. It has remained in my family ever since."

The detective nodded, holding his little notebook and pen. "Then perhaps you might be able to suggest how someone would be able to get into room 219 without going through the guestroom door?"

"I guess an agile fellow could make it up to the balcony?" Dimitri smiled.

Again, the detective didn't return the sentiment. "I'm thinking he'd have to be very agile to shimmy up that pole to get onto that small balcony. There's not even a ladder to extend."

"I couldn't do it, that's for sure." Dimitri chuckled. "But alas, I'm not as fit as some others. I did, however, recently watch a documentary on parkour. Have you ever seen it? It's like a sport—running and jumping through an obstacle course, but using the existing environment. Walls, stairs, railings. Looks like fun."

Detective Taton interrupted. "You're telling me you think a parkour enthusiast broke into Kevin Muller's room and murdered him with a knife from your hotel's kitchen?"

Ah, there it was, the mention of the murder weapon. But the detectives were slick—they didn't flat out ask about it, just mentioned it. Maybe hoping Dimitri would incriminate himself?

Dimitri hid his smile behind his hand as he slowly stroked his chin. "I'm saying no such thing. I have no idea how anyone got into the room, much less have any idea why someone would murder the guest." He lowered his gaze to his hands. But he did know someone who had every reason to want the man dead.

"I noticed you were in the kitchen when we arrived." Detective Taton crossed his arms over his chest.

Dimitri lifted his gaze. "Yes."

"Why?" Detective Taton asked.

"Why?"

Detective Savoie nodded. "Yes, why were you in the kitchen? You're an owner of this hotel, but I hear that you spend quite a bit of time in the kitchen, at least lately."

"My father has requested I learn every aspect of the hotel business. This happens to be the time I'm learning all about the kitchen duties and what all that entails: menu planning, food ordering, purchase orders for drinks, staffing, and various other aspects I won't bore you with."

Detective Taton sat up straighter. "Speaking of staffing, what can you tell me about Ethan Morrison? What does he do here?"

Good thing he'd pulled Ethan's employment

152

folder and read the whole thing earlier this morning. "He's one of the newer hires under the work-release programs from the probation office. Those petty criminals who have turned their lives around and are looking for a second chance."

Dimitri leaned back in his chair and stared at the detectives. "I'm sure you're aware Ethan has a record. He's been an exemplary employee here for over a year, working in the kitchen as a dishwasher and vegetable washer."

"So he would have access to all the kitchen utensils—forks, spoons, knives?" Detective Taton asked.

Dimitri resisted the urge to roll his eyes. "Yes, he would."

"As would you?" Detective Savoie asked.

"Of course."

"Back to the question about entry into room 219 . . . aside from a parkour practitioner, can you think of any other way someone would get into the room?" Detective Taton asked. The two partners were like a well-choreographed routine.

Dimitri paused. Not everyone knew about the tunnels and passageways, but they were there inside the Darkwater. If he didn't mention them now, and the police found out that's how the murderer got into the room, he'd be more of a suspect. Everyone who knew about the passageways would be.

Adelaide would be more of a suspect than she was now.

"Dimitri?" Taton asked.

He let out a slow breath again. "Yes."

"Yes?" Savoie asked.

Dimitri stood. "I think it best if I show you, detectives."

Without hesitation, both men were on their feet. "Lead the way."

Dimitri led the detective across the lobby and into the service elevators. "Remember, over the decades, this hotel has been renovated many times. During one such renovation at the onset of the Civil War, there was a need for hiding places to keep valuables out of the hands of the Union soldiers and officers. Many of the public places built in hiding rooms."

The detectives remained silent as they followed Dimitri from the elevator to a hallway on the second floor.

"Such rooms were later connected, forming passageways through buildings. Eventually, some of these passageways were widened and extended to connect with tunnels running throughout the city." Dimitri opened the door.

A gust of cold, damp air rushed out to greet them.

"The Darkwater Inn has such passageways that extend through the length of the building, mostly."

Detective Savoie's eyes widened as he stepped into the darkness. "And this runs along room 219?"

"Yes."

Detective Savoie stepped back into the hallway. "I need to call our crime scene unit back out to scour these passageways." He pulled his cell and texted quickly. "Why didn't you tell anyone before now?"

"It's not something we broadcast, for obvious reasons. If I might request that you be as discreet as you can in your investigation? Most of the hotel employees aren't even aware of the passageways."

"Who does know about them?" Taton asked.

Dimitri had known this was coming. "My father and I, of course. Adelaide and her assistant. Security. Some of the housekeeping employees who've been here for over twenty years." He shrugged. "There are probably a couple who suspect, having heard the rumors over the years, but they don't know how to access the passageways."

Detective Savoie had his little notebook out again, writing furiously. "While we're waiting, do you have an explanation for how your fingerprints got on the murder weapon?"

Wow. That was out of the blue. If he'd planned on catching Dimitri off guard, it worked. Had Dimitri not already known about his prints being on the knife, he'd be stuttering and stammering. Instead, he calmly tilted his head and studied the detective. "I couldn't say, for sure. As you've already pointed out, I've been in the kitchen a lot recently and have touched almost all the utensils in the course of my job. I would dare to say that's the most logical reason why my fingerprints would be on a knife from the hotel's kitchen."

"The murder weapon." Detective Taton's stare could penetrate the most hard-nosed criminal and make them squirm.

Dimitri remained silent, just stared at the detectives. He would not be baited into an emotional outburst.

"Did you know Kevin Muller, sir?" Detective Savoie asked.

How had he and Adelaide been friends for so long? The detective couldn't have much in common with her. "No, I did not."

"You never met him?" Detective Taton asked.

"No."

"Didn't see him in the hotel? In the restaurant? The bar? He was here with a group for four days—maybe you saw him in the meeting space?" Detective Savoie continued the questioning.

The detectives were thorough, Dimitri would give them that. "No, Detective. I don't recall seeing the man you've identified as Kevin Muller ever before, here or elsewhere."

"I see." Detective Savoie wrote more in his

156

notebook. "And where were you between 11:15 and 12:30 on Thursday night, Friday morning?"

Without missing a beat, Dimitri replied, "Trying out a new recipe in the hotel's restaurant."

"At almost midnight?" Detective Taton asked.

"Yes. I had to wait until the dinner service that ended at eleven was cleaned up."

Detective Savoie jutted out his chin. "I'm guessing you don't punch a timecard to verify your hours, seeing how you're an owner and all."

Dimitri snorted. "Of course not. But if you'd like to verify my whereabouts, the waitresses didn't leave until after eleven."

"All of which are your employees, yes?" Detective Taton pressed.

Oh, this detective knew how to get under his skin. "Technically, that would be correct."

The detective smiled. "I see."

"However, there was also a delivery from our liquor supplier right around midnight."

"They make those so late?" Detective Savoie looked up from his notebook.

"Sometimes. Since we're a hotel and open twenty-four-seven, they know they can deliver after normal hours. We are in the city that never sleeps, right? They made their delivery and had to have a manager's signature of acceptance. I signed the purchase order." Dimitri grinned, flashing all his pearly whites. "I can provide you with the company name and that of the driver so you can verify the signature and the time."

"Yes, we'll need that." Detective Taton looked less than pleased.

Detective Savoie's phone chimed. He glanced at it. "Our team is here to inspect the passageway. Where would you like them to come?"

Despite being bested in the questioning, the detective was discreet. For that, Dimitri was extremely grateful.

His father would blow a gasket that not only were the police aware the passages existed, but that they would be open to scrutiny and dissection. He'd find a way to blame Dimitri for the umbrage, of course. Or Adelaide.

And Dimitri couldn't have that happen, no matter what it cost him.

# FOURTEEN

## BEAU

This had to be the worst part of his job that he'd ever experienced, but if he hoped to solve this case and be up for promotion, he had no choice.

Addy's eyes were a little wider than usual as she sat behind her desk and stared.

"You know this isn't personal, right?"

"Of course, you're just doing your job." But Addy's tone came out flat.

Beau couldn't help it. He had to do his job. Thank goodness Marcel was tied up watching over the team in the secret passages. "I'm guessing as general manager, you're aware of the passageways hidden inside this hotel?"

She cleared her throat and nodded.

"And you didn't think it important to mention when we were working the crime scene?"

"To be honest, I wasn't thinking about secret passageways. There was a dead body in one of our hotel rooms. One of our guests had been murdered."

He stared at her, hard. Another detective wouldn't have noticed the slight change in her speech as she said *guests*. "Understandable, but as I was reviewing the security footage, neither you nor your chief of security thought to even mention about the passageway into room 219? With no obvious entry or exit of the murderer through conventional methods, surely you had to at least consider the possibility that the passage could be the way the killer entered the room?"

"I really didn't."

He couldn't allow himself to feel sorry for her. He had to treat her as he would any other suspect. "I just hope that no evidence has been destroyed with the delay in telling us the truth."

"I'm sorry. Really."

Flipping the page in his notebook, Beau moved on. "Did you know Kevin Muller?"

She swallowed. Was that from nerves or was she hiding something? "I never met anyone named Kevin Muller. The first time I even heard the name was when Erika told me the name of the guest who had missed checkout, just before we went to unlock the room."

"Had you seen him around the hotel? With the group? In a meeting room?"

She hesitated again. "I told you, Beau, I never met a Kevin Muller. Period."

He didn't have to know her well to know that she was hiding something. He'd have to knock her off balance, as much as he didn't relish the idea. "Do you have any idea how your fingerprints would have gotten on the knife that killed him?"

The slight shift of her gaze. The almost undetectable catch in her breath.

She already knew about her prints being on the knife. How?

"I eat in the kitchen all the time, using utensils and so forth. Anybody could've picked up a knife and fork that I used before it was washed and stolen it."

"Do people often steal silverware from the hotel?"

She lifted a casual shoulder. "You'd be amazed. People assume the biggest items stolen are robes or linens, but silverware and pillows are right up there."

"Pillows?" That surprised him.

She nodded. "And back before the artwork was hard-mounted to the walls, people would put those large paintings in their suitcases and carry them right out."

"Really?"

She smiled, her breathing regulating as she nodded, clearly relaxing. "That's why we don't put vases or the like in the regular rooms. They kept getting stolen."

"That's crazy." He flipped to a new page in his notebook. "Any speculation on how yours, Dimitri's, and Ethan Morrison's fingerprints all got on the *same* knife? The one that was used to stab Kevin Muller nine times?" He could tell by the paling of her face that he'd done as he'd intended: lulled her into a false sense of security and familiarity, then pushed her with a probing question.

Didn't mean he had to like it.

She blinked several times before responding. "I guess mine probably got there when I ate something in the kitchen."

"And Dimitri's?"

"When I eat in the kitchen, Dimitri usually serves me. He tells me what I'm eating so I can sample if it goes on the menu or if the recipe needs tweaking in some way."

Plausible. "Ethan's?"

"One of the regular kitchen workers usually clears the dishes. I'm guessing Ethan was the one to clear that time."

"So you're saying that Dimitri served you dinner, you ate, Ethan cleared, and that's how all three of your fingerprints ended up on the knife?"

She stiffened, obviously offended by his tone. Or maybe it was just his questions. Either way, it couldn't be helped. He had a job to do and she had to understand that.

"That's just my guess. I don't know for certain."

"Then you think someone—what? Stole that particular knife and used it to kill a guest in your hotel?"

"I don't know, Beau. I don't know who took the knife. I don't know who stabbed him. All I know is it wasn't me."

"Wasn't Dimitri either, because his alibi checks out."

A hint of a smile curled the corner of her lip. "Well, of course it wasn't Dimitri."

Beau resisted the urge to give in to the jealousy. He had to remain objective to do his job, even when he wanted to rip Dimitri's polished throat out. "Where were you between 11:30 Thursday night and 12:30 Friday morning, Addy?"

She leaned back against her chair, her jaw dropping slightly. "You really think I could have murdered someone?"

"It's my job to rule you out."

She gave a half smile. "But you aren't a hundred percent sure it wasn't me who stabbed a man to death?" But there was something in her eyes . . .

"Just answer the question, Addy."

"How quickly you forget, Beauregard Savoie. I was with *you* a little after midnight. I'd eaten a late supper in the kitchen, then decided to go for a run out in the Quarter, which is where I ran into you."

She was right. It had been that night. If he hadn't been so focused on treating her like any other suspect, he would've remembered.

"I'm guessing that you realize there's no way I could've murdered someone, then met you—

what, fifteen to thirty minutes later—calm and in clothes that clearly had no bloodstains."

Of course, she did live at the hotel, and Walt put the time of death between 11:30 and midnight. He'd run into her after midnight. If she killed Muller right at 11:30, she could've showered and changed clothes, then run out so people would see her to be her alibi.

"Beau? Surely you can't think . . ."

No, this was Addy. She couldn't hurt anyone, let alone stab someone nine times. It just wasn't in her.

"No, of course not, but I have to ask the questions. It's my job."

She nodded. "I understand, but it's my job to look out for the hotel's best interests."

He grinned. "Then we're on the same side because solving this homicide is in the best interest of the hotel and the New Orleans Police Department."

But inside, Beau couldn't deny recalling he'd thought there was something off with Addy that night. Something off that had nothing to do with the exhausting day she had or missing supper with her dad.

Something had rattled Adelaide Fountaine— something serious—the night of the murder. Something she didn't want to tell him, which made him all the more determined to find out what it was.

# ADELAIDE

"Did they tear up the passageway too terribly bad?" Adelaide leaned forward in the chair facing Dimitri's desk until her elbows rested on the desk.

"Surprisingly, no. They took samples of most everything, but didn't do much permanent harm."

"Good. I know how your dad is about those secret passages." She leaned back and smiled at Dimitri. "And I heard your alibi panned out."

"As did yours. Running into the detective handling the case kind of cements your alibi." His returning smile made her feel warm inside. "They took Ethan down to the station to question him because he had a record, so he wanted his lawyer present."

"He didn't kill anybody either."

Dimitri nodded. "I know, but somebody did, Adelaide. Someone who used a knife that put us in the crosshairs of the police."

"Do you think using that particular knife was intentional?" It was the question she'd been going over and over since Beau left, playing like a video on auto-repeat. "That someone deliberately tried to set up one of us as a suspect?"

"It would seem that way. That, or it was mighty convenient."

Tracey's warning sounded inside Adelaide's head. "Hey, I mentioned something about you finding a boa in your mailbox to Tracey, and she thinks someone might be trying to use voodoo on you."

Dimitri burst out laughing. "Come on, Adelaide! Surely you don't buy into all that nonsense." He sobered. "You know I don't believe in hocus-pocus stuff. My belief is in Jesus Christ."

"I know, and I understand. Yet there are many in New Orleans who do believe in voodoo and hoodoo as a spiritual connection." How to approach this without offending him? "Just because you don't believe in something doesn't make it less real."

"You believe in spells and hexes and *gris-gris* and the like?" His eyes widened as he leaned forward in his chair. "Considering your upbringing and what you know from your study of the Bible?"

Oh, she had to be very careful here. "I believe in Jesus Christ. I might be angry at Him and not on speaking terms with Him, but I believe in what Scripture tells me."

"See—"

She held up a hand. "And that's a reason why I do believe in voodoo and the like. Scripture warns us against communicating with the spirits. It tells of demons and the evil loose in the world. If such things didn't exist, the Bible wouldn't warn us against it. Wouldn't tell us to stay away, yes?"

"Well, yes. I suppose."

"I'm just saying to be careful. Tracey said snakes are used in various ways in voodoo. It's unlikely the pranks of teens, considering the price of boa constrictors." She crossed and uncrossed her legs. "First the snake, now the knife . . . I'm just asking you to be careful. The two could be connected."

Dimitri opened his mouth, paused for a second, then snapped it shut. He nodded. "You're right. The timing of the snake in conjunction with the murder is suspect. I'll be more vigilant."

As usual, Dimitri was the sort of man who could be reasoned with.

"I heard Geoff had to run off a few reporters who tried going undercover to get information on the murder." He shook his head. "They are a determined bunch."

"I guess a murder is news."

"And that it's tied to the hotel, and Father, are added bonuses."

"Have you heard anything more from Claude?" she asked.

He shook his head and lifted a pen, twirling it through his fingers. "Nothing, but then again, I don't expect to hear from him. He'll show up Monday or Tuesday morning like he's said and want an update. Once he's assured everything is handled and it's business as usual, he'll forget his threats and move on."

"That's a big if everything's concluded by then."

"I have faith in Detective Savoie." Dimitri dropped the pen and leaned forward. "Don't you as well?"

She did, but . . . Adelaide nodded. "He said he'd be back this afternoon when Corey and Richard are on duty to question them."

"Corey and Richard are . . . ?"

Adelaide shook her head. Dimitri had better start learning the employees' names. Especially if his father fired her and expected him to take over. "Corey is the bartender and Richard is the—"

"Elevator attendant who was on duty Thursday night into early Friday morning."

Her smile spread quickly. "Correct." Just as quickly, she frowned. "Beau wants to question them about the woman Kevin took to his room."

"Beau. You're very familiar with the good detective."

The heat crept up the back of her neck. "I've told you before that we're friends. Beau's family and mine are somewhat intertwined. We've been friends since we were children."

"So, you do trust him?"

She paused, remembering how Beau had questioned her. It hurt, but she understood he'd just been doing his job.

It still stung, though. "I do. He's honest and fair. He hasn't had the easiest life."

"Hasn't he?" Dimitri leaned back and lifted his pen again, twirling it.

"His father was a cop. A good one, from what Dad tells me. A lot like what Beau has grown into: a noble man of integrity."

"So what happened?"

She shifted, stretching her legs out in front of her. "When he was twelve, his father was killed in the line of duty. A young kid pulled a gun on him during a robbery that Mr. Savoie had responded to. Beau's father tried to talk him out of the gun. They struggled and the gun went off, killing Beau's dad instantly. Beau and his mom never had a chance to say good-bye."

"Oh, man, that's really horrible."

Adelaide nodded, remembering as best she could. "I was eight at the time, so I don't remember a whole lot. I remember the funeral and Mrs. Savoie crying." She closed her eyes, seeing the tween Beau at the funeral in his stiff-looking suit and flower on his lapel. "But not Beau. He didn't cry. He later told my dad that he had to be strong for his mom." Tears welled in her eyes at the memory.

"How awful. Twelve . . . that age of a boy standing on the brink of heading into manhood, when a boy really needs his father."

"I think that's why my dad stepped in. Began

inviting Beau hunting and fishing with him. I didn't realize it then, but he took Beau under his wing to make sure he grew up with a man in his life so Beau wouldn't turn out bitter."

"Your father is a good man."

Adelaide grinned. "Don't let him hear you say that. His head's big enough already."

"I'd really like to meet him in person. After all of this is settled."

"I think he'd like you too." She stretched, pushing the morning's stress from between her shoulders. "And then five years later, Beau's mom was killed in a car accident." She pressed her lips together. "A drunk driver ran a red light and T-boned her. A shard of metal sliced her jugular. She died quickly, just like Beau's father. No good-byes, no closure."

"Oh, wow. Tough childhood."

She nodded, but images of her own mother, alive, filled her mind. The screaming, then crying. The showing up at school to take Adelaide home, only to have to have her father called to come get her mother. The embarrassment. The stigma of hearing *Addy's alkie mom* from her classmates.

She pressed her lips together. "I guess we all have our childhood demons to deal with."

"I suppose we do. Look at Claude. He was so cruel my mother ran off as soon as she could get away. And I don't blame her. I just wish she'd taken me."

"I'm sorry, Dimitri."

He shook his head. "I'm sure she wanted to take me, but Claude threatened her. That's what bullies do, yes?"

"They do." Her mom hadn't been a bully, but she'd made Adelaide's childhood unstable and at times, miserable. She'd felt so guilty after her mother finally died because all she felt at the funeral had been relief. Grateful to not have to live in turmoil anymore. Comforted not to have to deal with a person bent not only on her own destruction but also those closest to her as well.

Dimitri tapped the pen against his desk mat. "Beau questioned me about knowing Kevin Muller. I'm assuming he asked you as well."

"He did."

"What did you tell him?"

"What I told you. That I had never met a man named Kevin Muller, and the first time I'd ever even heard the name was when Erika told me who was in room 219."

He dropped the pen and shook his head.

"I told him the truth."

"Adelaide . . ."

She straightened, squaring her shoulders. "That is the truth. I never met a Kevin Muller."

"But you know Kevin Muller and Brayden Colton are one and the same. You're lying by omission."

Shooting to her feet, Adelaide pointed at him. "It's not a lie. He asked a question and I answered it truthfully."

Dimitri stood as well but stayed behind his desk. "If he had asked if you'd ever seen Kevin Muller before, what would you have said?"

"That I have never met Kevin Muller before."

"You're being evasive."

"I'm protecting myself. And my father." And Beau too. "I have a right to protect myself and what happened to me in the past."

"I doubt Detective Savoie would see it that way, wouldn't you say? This is a homicide investigation."

"I didn't kill him. Sure, I'm glad he's dead. I'm glad someone took a knife and stabbed him until he couldn't hurt anyone else. There, I said it. Are you happy? Does it make you feel better? Yes, I hated him. He raped me. He took my innocence and my trust and made me feel like I didn't matter, so I'm actually very happy he's gone and I'll never have to worry about him again. But I did not kill him." She stopped, struggling to catch her breath. Her entire body trembled.

Dimitri was around the desk in a flash, taking her into his arms and holding her tightly.

She leaned into his strength . . . his warmth.

"Shh. I didn't mean that I could ever believe you'd stabbed him. Shh." His words were warmth on her forehead.

She took a step back from him, putting a couple of inches between them. Her breathing still came in spurts as she stared up at him.

"Adelaide." Her name was more of a growl, as if it came from his gut. He held her by her shoulders, providing the steadiness she needed.

She placed her hand on his chest, ignoring the thumping of his heart. Now wasn't the time or place and definitely not the situation to delve into her strange emotions. "I have to go."

Adelaide rushed from his office, her heart racing the quick pace of her heels.

# FIFTEEN

## BEAU

Corey Devereaux's intellect surprised Beau and Marcel. Surprising a detective wasn't a common occurrence, but the Darkwater Inn's favorite bartender did just that. Beau hadn't expected to find a man holding an associate's degree who was back in college to earn his bachelor's tending the bar. It was quite refreshing to find a bartender who was not only quick on his feet but also extremely observant.

Now that the preliminary questions were out of the way, Beau and his partner moved on to the reasons they'd called him in before noon on Twelfth Night. "Tell me what you remember of this man." Marcel pushed the photo of Kevin Muller across the slick bar.

Corey studied it for a moment, never stopping in his task of polishing the brass adornments on the bar. "He was in the bar Thursday evening, early . . . from about seven until ten or so. Clean-cut kind of guy, like the other pharmaceutical reps in the group. But this one, he was arrogant. Had that air about him."

174

"Arrogant?" Beau tightened his hold on the pen. Finally, someone who actually remembered Muller and what he'd been like alive.

The bartender nodded. "Came off as if he thought he was better than everybody else around him. Those kinds of people ooze the stench of arrogance. He had it in spades. The way he cajoled his friends to buy the rounds they were putting down. Jack Daniels, single barrel. Not cheap, but that's what they were drinking."

Neat trick. "How'd he manage that?"

"Oh, same game that's been around as long as there have been drinks served. *I bet you a shot that I can get that girl to dance with me* or get her number or whatever."

"This guy won those types of bets?" Beau glanced at the picture again. Kevin Muller didn't seem to be overtly attractive or appealing, but what did Beau know?

The bartender nodded. "Sure did. Got one of the snooty girls' number. One of the ones here with a bachelorette party from the Garden District."

Beau knew the type well: old money with Daddy's doting indulgences. He'd gone to school with plenty of girls who would've given their right arm to be invited to the Garden District, much less live there.

"For another round," Corey continued, "this guy got an eyeful of a gal's big beads, if you know what I mean."

Unfortunately, Beau did. It wasn't much of a secret during Mardi Gras parades that the bigger the breasts shown, the bigger the beads thrown to them.

"He even managed to get one of our regulars to make out with him right here in the bar, knowing that I disapproved." Corey tossed the dusting rag over his shoulder and leaned his elbow on the bar. "'Course, that made one of the few ladies in his group rather upset."

"How so?" Marcel asked.

"She told him perhaps it was time for him to go call his pregnant wife. She tossed back his last single barrel, slammed the glass down, then shoved him out of her way as she stormed off."

Marcel straightened. "Did he seem angry?"

Corey laughed and flicked the rag off his shoulder. "Dude, she'd just announced he was married and his wife was pregnant while he was hitting on women right and left. What do you think?"

Beau figured Muller had probably been all kinds of mad. "Do you remember what he did or said?"

"He made some remark about the girl's, um, wide rear as she walked off. He and his buddies laughed."

"What about the girl?" Beau glanced to his notes. "If she's a regular, you must know her name."

Corey hesitated, running the rag over an area of the bar he'd already polished.

Beau and Marcel waited. One second passed. Two. Three—

"Zoey's a good girl. She's made some bad choices, sometimes still does, but overall, she's a good person. Has a good heart."

The bartender clearly had things he needed to tell the police, but didn't want to.

Just like Addy. Beau cleared his throat. "I understand. She's a friend of yours. What's her last name?"

"Naure. N-a-u-r-e. Zoey Naure."

Beau scribbled in his notebook. "I don't want to make any trouble for her. I just need to know what happened."

"Zoey left with him soon after the other woman stormed off. They were headed to his room."

"Was that common for her?" Marcel asked a little softer, following Beau's example.

The bartender rubbed the same part of the brass in front of him for a few moments before lifting his gaze to meet the detectives' gazes. "Look, she'd been busted a couple of times for prostitution, but she isn't turning tricks anymore."

Ah. Beau understood now. "But it's possible she might have gone to his room with him as a *business deal?*"

"She swore she was out of the business for good."

"I'm guessing you don't know that to be one hundred percent truth, right?" Marcel asked.

Corey tossed the rag on the bar. "No. I'd been talking to her for months, trying to get her to work on getting her life back on track. Despite how much she said she wanted to leave that life behind, she'd slipped up more than a time or two."

A prostitute would explain the short time—Beau flipped through his notes on the case—of about forty-five minutes that she was in Muller's hotel room.

"Did she come back to the bar later that night?"

Corey shook his head. "I didn't see her, but we got busy with that group and the regular tourists."

"Have you seen her since? Talked to her?" Marcel asked.

"I was off yesterday. She and I aren't friends, per se. Just a girl I know from the bar who I'm trying to help out."

"Have any idea where she lives?" Marcel asked.

Corey shook his head. "Sorry."

Beau handed him his business card. "If you see her again, give me a call, please."

"Sure."

Beau held the card as Corey tried to take it. "I'm not trying to cause her any trouble. I mainly just want to know about the guy."

"I'll give you a call."

"Thanks." Beau started to turn away, but stopped. "A couple more questions."

"Okay."

"Do you know Ethan Morrison?"

"Guy that works in the kitchen here?"

Beau nodded.

"Yeah. I've talked to him a couple of times when he's come in here after his shift. Seems like an okay guy."

"Do you remember if he came in here Thursday night? Late?"

"Not that I recall, but as I said, we were busy later that night."

Beau slipped his notebook back into his pocket. "What about Dimitri Pampalon?"

Corey frowned. "What about him?"

"What's he like?"

"Nice. Takes the time to really talk to people and listen to them. Goes out of his way to be kind. Total opposite of his father."

"I take it his father is sort of a jerk?" Marcel asked.

Corey laughed. "Sort of? The man defines the word. Cold and callous to everyone. Doesn't matter your position in the hotel, he'll chew out a maid or supervisor just the same. Even snaps at his own son." The bartender shook his head. "I don't know how Dimitri puts up with him, honestly. Forget the money and hotel, it's not worth it to put up with the old man's cruelty."

Beau couldn't imagine Addy working for some-one like that. "What about Adelaide Fountaine?"

Corey smiled with his whole face. "You'll be hard-pressed to find anyone at the hotel to say anything bad about Adelaide. She's kind and considerate, fair and just." He grinned wider, if that was possible. "She's beautiful to look at, but just as beautiful on the inside."

"I think so too." Beau couldn't help smiling back. "Thanks again. Do call me when you see Zoey again."

"I will." Corey slipped the card in the back pocket of his jeans and turned away, moving to the other end of the bar.

"Why don't you call the station and run a background check on Zoey Naure before we interview the elevator attendant?" Beau pocketed his notebook.

"Sure." Marcel pulled out his cell.

Glancing around the hotel lobby, Beau spied Addy and Dimitri at the front desk, heads bent together. They sure looked chummy together, comfortable with one another. He could choose to believe that was because of their positions at the hotel, but his mind's eye kept going back to the image of Addy in Pampalon's arms.

As if she could hear his thoughts, Addy lifted her head and settled her gaze on Beau. She smiled, and Beau forgot how it felt to see Dimitri kiss her temple on the security video.

"They'll text you when they get the background." Marcel joined Beau as they headed toward Addy.

She stepped from behind the desk. "Finished talking with the employees?"

"We still need to speak with the elevator attendant."

"Richard Norris." She started walking down the hall toward her office. "Come on, I just saw him heading to clock in."

Beau and Marcel fell into step beside her.

"How's the investigation going?"

"We can't really discuss it with you."

Beau could sense more than see her stiffening. "Addy, you have to understand."

"I do. I do." She let out a sigh and paused at her office. "I don't have to like it though, right?"

He nodded. "I don't exactly relish this either."

She pointed at the open doorway down the hall. "The employee room is there. Check and see if Richard is still getting settled before his shift. There shouldn't be anyone else in there. If he's not there, he'll be at the elevators."

"Thanks, Addy."

She gave a little half wave, then slipped into her office.

"I forgot y'all are tight. I'm sure the Captain would pair me up with someone else if this is a conflict of interest for you," said Taton.

"Don't be stupid. It's fine. I'm doing my job."

Beau moved down the hall to the task at hand, even though his chest tightened to the point of cutting off his breath for a minute. He nearly collided with the young man exiting.

"I'm sorry." The young man—who couldn't be more than twenty-one or -two—reached out to steady Beau.

"Richard Norris?"

"Yes?"

Beau waved the man back inside the employee room while flashing his badge. "I'm Detective Savoie and this is my partner, Detective Taton. We have a few questions for you."

Norris went pale.

"Here, sit down." Beau led the kid to one of the couches.

The employee room, whatever that really was, held a row of lockers on one wall, doors for men and women on the opposite side, and three large couches in the middle of the room. Not really a break room, more like a true resting space with lockers for employee belongings.

While Marcel hovered, as he did so well, Beau sat opposite Norris. "You okay?"

"Yes, sir."

"We have a few questions for you about Thursday night."

"The murder, right?"

Beau nodded. "Yes. I understand you were the elevator attendant on duty that night?"

"Yes, sir."

He handed the young man Muller's photo. "Do you recognize this man?"

Norris nodded. "He's the guy that was murdered in 219."

"Right. Do you remember seeing him Thursday night?"

"Yes, sir."

Beau pulled out his notebook. "Tell me what you remember about him on Thursday night. When you saw him. Who he was with. Anything that was said."

The kid's knee bounced. "I remember taking him up to his room shortly after four, when the whole group broke. Most of them went up to their rooms to change or whatever."

"Do you remember if he changed?" Marcel asked from behind the kid.

Norris startled, but nodded. "He went in with a suit but came out in jeans and a shirt. No tie."

"About what time did he come out? Your best estimate." Marcel pressed.

"I'd say around five-thirty-ish. There were a lot of them heading out. Some of them had signed up for the night cemetery tours. Some talked about bar hopping through the Quarter."

"What about him? Do you remember if he mentioned what he was doing?" Beau asked.

"I do. He was on the phone when the elevator got to the second floor. He told whoever was on the phone that he was meeting some of the guys in the restaurant. He said he was getting on the elevator and would probably lose reception. Told whoever he was talking to that they should get some rest and he loved them."

Beau made a note on the side of the page: Richard Norris eavesdrops.

"Once he hung up, I tried to talk to him, but he ignored me. Looked at me like I was dog poo on his shoe. He didn't say anything else to me on that trip. Real jerk."

Right in line with what Corey had said. Wait. "That trip?"

"Yeah." More knee bouncing. "He and a really hot chick rode up to his room later. Around ten-ish, I'd guess."

"Do you remember anything about that elevator trip?" Marcel asked.

Kid grinned at them. "Well, yeah. I mean, they were the only two in the elevator at that time, and, well, like I said, the chick was one hot redhead."

Beau let the comment slide. "What do you remember?"

"He was all over her, man. And I think he got off on me being in there with them. He'd be kissing her, but staring at me." The kid's eyes widened. "One time, he yanked her dress up and grabbed her a—er, behind, staring and grinning right at me."

Beau knew what he meant and knew the kind of man Muller seemed to be. He couldn't stand those types.

"But we got to the second floor right then, so he shoved her out of the elevator in front of him, tossed an empty condom package at my feet, and grabbed her again, almost running her down the hall to his room. But she was giggling, so I guess she liked that rough stuff."

"Did you see him again?" Marcel asked.

The kid shook his head. "Not the rest of the night."

"What about her? Did you see her when she went back down to the lobby?" Marcel asked.

Norris nodded, his knee still bouncing like crazy, starting to wear on Beau's nerves. "Yeah. Girls like that usually chat with me. She had before when she was here a couple of months ago, but she didn't that night. I think she'd been crying."

That piqued Beau's interest. "Crying?"

"Yeah, her eyes were all red and watery. She didn't talk to me, did her best not to even look at me. And she wasn't wearing her dress."

"What?" Beau's fingers squeezed the pen so tight it could've snapped.

"Yeah, she had been wearing this dress with one of those almost see-through things that goes over it. When she left, she didn't have the dress on, just that cover up thing."

Interesting.

"She didn't say anything."

However, Norris was an eavesdropper and observer. "But do you have any idea where she went?" Beau asked.

"She went straight from the elevator out the front door, hugging that thin cover up thingy she was wearing."

"Did you see her again?" Beau asked.

"Nope. Haven't seen her since."

"Or him? Maybe later that night?" Marcel asked.

Norris shook his head.

Beau tapped his pen on his notebook. "I'm sure you know that group's planner, right? Young blonde lady."

"Bigger girl?" Norris nodded. "Yeah. She went up to that guy's room after the hot chick left."

Marcel moved from behind the kid, looming into his personal space. "She rode up in your elevator?"

"Nah. The other one. But she rode down in mine."

"About what time?" Marcel asked.

"I guess a little after eleven-ish."

Beau had about enough ishes for one interrogation. "How did she seem?"

"She was really crying, tears and everything. She was sniffling when she told me not to grow up to be a cheater."

"Did you happen to notice if there was anything odd about her appearance?" Marcel asked.

Norris grinned. "Like her dress was missing? Nah, man. She had on this white top with black buttons. Real stuffy looking, to be honest. Not my type."

Beau didn't comment on that. Some things were just better left unsaid. "Anything else?"

"Nope, she rode up to the third floor and headed to her room, I guess."

Beau slipped his notebook in his pocket just as his text alert vibrated his cell. "Thanks." He handed his business card to the young elevator attendant. "If you remember anything else you think might be important, give me a call."

"Yes, sir." The kid shot to his feet and headed from the employee room.

Beau checked his text message: Zoey Naure, 1 DUI, 3 prostitutions.

He scrolled to the next message, which had Zoey's last known address. Smiling, he headed down the hall. Time to visit the alluring Zoey and get her statement.

And find out what happened to her dress the night Muller was murdered.

# SIXTEEN

## DIMITRI

He could have sworn he'd set the alarm when he left, but his father's housekeeper had arrived this morning to find the downstairs a mess and the alarm off.

Dimitri whipped his car into the driveway and parked behind Tilda's blue Mustang. He smiled as he got out of his car, as he always did when seeing Tilda's car. The sight of a white-haired, sixty-something Creole woman in a '69 Mustang GT, top down, singing at the top of her lungs . . . well, it made Dimitri smile. Tilda said she'd always wanted such a car, and she'd saved up to buy just the one she'd wanted.

"Thank goodness you are here." Tilda stepped onto the veranda, followed by her niece, Elise, who had been coming to assist her aging aunt over the last several months. "I wanted you to decide whether or not to call the police since Mr. Claude is out."

"You did the right thing, Tilda." Dimitri could practically hear his father's tirade if he was told about the break-in. It would be, no doubt,

Dimitri's fault in Claude's eyes. If nothing had been taken, he could avoid a police report all together.

Stepping into the entryway, he could understand why Tilda and Elise stopped and called him. The antique entry table had been turned over, one of its legs broken. The mirror that hung over it, crashed to the floor. Shards of mirror littered the Italian tile.

He continued on into the den. The couch and high-back chairs had been ripped, stuffing strewed about the room. Pictures pulled from the wall and lying on the floor. The marble fireplace had chunks gouged out, probably by the poker.

Dimitri quickly checked the other rooms in the downstairs and let out a sigh of relief. It appeared nothing else had been touched. He rushed upstairs to check his father's suite.

He froze as he entered his father's bedroom through Claude's private study. In the middle of the bed laid a bloody corpse of a chicken without a head. Nothing else seemed amiss.

Quickly, he checked his own suite. No dead chicken rested on his bed, and there was nothing obviously taken, but Dimitri couldn't help the feeling of violation—that someone had touched and moved some of his personal items.

"Dimitri, are you okay?" Tilda's voice rose up the staircase.

He couldn't let the older woman see this.

"I'm coming." Glancing around, he looked for something to put the chicken and the bedding in to dispose of them.

"Auntie asked if—" Elise froze in the doorway to Claude's bedroom, her stare fixed on the dead chicken.

"I'll take care of this. Let your aunt know nothing up here is disturbed."

"But Mr. Dimitri, that's a dead chicken."

"I'm well aware, but I don't want your aunt to be afraid. I'll get this cleaned up while you and Tilda tackle the downstairs. I can't see that anything was taken, so I see no need to call the police."

Barely nineteen, Elise wasn't easily intimidated. She narrowed her eyes at him. "Are you sure, Mr. Dimitri?"

"Yes. Thank you. Please help your aunt, and anything that's broken, just make a list and I'll see that someone gets on making the repairs or replacing." He grabbed the corners of his father's duvet, bringing the four together and covering the dead chicken. Under his breath he mumbled, "Preferably before Father returns."

"Mr. Dimitri, I can help you."

He stopped and stared at her.

"You go. I'll take care of this. I'll also find the exact bedding to replace this. We will have it all seen to before Tuesday, if that's soon enough?"

A day's grace period before his father returned.

"Yes. Thank you." He relaxed his shoulders. "Thank you, Elise."

She nodded. "Just don't let Auntie know about this up here. She gets a bit—oh, what's the word?—spooky over such things."

"I understand." He reached for the bundle. "I'll get rid of it."

"No." The sharpness of Elise's tone stopped him. She reached out and put a hand over his. "I know you probably aren't aware of most things such as this, but it needs to be taken care of in the right way."

"The *right* way?" Dimitri straightened and stared down at the young woman as she withdrew her hand from his.

"Forgive me for being so familiar." Her smile was easy across the smoothness of her Creole-darkened skin. "But I'm concerned for you and your father. That chicken was part of a ritual against your father."

"Come again?" He couldn't be having such a similar conversation to the one he'd just had with Adelaide.

"Someone broke in here to perform a ritual against your father. I'm not sure exactly of the spell, which is why the chicken needs to be disposed of properly. I'll try to find out what the hex actually was for, then work to undo it."

Dimitri shook his head. "Voodoo again?" Adelaide had warned him. Had she been right?

"Again?"

"I found a boa constrictor in our mailbox the other day."

"A snake?" Elise's chocolate-colored eyes widened. "Someone is very determined to cast rituals against your father."

"You know about this stuff?" He couldn't believe he was actually listening and considering that this could be happening.

"Dimitri? Elise?" The old housekeeper's voice rattled up the stairs.

"I'm on my way down, Tilda," Dimitri called. "Go ahead and start cleaning up the den, please." He turned back to Elise.

"I do know about things such as these. You go ahead and go back to work. I'll help Auntie clean up and set about repairs and replacements, then I'll see what I can find out about who is trying to cast spells on your father, and for what."

"I don't know what to believe anymore."

Elise smiled and reached for his arm again. She gave it a gentle squeeze. Heat rushed up his arm and into his chest. He didn't know who was more surprised, him or Elise, as she gave a little jump before rubbing her fingers.

"Let's just wait to see what I can find out before you have to believe anything."

He remembered the little sachet that had been in the mailbox with the snake. "Hang on, I have something else to show you." He rushed to his suite, grabbed the cloth sack from where he'd left it behind his computer, and returned to his father's rooms across the hall.

"I found this in the mailbox with the boa constrictor." He handed the sack to Elise.

"Ah. A *gris-gris*." She carefully opened the little sachet and peered inside.

"A what?"

"A *gris-gris* is a charm or amulet used in voodoo to cast a hex or spell, depending on what's in the item and what was cast." She closed up the sachet.

"So what does mine mean?"

"I'm not entirely sure. I'll need to check some things, consult a friend or two. I'll let you know as soon as I get an answer."

"I'd appreciate it." Although he knew the blood Jesus Christ shed for him protected him, he couldn't deny he felt unnerved by it all. Very unnerved.

"I won't have a chance to look into this until after Auntie and I have done what we need to for the house. Probably tonight or tomorrow."

"I understand. Anything. Thank you."

"Of course." Elise slipped the cloth sack into the pocket of her loose-fitting jeans.

"And if you could keep it from your aunt, I'd really appreciate it."

Elise smiled again and reached for the bundle.

"Of course. As I said, she gets spooky over voodoo."

She wasn't the only one.

## ADELAIDE

"Happy Twelfth Day."

Adelaide looked up from the spreadsheet that had her about ready to pull all her hair out to see Tracey in her office doorway, holding a baker's box. As always, Tracey looked perfect. Hair that looked soft as silk falling over her shoulders like warm chocolate. Her makeup as flawless as her skin. Even her dress, which hugged her curves and looked so comfortable, looked as if it had been made for her. Typical Tracey.

Adelaide loved every bit of her. She smiled and waved her friend in. "Oh, you are such a sight for sore eyes. Please tell me that's a king cake." She stood and stretched.

"But of course." Tracey set the box on the little table off to the side of Adelaide's desk. "What kind of friend do you take me for?"

"The best, of course." Adelaide lifted the cardboard top and pinched off a piece of the oozing sweetness, slipping it into her mouth and closing her eyes as her taste buds appreciated the bakery deliciousness. "Oh, I love you."

Tracey chuckled and plopped down on the chair. "I can't stay but a minute. I wanted to bring you the cake, but also needed to come by and give you a little heads-up."

"Oh?" Adelaide pinched off another bite before shutting the box and joining her friend.

The noonday sun shone down on the city. From Adelaide's window, she could see the sparkle of green, purple, and gold decorations filling the French Quarter. Tonight, the beginning of the carnival season would kick off. The streets would explode with tourists and locals alike, all out to celebrate and party.

Tracey tapped her bright red nails against each other. "A friend of a friend of a friend told someone, and it's getting around that the man murdered here wasn't exactly a nice guy."

"Well, we already knew that."

"Yeah, but there's a girl claiming he was a little rough with her, in an intimate sort of way. Really rough, to be honest, and that's the talk going through the Quarter." Tracey's dark eyes turned serious in the brightness of the sun's beams bursting through the window.

Suddenly, the king cake bites seemed to grow in the back of Adelaide's throat until she almost couldn't breathe.

"Hey, calm down." Tracey leaned over and took her hand. "I'm just telling you because if the police catch wind of the story, and they probably will, they might be inclined to check into his past."

Adelaide's stomach dropped to her toes. "But I never pressed charges."

"No, and there's probably nothing to connect you to him. There's probably no reason to be concerned, but on the off chance there's something, even a single piece of paper from the campus police's old files that has your name, I didn't want you to be blindsided."

This was it. Everything was going to blow up. Right now, when the threat of Brayden had been eliminated. Her secret would get out. Her father would—

"I think you should tell Beau everything, Ads."

She'd worked so hard to keep her secret safe. And now, once again, Brayden Colton or Kevin Muller would destroy a part of her. Piece by piece, until there was nothing left of her. Until she was just gone.

Tracey squeezed her hand tighter. "Please, tell him. He'll understand. He's your friend. He'll listen and understand."

Adelaide pressed her lips together and shook her head. She remembered Beau's questions. Remembered him telling her it wasn't personal, that it was his job and he had a job to do. "I can't, Trace. Trust me, he's not my friend right now. He's the detective working the case. If I tell him, I give myself a motive for murder to go hand-in-hand with my fingerprints being on the murder weapon."

"I think you're misjudging him." Tracey gave her hand a final squeeze, then stood. "When push comes to shove, I think Beau will have your back."

Adelaide pushed to her feet as well. "I don't. He's questioned me, Trace. Treated me like any other suspect. It would be a mistake to tell him now."

A big mistake that could break her heart into a million little pieces that would never fit back together again.

"One other thing." Tracey stopped at Adelaide's office door. "Has Dimitri mentioned anything about a headless chicken in his bed?"

"What?"

Tracey grinned. "Just something I heard. Someone was asking about spells with boa constrictors, *gris-gris* with ashes and rat bones, and a headless chicken in the bed."

"And you automatically thought of Dimitri?"

"The boa. Guess someone else is getting even more hexed than him." Trace waggled her fingers. "I'll talk to you tonight. Think about what I said." She disappeared out the door.

Now Adelaide couldn't get snakes and headless chickens out of her mind.

# SEVENTEEN

## BEAU

"New Orleans police." Beau held his shield up to the keyhole. "I'm Detective Savoie and this is my partner, Detective Taton. We need to speak to Zoey Naure." He stood on a porch that needed more than a couple of planks replaced, under the midday sun sprinkling in through holes in the porch's roof.

There was only a slight hesitation before the click of the deadbolt echoed. The door with peeling paint opened a couple of inches to reveal a very attractive redhead. Richard Norris, little eavesdropper and future menace to womankind that he was, hadn't exaggerated Zoey Naure's natural appeal.

Dark red hair that was straight as a board but looked soft as satin; big, round, dark eyes that drew the attention from her almost transparent skin; and a lithe physique with curves in all the right places gave her an ethereal effect. Stunning.

"I'm Zoey, what's this about?" She leaned against the doorjamb, her body language clear that she wasn't going to invite him inside.

"We have a few questions for you." Marcel would start while Beau observed.

"I haven't done anything wrong."

"I didn't say you had. I just have a couple of questions in an ongoing homicide investigation."

"Homicide?" Those eyes of hers widened even more.

"Yes, ma'am." Marcel paused. "May we come inside?"

She glanced over her shoulder, then stepped onto the porch and shut her front door behind her. "I can answer any questions out here, officers." Bare feet stuck out from the bottom of her faded jeans. She pulled the arms of the hole-filled sweatshirt she wore down to cover her hands.

Marcel didn't correct her on their titles. "As you wish, ma'am."

Beau pulled out his notebook and photo, then checked the stability of the supporting beam before leaning against it. He showed her Muller's photo. "Do you know this man?"

Her eyelid twitched. "I've seen him once, so I don't think that qualifies as really knowing him."

Coy, how evasive. He could be cute too. "Tell me about your encounter with him, please." He flashed her the smile Addy said could calm raging seas.

It didn't seem to have that effect on Zoey. Her lips curled into a pout as she handed the photo back to him. "I met him in a bar on Thursday night."

"That's it? You just met him? Did you dance? Share drinks? Talk?" Marcel let his voice trail off, but the implication was clear.

Her face reddened and she crossed her arms over her chest. She leaned against the door-jamb, as if willing herself to disappear into the weathered wood. "He approached me, introduced himself and asked if he could buy me a drink. I let him."

Beau wrote, keeping his eyes on his notebook. He didn't want to embarrass her, but he needed the truth. "Then what?"

"He was an attractive man, so when he tried to kiss me, I let him."

"And then?" Beau caught a glimpse of her microexpressions. Eyes shooting to one side. Quick, inaudible intake of breath.

Her eyes narrowed. "A woman came up and told him that perhaps it was time he called his pregnant wife. She shoved him, told him she wished she'd never met him and wished that he was dead, then stormed off."

*She wished he were dead?* That was something Sidney Parsons hadn't admitted to in her statement. A barely veiled threat. He might need to revisit with the pharmaceutical company's event planner.

For now, he needed to get more information.

Beau turned his attention back to the young woman in front of him. "And what did you do?"

She shrugged. "It caught me off guard that the woman he was clearly cheating on his wife with was jealous of his flirting with me. I laughed it off."

He didn't say anything, just stared at her.

"Look, I know that makes me kind of a bad person, but I wasn't cheating on anyone. I don't know his wife. I didn't set my eye on him, he came on to me."

"We're not judging." Marcel's tone was lower, but Beau could tell his partner was, in fact, judging Zoey.

And she knew it too. "Yes, you are. You're sitting there, already knowing about my past arrests and thinking I'm just some woman who'll let some poor sap cheat on his pregnant wife with me for money. Well, we all have to make a living. You may have my record and think you know me, but you don't. You don't know my obligations. You don't know what I have to do to survive." Tears mixed with regret in her eyes.

Beau knew all too well that time was unrefundable. As much as people, and he personally, would love to go back in time and take just one moment, one decision back, that wasn't possible. Maybe Zoey had reasons to protect her secrets just as much as he did. "Look, we're not here to judge you now or for what you've done before.

We're just here to investigate a homicide and get to the truth."

"The truth? The guy was a jerk. A blood-sucking leech. He had to handle his pregnant wife with kid gloves because her father has a vested interest in the company he works for. And he likes things rough, that he says his delicate wife can't take." She blinked away the tears. "After one hour with him, I understand what she means."

"How's that?" Marcel asked.

She jerked her attention to him, as if she'd been talking to herself and his question reminded her she had an audience.

"I understand what you mean generally, but specifically?" Marcel pushed on.

Zoey frowned and tightened her arms, hugging herself. "He liked to take charge, liked his way. I think he wanted me to be scared of him, of what he was doing. He ripped my dress right off of me, grabbed me by the arms. Tried to slap me. I told him that wouldn't fly with me and slapped him back. He seemed to try to decide if he liked that turn or not, but I was done. I grabbed my sweater and left him." She wiped her nose on the sleeve of her sweatshirt.

Beau wrote furiously. "He just let you leave?" Didn't sound like the Muller he'd been learning about.

"Well, he tried to block me from leaving.

202

Grabbed my hair and tried to yank me back. I punched him square in the gut."

Beau raised his brows at her.

"Yeah, I know. Not my smartest move. He raised his fist and I grabbed my can of mace from my purse. Told him if he came near me again, I'd kill him."

A threat—and less than an hour later Muller had been murdered.

Zoey sniffed. "Did he go out and hurt someone after I left?"

He glanced up to see her widened eyes full of regret. He shook his head. "No. About what time did you leave his room?" He already knew, but needed to make sure everything matched up.

"A little before eleven, because he complained I didn't give him the full hour—um, attention he wanted."

So, she had been paid. Beau swallowed the sigh. He could charge her with prostitution again: she *had* admitted to threatening to kill him.

"I passed his girlfriend from the bar in the hallway. She called me a name under her breath. I figured those two deserved each other. He didn't hurt her, did he? I didn't really want to cause a problem between them, but I needed some quick cash and he had seemed okay enough until we got into his room."

Beau stopped writing and stared at her, recalling what the elevator attendant had said about Muller slapping her and her giggling.

"Look, some guys are jerks like that because some women like that. Maybe his girlfriend was that way. She sure came across that way in the bar, the way she shoved him and all. Maybe that was just how it was between them." Zoey shifted her weight from one foot to the other. "Did he kill her?"

"No. He's the victim," Marcel said.

Her face went colorless just before a child's cry sounded from inside the house.

## DIMITRI

"Perfect. Perfect." Dimitri looked over the cupcakes he'd carefully crafted in green, purple, and gold, topped with handcrafted sugar masks and spun sugar for the feathers. The in-house krewe would be pleased with their dessert tonight.

He slid the last cupcake into the display and shut the refrigerator door before setting the perfect temperature to keep the treats cool enough for the sugar decorations to stay in place and well formed, but not too cold to dry out the cupcake itself. It was a delicate balance.

Like keeping Adelaide's secret.

On one hand, he'd earned her trust and would do his best not to betray it. Doing so would cause her to hate him, and he didn't know if he could live with himself if that happened. Yet he also knew withholding such important information from the police could cast a guilty light on her if they found out.

No, there was no *if.* Dimitri knew it was only a matter of time until the truth was uncovered. Detective Savoie was too good at his job not to uncover the truth.

That made Dimitri even more confused: why wouldn't Adelaide tell Detective Savoie, who, by Adelaide's own admission, was her friend? Why wouldn't she trust her friend with such information? Fear? Anger?

What did she have to fear from the man now that he was dead? She had every right to be angry at what happened to her, but it was so long ago. Surely the anger and fear had lessened over the years? Or maybe he just didn't understand. Unless she also wasn't being truthful with Dimitri.

Or maybe she didn't want to tell the detective because he was more than just a friend, despite her claims.

"Dimitri."

He spun around, startled not only because he hadn't heard her come into the kitchen, but also because he'd been thinking of her. Still, just her presence lifted his spirits. "Good evening, Adelaide."

She smiled. "Happy Twelfth Night."

"Same to you." If she only knew how lovely

she looked in her black slacks and off-shoulder purple blouse.

"I saw the set for the krewe tonight. You've outdone yourself."

He gave a lavish bow, then chuckled. "It was nice to concentrate on recipes and sugary concoctions."

She nodded as she grabbed a piece of celery from the cutting pile. "I know what you mean. I almost enjoyed working on the spreadsheets." She took a bite of the celery and chewed slowly. "Almost."

Dimitri hid his smile. He'd started leaving out little piles of her favorite finger foods when he realized she dropped by often, always wanting to grab a piece of celery or handful of almonds. "Just almost?"

"Well . . ." She laughed and popped a cherry tomato into her mouth.

"Have you heard anything new?"

He didn't have to specify to what he was referring. She swallowed. "Geoff's friend said that they aren't as actively pursuing information about our prints on the knife at the moment because of the alibis, as well as there was smudging over the prints."

"What does that mean?" Dimitri grabbed a bowl of ranch dressing from the fridge and slid it over to Adelaide.

"It means they think someone with gloves

handled the knife after our prints were on it." She dipped a tomato into the dressing.

This was great news! "The killer wore gloves."

She nodded and swallowed. "So Geoff's friend said that we're still suspects, but they are looking further than just us three."

Dimitri pulled a water bottle from the refrigerator and handed it to her. "That's good to hear." Although he didn't relish someone having access and the foresight to take a knife that had their prints on it and use it to kill someone in the hotel, but he wouldn't mention that to Adelaide. Not when she wore relief as casually as the purple blouse.

"It is. Geoff said they were concentrating on finding motives."

Dimitri's chest seized. If they found out about Adelaide's past with Kevin— "Do they have any other suspects?"

"According to Geoff's friend, right now Sidney Parsons is a suspect, as is a Zoey Naure. He did say, however, that the Natchitoches police were running down some possible leads on personal items they recovered from his home and office." She took a long drink of water. "My friend Tracey warned me that the police might be digging around in his past." Adelaide stared into the water bottle. "She's concerned that there will be something that will tie me to him from back then." Her voice was barely a whisper.

"It's my concern as well, *mon chaton*." They were running out of viable suspects, and while they might not be pushing the fingerprints on the knife at the moment, if they uncovered Adelaide's experience with the victim, they likely would come after her.

She shook her head. "I don't think there's anything that will connect me."

Dimitri ground his teeth. Why couldn't she see the dangerous game she played? "By not saying anything now—"

"Yes, I know. It will be worse for me if Beau finds out."

He nodded. "I'm guessing that's the same advice your friend Tracey has given you?"

"She has, but that doesn't make it the right advice. From either of you." She gripped the plastic bottle so tightly that it crinkled. "If it comes to that, I'll deal with it, but for now, I'm not in a position where I should say anything."

Dimitri did a small mock bow. "It is, of course, your call."

She gave a curt nod. "But there's something else I wanted to ask you."

"Yes?"

"Have you recently found a chicken with its head cut off in your bed?"

How did she know about that?

Adelaide's eyes grew wide. "Oh my goodness, you have! I can tell by the look on your face."

"How do you know that?"

"I thought Tracey was talking about someone else, but it was you."

"It was actually in my father's bed. We just found it this morning."

"Tracey said someone was asking in the Quarter, in her circle of people, about spells and stuff with boa constrictors and headless chickens in beds."

"What did she say?"

"Nothing, really. Just that someone had been asking around."

Maybe it was Elise, but it could be the person responsible. "Could you ask Tracey to keep listening and let you know if she hears anything?"

"I will." She reached out and took his hand. "I'm starting to get worried for you, Dimitri. First a snake, then our prints on the murder weapon, and now a dead chicken in your dad's bed. I don't know what it all means, but I don't think it's something good."

"Me either." He'd call Elise as soon as he could.

# EIGHTEEN

## ADELAIDE

"Good, I'm glad you weren't in your office." Tracey burst into Adelaide's suite at the Darkwater.

"I'm glad I gave you the code to get into my suite for emergencies." Adelaide laid the suit jacket she was about to slip on over the back of the chair.

"Sorry, but I—" She took in Adelaide's dress and let out a low whistle. "Wow, where are you going all dressed up?"

"It's Twelfth Night and we have a Mardi Gras krewe in-house. Considering what's been going on around here, I thought it might be appropriate for me to drop into their gala tonight. Just to make sure everything's going well and there are no issues."

And maybe she could relax, just a little. That would be really nice for a change.

"Oh. Right."

Adelaide grinned and shook her head. Her best friend was so easily distracted. It was one of her most endearing features, just not tonight. "I would think you'd be busy at work yourself on such a festive night."

"I have tours back-to-back, but I needed to tell you what I found out." She slumped onto the couch.

Adelaide sat on the edge of the chair opposite the couch. "Okay, tell me."

"When I started asking around, imagine my surprise to find there was someone else asking around about snakes and *gris-gris* and dead chickens."

"Really?"

Tracey nodded. "Yes. Turns out, she's the niece of the Pampalons' housekeeper."

"What'd she say?"

Tracey kicked off her heels and curled her feet under her. "Her name is Elise, and after much discussion where she could no longer avoid my powers of persuasion, she finally admitted that she'd told Dimitri she'd look into what he'd been finding."

"There was more than the snake and chicken?"

Tracey nodded. "Apparently there was also a *gris-gris* with ashes and rat bones."

Adelaide crinkled her nose. "Oh, gross." Her stomach tightened. He hadn't mentioned that to her. "What does that mean?"

"That's what Elise was trying to find out. She had one of the older women look up the ingredients in the *gris-gris* and track it."

"Could they tell?"

"It's a binding hex. To bind Dimitri to whomever was casting it."

Adelaide's chest constricted. "I'm not sure what that means."

"There are different types of binding. Some are for whatever one person in the spell feels, the other will as well. Another one makes the separation of the people in the binding not able to be too far apart or they'll get ill. But this one in particular, the one on Dimitri, looks to be a hex where he will be inclined to side with the person who cast it."

"And that involves a snake and dead chicken?"

"Oh, no. Well, the snake maybe, since it was alive. The *gris-gris* sachet was with the snake, the items in the amulet drawing strength from the snake's power."

Adelaide shook her head. This was getting crazier and crazier sounding. Maybe Dimitri was right to just give none of this any weight.

Tracey continued to explain. "But the chicken with its head cut off and left to bleed out, that's an outright hex for harm to whomever it was left for."

Adelaide stared at her best friend. "Someone wants harm to come to Dimitri?" Her chest tightened even more, as if it was in a vise grip.

Tracey shook her head. "The chicken was left

in Dimitri's father's bed. The harming hex is for him."

That was more than a little understandable. Claude Pampalon was rude, arrogant, and could be downright mean.

Adelaide's mind raced. It was so much to take in. "So, this Elise, her aunt is the Pampalons' housekeeper?"

Tracey nodded. "She's really nice."

"She's not the one casting these things, right?"

"Right. She helped Dimitri get rid of the chicken and put things to right so his dad would never know. Now she's been poking around, trying to find out what's going on. She found out about the binding hex on Dimitri."

"Why would she help Dimitri like that?" If his dad wouldn't like it . . . Claude Pampalon was a powerful man and didn't tolerate less than 100 percent loyalty from his employees.

Tracey smiled. "Sweetheart, that girl has a crush on Dimitri like you wouldn't believe. Just saying his name made her pupils dilate."

A twinge of something Adelaide didn't quite recognize tightened her gut. She rubbed her temples. "I don't understand why someone wouldn't just come to Dimitri and talk to him instead of doing some type of voodoo or whatever." She couldn't believe she was having this ongoing conversation about voodoo, hexes, and such.

"I don't know, but Elise seems to think she's uncovered the woman responsible for all the hexing and binding to do with Dimitri and his father."

"Who?"

"A woman named Lissette Bastien. Do you know her?"

Adelaide thought carefully but had never heard the name. She slowly shook her head. "Who is she?"

"I don't know." Tracey uncurled her feet and put her shoes back on, then stood. "I didn't have time to look into her or anything. I just wanted to come by and tell you before I headed out to work."

"I appreciate it." Adelaide walked Tracey to the door. "I'll see what I can find out."

Tracey gave her a quick hug, then held her by the shoulders and stared into her eyes. "You take caution now, do you hear me? I love you, and I want you to be careful."

"You too, Trace. You're the one out there in the cemetery during the crazy season." She glanced at Tracey's red heels. "In spikes, none the less."

Tracey laughed, full and throaty. "Of course, my sweet. I have to look the part during festival season, you know."

"True. Speaking of, did they ever find the kids who were vandalizing?"

Tracey sobered. "Not yet. We're hoping the

private security will detract them from doing any more damage."

"I hope so too."

Tracey gave her another hug. "I'm not kidding about being careful, Ads. There are a lot of crazies out there, and now that voodoo is in the mix with Dimitri, just be alert, okay?"

"I will. Promise. And you too."

"Promise." Tracey blew her an air kiss, then left.

Adelaide checked the time: 6:05. Dinner wouldn't be served for the krewe until 6:30, so she had a little time. She sat down in front of her laptop and opened the browser. She typed in *Lissette Bastien* in the search bar and hit enter.

Only two returns. One was an older woman living in France. Adelaide felt pretty certain that wasn't the one casting any hexes in New Orleans.

The only other match brought up a photo of a lovely young woman. Twenty-two years old. Adelaide brought up the image associated with the name. Beautiful girl with long, straight dark hair. But it was her eyes that truly stunned. So light blue they were almost reflective. They reminded Adelaide of someone else's eyes, but for the life of her, she couldn't think of whom at the moment.

No employment listed, but her last known address was on Saint Roch Avenue.

One of the seedier neighborhoods of New Orleans.

# BEAU

"What did we get from the Natchitoches police?" Beau leaned back in his chair and stared across the back-to-back desks at his partner.

Marcel opened the satchel in front of him and pulled out a folder. "Grieving wife claims no one had any beef against him. According to the officer notes, she was unaware of any infidelity."

Beau rolled his eyes. Why was the spouse always the last one to know?

Turning the page in the file, Marcel continued. "Coworkers were aware of his affair with Parsons, but she wasn't the first. Apparently there'd been a few others, some that didn't end so well."

"Do tell." Beau pulled out his own notebook.

"Two filed sexual harassment claims to the company. They were settled in-house and the ladies were promoted, but to other office locations."

"Real dirtbag."

Marcel nodded. "Yeah. But his sales stats were high, so the company kept him."

"Ode to the almighty dollar, of course."

"Right." Marcel flipped the page. "According to his employee file, he had a few disciplinary actions, but no specific details are listed."

"Of course not. The company wouldn't want a

record that they were aware of his sexual predator ways but didn't fire him because he made them too much money."

"Probably." Marcel flipped through more pages. "His income doesn't support the lifestyle he and his wife were living. Mortgage over fifteen hundred a month, a car note ranging in the seven hundred range, lots of revolving credit accounts."

"Criminal activity to bring in extra cash?"

Marcel shook his head. "Remember Zoey told us that Muller said he had to handle his wife with kid gloves?"

Beau flipped back in his notebook to the section of their interview with Zoey. "Muller told her that his wife's father had a vested interest in the pharmaceutical company where he worked." Beau looked at his partner. "I'm guessing that's the truth?"

"Yep. According to these notes, Muller's father-in-law is one of the company's board members."

Beau shook his head. "Why on earth would her father put up with such behavior? As a board member, he'd know about such things. How could he let his daughter stay married to such a total jerk?"

Marcel leaned back in his chair. "We see it all the time, man. The wife doesn't believe her husband is capable of such actions. If her father told her, she could very well have defended

Muller to her father. The poor man would be between a rock and a hard place."

"If it were my daughter, he'd be in more of a hard place than not."

Marcel snapped his fingers and pointed at Beau. "Hey, it's possible her dad wanted him dead, for the way Muller treated his daughter."

"That could be something." Beau couldn't help but feel a surge in his gut. They were on the right track, he could feel it.

Marcel lifted the phone. "Let me call our contact in Natchitoches PD and see if he can discreetly check if her father was in town and accounted for on Thursday night."

While his partner made the call, Beau stood and stretched over the desks. He grabbed the satchel Natchitoches officers had sent over. Inside was a laptop and what looked like a leather book, about five by seven. A traveler's notebook. He opened the book and sat down.

It was filled with handwritten notes, clippings and memorabilia. Flipping through it, Beau felt a sense of getting to know Kevin Muller on a very personal level. Bar receipts shoved in the pockets haphazardly. Phone numbers.

Lots and lots of phone numbers with numbers beside them. Numbers ranging between two and nine. Woman rating?

Some clippings from newspapers that dated back well before he got married were tucked into the plastic zippered pouches. All of debutantes and young women who had very prestigious and important fathers.

"Our contact will check it out and get back to us today if at all possible." Marcel stood, then looked over Beau's shoulder.

"Good." Beau turned the page.

"What's this?" Marcel asked.

"A peek into the mind of Kevin Muller. This guy was as scummy as Zoey said, as calculating as Sidney said, and just as much of a sexual raider as the women who filed their sexual harassment suits." Beau shook his head and kept flipping the pages.

"Wow, this guy was a real piece of work." Marcel lifted the folder from his desk. "Natchitoches reports this was in Muller's personal effects in his locker at his office. They bagged up everything and sent it over. I'm guessing they didn't even look through that."

"I bet not, and I'd say this was probably locked up where only Muller had access until his death. Not something he'd want his wife to see." Beau turned the page. More numbers. He paused as he read a scribbled part of a poem, the writing nearly indecipherable as if written in the dark:

*Storms of life ravage*
*years pass*

*She grows older*
*learning*
*But still close to the nest*
*Lest she fall.*
*The taste of the future sits*
*on the tip of her tongue—*
*sweet, yet tangy*
*inviting, yet scary.*
*She takes a cautious step*
*into unknown territory*
*a place where her certainty is unsure*
*her confidence*
*not proven.*

Beau's thoughts on the almost-familiar prose were interrupted by his partner. "I've left a message for Nolan to run a search on Muller's laptop tomorrow. He'll be in early on Monday."

Beau turned to another page, then stopped. It wasn't the norm for the rest of the book. This clipping wasn't in a pocket or a pouch, but shoved between the pages. It was more than just a clipping—it was an obituary. An obituary of a very beautiful, very young black woman with a smile so mysterious that Beau's knee-jerk reaction was to gasp.

Marcel moved to look over his shoulder again. He let out a low, soft whistle. "Wow, she's beautiful."

Beau could only nod. Even in a photograph,

she was mesmerizing. He glanced at her name: Jada Aubois.

"Maybe she's one who broke his heart." Marcel moved closer to read the fine print. "Says she died suddenly and unexpectedly. She was only eighteen." He turned and sat on the edge of Beau's desk.

Beau continued to read. "Jada was a freshman at Northwestern State University in Natchitoches, majoring in computer programming and technology."

"What a waste. Beautiful and smart."

"She is survived by her mother, Esther Aubois and her brother, Geoff, both of New Orleans." Beau could only stare at that sentence.

"Geoff Aubois?" Marcel stood, almost bouncing.

Beau could only nod. "The chief of security at the Darkwater Inn."

# NINETEEN

## DIMITRI

The St. Louis Cathedral's bells rang out with an eerie echo in the fog over the Mississippi River. Sunday's sunrise tickled the January clouds pink, a promise the fog would dissipate soon. The French Quarter still slept as the churches spilled the parishioners from early mass out into the downtown area.

Dimitri rushed to Decatur Street, hoping Elise had waited for him. The famous Café Du Monde wouldn't be too crowded with locals on a Sunday morning, but tourists packed the place. Naturally, many were in town for Twelfth Night, and many more would come to celebrate the festival season leading up to Mardi Gras.

"Dimitri!" Elise called out, sitting at one of the tables under the green awning, closest to the black wrought iron fence.

He made his way through the crowd and joined her. "I'm sorry to be late. Mass ran a little later than I expected."

She smiled. "It's okay, but there's only one beignet left for you. I ordered you an au lait, but it might be a little cool." She pushed the cup and saucer toward him.

The Acadians from Nova Scotia had brought both the fried sweet dough concoction as well as the roasted chicory, which lent an almost chocolate flavor to the bitterness of strong coffee. Most people preferred the coffee to be prepared Au Lait—the coffee mixed half and half with steamed milk.

"Thank you." He reached for the last beignet. The fried dough was still warm enough, and he washed it down with a sip of coffee. He wiped the ample powdered sugar from his fingers.

"How was church?" Elise might only be nineteen, but her eyes told of a knowing beyond her years.

"Nice. You should come with me sometime." He took another bite.

Elise's smile widened. "I think I'd like that. I really would." She ducked her head to take a sip of coffee. "I go with Auntie sometimes. Not as often as she'd like, but enough to keep her complaints to a minimum."

"Tilda's a good woman." Dimitri took a sip of the quickly cooling coffee.

"She is." Elise waved the waiter over. "Another coffee au lait for me, please."

"Me as well," Dimitri nodded.

"Another order of beignets?" the waiter asked.

Dimitri shook his head. "Just the coffees, please."

The waiter disappeared into the line with the other waiters and waitresses.

"So—you have information?" Dimitri finished the last of the beignet and washed it down with the coffee.

Elise set down her white ceramic mug, keeping her fingertips on the rim. "I've made several inquiries regarding your reptile and fowl problem."

"And?"

"There's a girl who has cast a spell to cause your father problems. Physical pain, discomfort, and the like."

His father could be overbearing and cruel at times, but to a girl? "Why?"

Elise shook her head. "The spell isn't tightly cast."

"What does that mean?"

"No specific or significant harm was tied into the spell. The best I can figure out is that she wanted to cause him trouble, but not really hurt him."

"That doesn't make much sense." As if Dimitri believed in any of it, but he couldn't ignore what Adelaide had pointed out. "Why even bother?"

Elise waited to answer until the waiter set down their coffees and rushed to the next table. "For some reason, she wants to cause him discomfort, but not real harm. My best guess is she wants to knock him off balance. Get him off his game, so to speak."

Dimitri shook his head. "I just don't understand."

"Now, in regard to the snake and the *gris-gris* . . . that was definitely intended for you. It's a binding hex."

"A what?" He wasn't even sure he wanted to know. Despite having been raised in New Orleans and hearing all the whispers about voodoo and everything else, Dimitri had never had it so close to his personal life.

"Don't freak out, Mr. Pampalon—"

"I told you, call me Dimitri."

Elise took a sip of coffee before answering. "The binding hex means you absolutely no harm. It looks like its intent is the opposite. From what I can tell, it's actually to give you the inclination to agree with the girl who cast the spell."

"Agree with her?"

Elise nodded. "That's what the ingredients tell me."

Dimitri had heard enough. "Who is this girl?"

"Her name is Lissette Bastien. Do you know her?"

He shook his head. "I don't think I've ever heard her name before, but I'm pretty bad with names." He lifted his mug.

225

Elise took out her phone, tapped the screen, then turned it to him. "Here's her photo."

Dimitri froze, cup midair, as he stared at her.

"You recognize her?" Elise asked.

Dimitri shook his head, unable to process what he saw.

"Then what?"

He set down the mug. "I recognize her eyes. They're my father's."


## ADELAIDE

She still had an hour before the lasagna would be ready to come out of the oven. Adelaide relished the thought of a long, hot shower. She'd been up early to assemble the lasagna, then had to finish two reports in the office. Now she could look forward to the day with her dad, taking down the Christmas decorations.

"Addy!"

She turned to see Beau and his partner making their way across the hotel lobby. A sigh escaped before she planted on a smile. The shower would have to wait. "What are you two doing here so early on a Sunday morning?"

"We're homicide, ma'am. We never sleep." Beau's partner's attempt at a joke wasn't impressive. Or maybe she was just really tired.

"Are you here to see me?" She had grown more than weary of police, murder, and investigations. Almost as much as voodoo, snakes, and chickens.

"No. We're actually here to meet Geoff. He said he was on duty this morning?" Detective Taton replied.

She smiled. "Yes. He's been working longer hours since . . . well, he'll be here." But why did they want to talk to him? If it was about something going on in the hotel, she should be made aware. "Did he say where he would meet you?"

Beau shook his head. "He didn't, now that I think about it."

"Come on, let me take you to his office." She led the way down the business hall, past her closed office, past the employee room where the delectable aroma of freshly made coffee seeped out into the hallway, to Geoff's office. She knocked softly on his door before pushing it open. "Geoff? Detectives Savoie and Taton are here."

Geoff stood from behind the desk. "Y'all come on in and have a seat."

Adelaide entered first and waved for Beau and Marcel to sit in the chairs.

Geoff motioned her to take his seat as he sat on the edge of his desk. "I'm assuming this is about the investigation, detectives?"

"It is," Beau answered. "But it has nothing to do with the hotel." He stared at Geoff for a long moment, then glanced at Adelaide, before looking back to Geoff.

"Oh." She jumped to her feet. This had to be a personal interview. But what about?

"Sit." Geoff placed his hand on her shoulder and gently eased her back into his chair before looking at Beau. "Whatever questions you have for me regarding the case, you can ask in front of Ms. Fountaine."

Beau and Marcel exchanged looks.

She began to feel more than uncomfortable. Clearly Beau didn't want to talk to Geoff in front of her. Technically, she was Geoff's boss, and if they needed to ask him something personal that he might not want his boss to know— "I'll just go so you can talk." She started to stand, but Geoff put his hand back on her shoulder.

"Stay. I insist." He looked at the detectives and crossed his arms over his chest. "Your questions, detectives?"

Beau paused, but Marcel had no problem diving in. "Can you think of any reason why Kevin Muller would have kept your sister's obituary in his personal journal?"

Adelaide swallowed the gasp and relaxed back in Geoff's chair.

Geoff's Adam's apple bobbed up and down. "I couldn't tell you why the man kept what he did."

"Your sister was a freshman at Northwestern

State University when she died, correct?" Marcel asked.

Geoff nodded.

"Do you know if she knew Kevin Muller?" Beau asked. "Maybe they were friends?"

"I couldn't say for sure, Detective. That's a nice-sized campus. I have no idea who she might have met there."

Adelaide had never heard that tone from Geoff. Still, she could understand how he might feel, having to relive such a painful part of his past. It'd be only natural for him to be snappish. She could relate. There were certainly parts of her past she didn't want to discuss.

"Did Kevin Muller attend your sister's funeral?" Marcel asked.

Geoff shot the younger detective a glare that could melt metal. "He did not." The roughness to his voice made Adelaide shift in the seat.

"If you don't mind my saying, your sister was very beautiful," Beau said.

"Thank you. She was." Geoff's voice hitched. "She was beautiful and funny and independent and a remarkable young woman with her whole life before her."

"I'm so sorry. May I ask what happened?" The gentleness and concern in Beau's voice drew a smile from Adelaide.

"She committed suicide." Geoff's voice was flatter than a soda left open overnight.

Adelaide reached out and took his hand.

He squeezed it back. "She had everything to live for, was so full of life and love. She was the best of us. The hope for the future."

"I'm very sorry," Beau said.

"Thank you. It was difficult. Her death undid us all, her family and friends." Geoff shook his head and he looked at the wall. "Mom mourned herself to death, dying of a heart attack just two years after Jada was gone. She couldn't bear to go on without her baby."

Adelaide's eyes filled with tears and she tightened her grip on Geoff's hand, hoping to ease his pain just a little.

"I know this is hard, but do you have any idea why your sister . . ." Marcel's question hung in the air.

"Why she took a whole bottle of sleeping pills?" Geoff shook his head. "She didn't leave a suicide note."

"Some kids just can't cope once they get out of their home and into college," Marcel said. "It's a shock to their system."

Geoff didn't reply, just stared at the wall.

"Were the sleeping pills prescription or over the counter?" Beau asked.

Adelaide nodded at her friend. That was a good question. Kevin Muller was a pharmaceutical salesman. If he gave the prescription sleeping pills to Jada that she used to commit suicide, that'd be a reason he'd keep the obituary.

Not that Adelaide believed for a moment the man possible of feelings of guilt. But if he'd been trying to cover himself . . .

"They were over the counter." Geoff destroyed that theory. "The autopsy found no other drugs in her system at the time of her death."

"So you can think of no reason Kevin Muller would have kept your sister's obituary after all these years?" Beau asked.

"I couldn't say, Detective."

Beau closed his notebook and slipped it into his jacket pocket.

"Don't you think it somewhat coincidental that a man who kept your sister's obituary from some six years ago is murdered in the hotel where you work?" Marcel asked.

"I couldn't say, Detective, being as I just learned he had the obituary. However, since I didn't know the man, I can't tell you why he had the obituary. He didn't come to Jada's funeral, nor to the house after. He sent no flowers or card that I'm aware of, so I can't speculate what the man's motivations were." Geoff eased his hand from Adelaide's and stood. "If there's nothing else, I have some things to attend to."

Both Beau and Marcel were on their feet.

"Of course." Beau reached out and shook Geoff's hand. "Again, I'm sorry for your loss."

"Thank you."

Adelaide stood, touched Geoff's arm, then moved around the desk. "Go ahead and do what you need to do, Geoff. I'll see the detectives out."

As soon as they had cleared the hallway, she confronted Beau. "That was a little pushy, don't you think?"

"It's our job, Addy." Beau's eyes pleaded with her to drop the matter.

She couldn't. "It's your job now to be insensitive to someone who obviously is still emotionally raw over the loss of his sister?"

"Ms. Fountaine, this is a homicide investigation." Marcel drew up to his full height, as if that would intimidate her.

It didn't. "Marcel, I know you're trying to do your job, but there's such a thing as tact and sensitivity. You'd do well to mature a little and learn both because they're sorely missing in your repertoire."

She turned back to Beau. "I know you have a job to do, but the manner in which you do it is entirely up to you. You should choose wisely." Adelaide waved toward the front doors of the hotel. "I think you both know the way out from here."

"Addy—"

She held up a hand. "Just go on, Beau. I'll pass along your regrets for not joining us to Dad."

Not wanting further discussion, she turned and headed to the elevators.

It might be best for her to have that hot shower right now.

# TWENTY

## DIMITRI

*This* was where Lissette Bastien lived?

Dimitri knew Saint Roch Avenue wasn't exactly the nicest neighborhood in New Orleans, but he hadn't expected it to be this bad.

Saint Roch's Shrine and Cemetery gave the neighborhood its name. The history was quite interesting, at least to Dimitri. Back in 1867, a yellow fever epidemic broke out. A German priest, Peter Leonard Thevis, came to New Orleans and turned to the patron of good health, Saint Roch.

History went that the good priest promised that if no one in the parish died from the epidemic, he would build a chapel in honor of Saint Roch. Interestingly enough, not one person from the Holy Trinity parish died from the fever in either the epidemic of 1867 or the one of 1878.

Today, however, the neighborhood wasn't what it once was. Streets were littered with shotgun style homes set close together, and the St. Roch Tavern stood close enough to the houses to be a problem.

Especially this particular house.

Dimitri got from behind the wheel and made his way to the house. The faint blue color of the porch, said to ward off evil spirits, had faded with years exposed to the Louisiana sun and neglect. The bowed front steps creaked under his weight. Various clumps of dried branches and herbs hung from the porch's ceiling. Two skulls rested at the base on either side of the front door. A line of crushed white powder that looked an awful lot like salt connected the two skulls.

Dimitri shook his head and lifted his hand to knock.

The door opened with a creak, but only a sliver. Just enough to make out the shadow of a slim girl with long hair wearing a T-shirt with jeans and only socks on her feet.

That was enough for him to recognize the girl that had been in the picture by the one eye he could see. "Lissette Bastien?"

She opened the door wide. "Dimitri Pampalon."

He stared at her for several moments before blinking. "I'm sorry, I don't mean to stare. It's just your—"

"My eyes. I know." She smiled. "Why don't you come in?"

He returned the smile and stepped across the threshold into a living room. Dimitri wasn't sure what he'd expected, but it wasn't the normal and boring sight before him. Two couches with an end table sat in front of a small coffee table. A TV on a stand in the corner. One wall had an abstract painting hanging over a couch, the other housed a hallway.

"Have a seat. Would you like something to drink? I have hot coffee." Lissette shut the front door and motioned Dimitri toward the couches.

"No, I'm fine." This was all surreal to him. The girl who had been said to be casting curses at him and his father stood before him, as ordinary as any other girl, sans her remarkable eyes.

She plopped down on the adjacent couch and smiled at him. "You're wondering about my eyes."

"They're very unusual. I've only seen one other person have such a color."

"Your father." She reached for her cup on the end table and took a drink.

"Yes."

"Claude Pampalon. Your father." She set the mug on the coffee table and pulled her legs up to her chest. "And mine."

"Yours?" This poor girl must be confused, but her eyes . . .

Yet she grinned even wider. "Ah, I see you've been left totally in the dark. Don't worry, you aren't alone."

Maybe he was the one confused. "I don't understand."

"Just hear me out, okay? I'll tell you as much

as I know, which is more than what I was told."

Dimitri relaxed against the couch and nodded. Surely there was a logical explanation. Like one a DNA test would go a long way in providing.

"My mother, Odette, used to work at your hotel. She worked in the housekeeping department back when they were called maids." She took another drink from her cup. "This was way back. From what Mom told me, she remembers Claude bringing you to the hotel after school. She said you'd sit in Claude's office and do your homework."

Dimitri nodded slowly as the memories crept across his mind. He did remember a woman he called Ette who worked at the hotel. He remembered his father planting him in his office, demanding he complete his homework perfectly before time for supper. If he failed to meet this demand, the consequences could be as harsh as a thrashing or as light as being sent home and to bed without supper.

"Mom said you were a darling and Claude doted on you." Her words brought Dimitri back to the present.

"I'm sure it looked to people on the outside that my father was doting. He wasn't. He was demanding and harsh. Cruel, even."

Lissette opened her mouth, hesitated, then shut it for a moment before speaking. "I'm sorry he treated you like that. At least he acknowledges you."

"About that—"

She nodded. "Let me continue. Mom thought Claude was everything she ever wanted. When he showed her attention, she couldn't resist."

"He and your mother had an affair?" Dimitri had suspected his father of such many times over after his mother left them, but never had any proof. Technically, his parents had never divorced, as far as he knew.

"They did. For roughly ten years, until I was five years old." She held her bottom lip between her teeth. "That would've been right when you started high school or thereabouts."

A lifetime ago.

She curled her legs under her on the couch, her long hair covering her shoulders like a shroud. "I have bits of memories of Claude visiting when I was child. Partial memories of him at Christmas. Having Thanksgiving dinner so late it was almost my bedtime."

"Father came here?" He couldn't keep the surprise out of his voice.

"No, he didn't. He wouldn't dare come here. Even back then when the neighborhood wasn't as bad as it is today, it wasn't good enough for Claude Pampalon." She let out a dry laugh. "Oh, my mother was good enough to sleep with and have a bastard child with, but not visit her house.

Oh, no. He would put us up in a suite in the Darkwater Inn."

"I didn't mean to disrespect your mother or your home." Dimitri had a hard enough time wrapping his mind around the fact that his father had sired another child. "You said the affair ended when you were five?"

She nodded. "Their relationship ended, and my mother never got over it. Never got over *him*." There was such venom in her pronunciation. "Mother didn't have many skills, so she ended up doing laundry and keeping house for some of the families in the Garden District. Claude, despite being my father, didn't feel a responsibility to help me and my mother out financially."

"Are you sure?"

She snorted. "Of course I'm sure. When I turned sixteen, I had to enforce my mother's power of attorney as her early-onset dementia robbed her of her common sense. Too bad it didn't rob her of her memories of your father."

Dimitri could only stare at Lissette.

"You see, that's where her mind was stuck— back when she was in love with Claude. When I was a baby." She shook her head, her hair partially covering her face. "She would tell me that Claude was coming over to visit her and Lissy— that's what she called me when I was a baby. She would talk about what she'd cook for him. How they'd eat together. How he would hold me

239

with such gentleness that her heart would almost explode." Lissette let out a half snort, half groan. "All the times they had together. It was enough to make me sick."

"I'm so sorry."

"In her lucid moments, she'd recognize me as her daughter. During those times I'd beg her to let me contact him and ask him for help. At least to help out with some of her medical expenses." She shook her head as her eyes glistened with tears. "But, no. She wouldn't allow it. Made me promise not to approach Claude as long as she lived."

She wiped away the tears with the bottom of her T-shirt. "Unlike Claude, who filled my mother with such dreams, then ripped them away from her, I kept my promise. I've yet to contact our father, but that's about to change. My birth certificate lists my father's name as *refused to state,* but I know the truth and I'll prove it. I know tests will prove he's my biological father, even if he didn't do a single thing for me."

"I can understand how you feel." He caught the disbelief in her face. "I can't relate to it, but I can understand feeling unwanted and abandoned." He stretched his legs out in front of him, sliding them under the coffee table. "I'm sorry for the childhood you had, but if you think having Claude Pampalon in your life would've made

240

it better, I beg to disagree. The man has never shown me one ounce of affection. Not a single *Good job, son,* even when I made dean's list at school. He ran my mother off when I was a child, leaving me reliant on him. I hated my mother at times because of him. At least you had your mother."

"That's true. I never thought about how it was for you. I grew up seeing you in photos with Claude and assumed you had a loving, doting father."

"That's a joke."

"Hey, at least he supported you." She offered him a smile.

"Supported me? That man has done almost everything in his power to destroy me. He's done his level best to cut out any self-esteem I might have by belittling and ridiculing me. I have no friends because of his rudeness and arrogance and abuse of power."

He shook his head as random memories flooded his mind. "And don't even dare let me think of having a girlfriend. He could run those potentials off with merely a glare and well-placed putdown. He might have provided for me financially, but trust me, I've earned every penny that man ever put out for me. In spades."

"I guess I had you all wrong." She took another drink. "Looks like Claude Pampalon messed up both of our childhoods."

He nodded. "Not just childhood. He's still pulling the puppet strings on me."

She sat upright, slamming her socked feet to the floor. "Let's not let him get away with it any longer, big brother."

Dimitri started to reply then remembered the snake and chicken. "Before we get all sappy over our relationship, why don't you tell me why you've been targeting me with voodoo or whatever? Then we can talk about DNA testing."

## ADELAIDE

"I can't believe Beau backed out of coming." Vincent Fountaine stared at Adelaide as he wound garland around the holder. "That isn't like him."

She weighed how to reply. "He *is* working a homicide, Dad." She shoved the Christmas wreath into its octagon-shaped bin.

"How's it coming along?"

"He can't discuss that with me." She gave her father a scrunch-face. "You should know that if you do enough research for your books."

"Ha. As if I don't."

"How's the latest one coming?"

"Turn it in next month. I'm letting it stew for a bit, then I'll do a final read-through before sending it off." He added the tinsel to the big plastic container, then reached for the tree's twinkling all-white lights. "Back to the case, what do *you* know about it?"

"They've cleared the room, so we were able to get a crime scene cleanup company to come in. They'll be finished by tomorrow afternoon." Hopefully before Mr. Pampalon returned. At least that would be something she'd done that wouldn't make him angry. "They didn't find anything to do with the murder in any of the passageways." Something else she wouldn't have to answer to her boss about.

"Those passages and tunnels are so intriguing. You should show them to me sometime. I could probably work them into a book."

She smiled as she finished putting away their stockings. "I'll see about doing that once everything calms down." If she still had a job.

"Addybear, are you okay?"

The old nickname warmed her heart. She moved into her father's embrace. "It's just been a rough couple of days, Daddy. I'm tired."

"That's it? There's nothing else?" Vincent held her chin in his hand and stared into her eyes. "I worry about you."

"I know, but I'm okay. Just tired, like I said. And not looking forward to Mr. Pampalon's return if this case isn't wrapped up by then."

Her father released her. "That man's an arrogant cuss. Always has been."

Funny that she'd never really heard her father

talk about Mr. Pampalon. "Do you know him personally?"

He shrugged, then closed the containers. "He wanted me to have a book signing at the hotel once he found out who I was." He shook his head. "Didn't want to take my no as an answer. He just couldn't understand why I didn't want people to know the town where I lived."

"Not everybody knows about the stalker, Daddy."

"Well, it's enough that I said no. I love what I do, but if it ever put you in danger again, I'd quit writing in a heartbeat."

She stacked the bins on top of one another and shoved them into the corner to be carried up into the attic before she left.

She wrapped her arm around her dad's waist and led him into the kitchen. "I was never in any danger, Daddy. You were. You were the one he wanted to kill because you'd offed his favorite character."

"He was mentally unstable. There are a lot of those types out there, Addy. It's a father's job to protect his daughter."

She let her arm fall. Despite all the advice everyone seemed determined she know, Adelaide knew this was why she hadn't told her father what happened to her and never could. His perceived guilt would eat him alive, and she couldn't—wouldn't—allow that to happen to him.

"Well, he didn't get near me and he's in an institution now." She turned on the kitchen faucet. "Let's eat. I'm starving."

"Me too. That lasagna smells wonderful, sweetheart."

She wore a smile, but her stomach and heart flipped places. If he ever found out, it would kill him.

That would kill her.

# TWENTY-ONE

## BEAU

Monday morning dawned cooler and brought a mist over the city, the gloominess casting a pallor over the beginning of the workweek.

"Detective Savoie, Allison Williams with channel 6—care to comment on the fingerprints found on the murder weapon?"

There had to be a leak in the department somewhere. He'd mention it to the captain, but for now, he gave out his standard "No comment."

"But Detective—"

Beau tuned out the reporter, trudged into the station, and headed to his desk. He peeled off his jacket and hung it over the back of his chair.

Marcel came from the break room and set a cup of coffee on Beau's desk before he took a seat at his desk with his own cup. "Morning. Made a fresh pot, so at least our first cups won't taste like burnt sludge."

"Thanks. I was bombarded by a reporter outside, asking about the fingerprints."

"Yeah, me too. I told the captain, who wasn't too happy."

"Well, neither am I. We need to seal the leak." Beau sat down and took a sip from the mug. Marcel could make a mean cup of java. "You know, I spent a good part of yesterday thinking about the case and Geoff's little sister."

"Oh? What'd you come up with?"

"I'm not convinced big brothers know intimate details of their little sisters' lives, despite what they like to think. Like who she might have been involved with but didn't want her family to know about." Beau remembered several times that Addy had met up with a guy she knew Vincent wouldn't approve of, so she didn't invite him to pick her up at the house.

"I can understand that. My sisters are older, but we usually don't discuss private details about our lives. Especially if there is romance or sex involved."

Beau nodded. "Exactly."

"What do you want to do?" Marcel took a sip of his coffee.

"I think maybe I should call the college. Ask around and see if there was any connection between Jada Aubois and Kevin Muller."

"From so many years ago?" Marcel shook his head. "I think it's a long shot, man."

"We've got nothing else at the moment. Do you have any other suggestions?"

"Call campus security and ask if there are any records on either of them. That might be a start."

Just when he thought his younger partner had blown off his idea, Marcel came up with a good jumping-in point. Beau opened a search on his computer for the phone number of the security department.

Marcel opened a folder on his desk. "Nolan came by earlier with some interesting results."

"Really? What?" Just one break, that's all they needed.

"He finished his inspection on Muller's laptop. Not much to help us. A lot of porn on there. Nolan underlined the words *lot* and *porn*." Marcel chuckled. "Guess that's Nolanese for the man was a deviant. He made special note that there was a good bit of porn relating to bondage and nonconsensual intimacies." Marcel looked at Beau. "Those are his phrases, not mine."

"What a prince," Beau mumbled, as his computer loaded the number for the university police on the Northwestern campus.

"Yep, the guy was pure scum." Marcel nodded. "I also heard back from our contact in Natchitoches. Muller's father-in-law was in Natchitoches the evening of the murder. Seems there was a holiday party, and he was there at least from ten until midnight, according to a multitude of witnesses."

"And another possible suspect bites the dust." Just one break, that's all they really needed. A point in the right direction would be nice.

Marcel continued. "Nolan also got other test results back. The DNA found on the linens in the hotel room came back positive for sperm from Kevin Muller."

Dejection weighted down Beau's shoulders. "From his encounter with Zoey Naure, I'm sure."

"There was female DNA, and it did come back belonging to Zoey Naure."

"That's not interesting." Beau took a drink of the coffee that bit as much as the disappointment.

"No, it isn't. But what *is* interesting is that the DNA of Muller was contaminated with DNA of another male."

"What?"

"Yeah. Nolan said the DNA of Muller could conclusively be determined because we have Muller's body. But there's a side note that the initial run of the semen brought back a result of belonging to a Brayden Colton."

"How does that happen?" Beau had never heard of such.

"I don't know and Nolan's trying to figure it out. He says he ran it multiple times and got the same result. The only thing he can surmise is that Kevin Muller's DNA somehow was marked in the system as belonging to a Brayden Colton almost a decade ago."

"Who is Brayden Colton?"

Marcel snapped his fingers and pointed at

Beau. "I'm about to check that out while you call the college."

Beau grinned as he dialed the number. He gave his name and rank to the person who answered, then asked to be connected with a supervisor in campus security. He was quickly corrected—Northwestern State University didn't have campus security, they had university police—before being put on hold. He glanced across the desks as Marcel leaned back in his chair, nodded.

"This is Captain O'Reilly, how may I help you?"

Beau quickly gave his name and rank before explaining. "I'm working a homicide, and we're looking into connections to some former students who may or may not have given a report, or been reported."

"Our digital records only go back twenty years."

"The former students would have been within that time frame."

"Okay, Detective, shoot me a name, and let's see if we get any hits." The university police captain seemed eager enough to assist.

Beau pulled out his notebook as he gave the first name. "Kevin Muller." He could hear typing over the connection.

Marcel hung up his phone, then lifted it again and punched numbers.

"Sorry, Detective. I'm not finding anything on Kevin Muller."

"He wasn't even a student?" All the records indicated he'd attended the school.

"I can only run a check on a name of someone who interacted with the university police in some way: complainant, suspect, witness, or the like. For enrollment, I'd suggest you check with the National College Clearinghouse. It'd be the quickest way and the path of least resistance."

Marcel slid a note in front of him that read: Brayden Colton doesn't exist. No SSN, no place of employment, no driver's license or state ID in any state.

How in the world could someone have a DNA profile in the system but not exist?

Beau locked stares with his partner who shrugged.

They'd have to figure it out. After his phone call. Beau went back to focusing on the man on the phone. "I understand. So Muller never had any interaction with your department?"

"I have no record over the past twenty years."

Hard to believe, considering how Muller treated women. Most of those types had been acting the same way for years. "Okay, next name. What about a Jada Aubois?" He spelled the last name for Captain O'Reilly.

"Yes, I have her in the system."

Beau sat up straight and grabbed his pen. "You do? Can you give me details?"

"Normally I couldn't, but since my records

show the student is deceased, I guess that means it's not an invasion of her privacy."

"Very true."

"She filed a sexual assault claim."

A sexual assault? That could definitely make a young woman suicidal. "Do you have a date she filed the complaint?" Beau jotted it down, making a note that it was less than a month before she killed herself. "Can you give me the details?"

"She claimed an upperclassman or someone older had met her in one of the student centers. She saw him there several times. According to her statement, one night it was raining and he offered to give her a ride back to her dorm. She agreed and got into the car with him. Her report says she was a little unclear what exactly happened next because she thought she was drugged—so her memory was foggy—but she knew that he raped her. She said she passed out, but woke up in her dorm the next morning."

How awful. Of course, Beau had worked in the sexual crimes unit before he made detective as part of his training, and the only things worse were crimes against children. "Do you have the investigation notes?"

"Just that the officer who took her statement referred her to the local hospital and the Natchitoches Police Department."

Beau dropped the pen and balled his hand into a fist. It was just that type of treatment that caused women not to come forward and report sexual assaults. "Did she happen to name her attacker?"

"She did." There was a pause. "I really want to help you, but I'm not sure I can give you this information, Detective. While she is deceased, I have no such indication on him. He could be entirely innocent."

"I could get a warrant for the information, Captain, but since we're both on the same side here, I'm asking you to help me cut through the red tape. You know how it is when you're working a case."

Beau grabbed his pen. He needed this to work—because who knew if he could actually get a warrant when there really wasn't a viable connection to investigate?

"I do understand. I guess we brothers in blue have to stick together."

Beau refrained from commenting.

O'Reilly continued. "In her report, she named a Brayden Colton as her attacker."

Beau couldn't breathe. The man who assaulted Jada Aubois was the same man with a DNA profile in the system who didn't exist? This was unreal.

Beau snapped his fingers to get Marcel's attention. "Could you please run his name, Brayden Colton, through your system and see if you get any other matches?" He turned his notebook so Marcel could read his notes.

"He's here on the Aubois case."

"That's it?"

"No, wait. There's one more. Hang on, it's not linked, so I have to enter the case number manually." Clicks came over the line.

"Can you believe this?" Beau whispered to his partner.

Marcel slowly shook his head. "This is getting freakier by the minute."

The captain came back on the line. "There, I found it."

Beau turned his notebook back around and grabbed his pen. "Go ahead."

"It looks like another sexual assault complaint, but the gal who filled it out later requested it be removed from records."

Probably got the same treatment: go to the hospital and the city police, the university police can't be bothered.

The captain continued. "We removed most of the complaint details as per her request, but we still had to document that a complaint had been made and withdrawn."

"That's why the record wasn't linked."

"Same scenario?"

"Basically. This one reported she'd met him at one of the coffeehouses on campus and had seen him there a couple of times before she got in the car with him. She reported he took her off campus and raped her. She also claimed to have been drugged when she woke up in her bed the next morning."

A sexual predator on the loose, and the university police did nothing.

"This is dated some time before Jada Aubois's statement."

Maybe long enough ago that the victim would talk to him. There had to be a connection between Muller, Jada, and now this Brayden Colton. Maybe this victim could put the pieces together for them.

"Can you tell me her name?" Beau held his pen over the notebook.

"Adelaide Fountaine."

## DIMITRI

"Thanks for coming. I appreciate it." Dimitri led Lissette past the lobby and to his personal office.

"Of course. Thank you for inviting me. I was a little surprised when you called."

He opened the door and motioned her to the couch. He sat at the other end, twisting to face her. "I told you when I left your home yesterday that I would look into my father's things and see if I could find anything about your mother."

She inched to the edge of the couch. "Did you? Find anything, I mean?"

He smiled, appreciating her obvious excitement.

"I did. I found records of her employment here for over fifteen years, as well as reservations here for you and her."

"See, I told you the truth."

"I never doubted you, only what you were doing to me."

She had the decency to blush. "I explained that I wanted you to be on my side when I demand Claude provide me with an inheritance that's rightly mine."

"I understand, and for the record, I agree. You didn't need to try to use any force to get me to agree. I stand for what's right."

"I'm sorry. I didn't know you. Didn't know what kind of man you were. For all I knew, you were just like your father."

"Bite your tongue." Yet he smiled. He truly did enjoy her company. "But if you are to be able to convince Father of anything, you'll need facts, not dead chickens."

"Facts?"

He nodded. "While your eyes make it pretty obvious that you are his daughter, he'll demand scientific proof."

"Like a DNA test?"

"Exactly like that." He pulled out a plastic vial from his pocket. "I had a friend collect saliva samples from Father's toothbrush. We can do a swab of the cheek of your mouth and send it off for testing."

Her eyes widened and she nodded. "Yes. Whatever it takes."

Carefully, he broke the seal of the other vial and swabbed the inside of her cheek, just like the nurse he'd gotten the kit from had shown him. He put it all just the way she'd instructed. "There, all done. We should get results within the week." Because he'd promised a nice cash bonus if the lab work could be rushed.

"Okay. So what else?"

"I've asked the company's accountant to prepare a report for me of our financial standing for the past twenty-three years. Your mother was owed compensation from the time she conceived you. The only way we can legally count that is to see what Father was worth then, and every year since."

Lissette frowned. "Won't he tell your father?"

"Perhaps, but I requested the report under the guise of getting a large scope of the entire business. Father should be pleased because he's been demanding for years that I prepare to take over this hotel so he can retire. If he questions my request, that's what I'll tell him."

"Smart."

"Lissette, it's critical that we not tip our hand before we have all our ducks in a row. If Father learns about you before we have proof that he's your father, he will utilize every resource at his disposal to disclaim you before you even have a chance to confront him."

"A DNA test doesn't lie."

"No, but lab technicians can be paid enough to lie for him."

"Seriously?"

He nodded. "Do you put anything past him?"

"No."

A soft knock sounded before his door creaked open and Adelaide stuck her head inside. "Dimitri—" She spied Lissette. "I'm so sorry. I didn't realize you weren't alone. I'll get with you later."

He stood. "No, Adelaide, come on in. I'd like you to meet someone."

Adelaide crossed the room, smiling.

Lissette's face wore worry like a comfortable sweatshirt as she stood and faced Adelaide. She looked even younger next to Adelaide's poise.

"It's okay. I trust her," he told Lissette before turning back to Adelaide. "I'd like you to meet Lissette Bastien, my little sister."

# TWENTY-TWO

## ADELAIDE

"Are you free for lunch?" Beau stood in her office doorway, holding a large paper sack.

Adelaide checked her watch: 12:42 p.m. "I guess it is about that time. What did you have in mind?"

He held up the bag. "Barbecue shrimp and grits from the Ruby Slipper."

Her mouth watered on cue. "Come on." She pushed open her office door and tossed her files on the desk before moving to the settee in the corner. She opened the mini-fridge and pulled out two waters, handing Beau one before sitting across from him.

The enticing scent of the food he set before her made her stomach growl. She grinned. "If this is an apology for the way you questioned Geoff, I accept."

"It is, and it isn't."

She opened the take-out container and inhaled. The sautéed Gulf shrimp floated in a scrumptious rosemary and amber beer reduction alongside stone-ground grits that were so creamy, the meal was slap-your-momma good. She popped one of the shrimp in her mouth and her taste buds exploded in pure delight. She chewed slowly, savoring every morsel.

Only after she'd swallowed and had taken a long drink of water did she realize Beau hadn't even opened his container.

She swiped her mouth with the paper napkin. "Okay, go ahead and say what you need to say before you ruin an excellent meal."

"There's been a new development in the case."

Adelaide balled the paper napkin in her fist. "Oh?" She took another drink from the water bottle.

Beau's facial features were stones. "We've found a link between Muller and Geoff's little sister."

She crossed her hands and rested them in her lap, even as her heart beat double time. How much did he know?

"Despite what your chief of security failed to tell us, we have a pretty good idea of why Jada Aubois committed suicide."

"Which is?" Adelaide struggled to keep her voice even. Her worst nightmare raised its ugly head and bared its teeth.

"Weeks before she died, she filed sexual assault charges with Northwestern's university police against a man named Brayden Colton."

Adelaide's heart free-fell to her toes as her face heated to almost burning.

"I see you understand where I'm going."

Her breathing became labored. Nausea threatened to reject the spicy bite she'd ingested moments before.

"Addy, I know you filed a complaint on him too, then asked for the report to be taken back. Why?"

Tears filled her eyes. No sense evading any longer, the truth had demanded exposure. "Because I was stupid. And scared. And I'd messed everything up." The words fell over themselves as she let it all out: meeting him in the coffeehouse, going with him, the attack, the next morning, and the university police's attitude of indifference. "I didn't know better. I just knew I couldn't stay there right then. So I came home and licked my wounds. I can't believe they didn't pull the entire report as I asked!"

"In his belongings, where we found Jada's obituary, there was a jotted poem. When I read it, the emotions felt so familiar, yet I couldn't place them." Beau let out a low breath. "It was yours, wasn't it?"

"Probably." She grabbed another paper napkin and dabbed under her eyes. Her makeup left streaks on the napkin. "Once I came home, Tracey made me see a therapist to work through my emotions. I did, and it helped. It really did. I was able to return the next semester without any-one being any wiser. That chapter of my life was over."

Beau shook his head. "I have no memory of any big change then. I remember you coming home for the semester. Your dad seemed so happy to have you home. I guess now I know he was relieved you were okay."

"No. I never told Daddy. He thought I was just taking some time off to adjust to college life. He still doesn't know."

"You never told him?"

"Don't sound so incredulous, Beau. I was nine-teen years old. I was Daddy's world. It would have killed him to see me as damaged. After what we went through with Mom—the hospital stays, the denial of being listed on the national transplant registry, his pain of his not being a match, her tormented death . . ." Adelaide swallowed back the painful memories. "There was no way I could hurt him by telling him what happened to me."

Beau remained silent for a moment. "I can see that. But why didn't you tell me? I've always been . . . we've been friends since we were little kids."

"I know." She swallowed, deciding to go ahead and get it all out. "I hadn't wanted to tell anyone, but you know Trace, she wouldn't let it go. I had to tell her. She went ballistic. Demanded I tell

Daddy. Go to the police. Hunt him down." She shook her head, remembering the fire in her best friend's eyes. "In the end, she agreed to keep it a secret as long as I went to a therapist."

"But I've been your friend just as long as Tracey. You couldn't tell me?"

The pain and pity in his eyes broke her heart. "I didn't want you to look at me with the pity I see in your eyes now. I didn't want you to see me as damaged either. I couldn't take that."

"I could never see you as damaged." Beau's voice was as soft as his gaze.

Her heart seized. "You can say that now, but back then?" She shook her head. "I felt broken and damaged. I was so demoralized, felt so violated. I can't even explain how I felt." She blinked back the tears. "And if Geoff's little sister went through that . . ." Adelaide couldn't even begin to comprehend how she would've reacted.

"You can understand why she committed suicide." Beau spoke in barely a whisper.

"I can. It wasn't an option for me, but I can understand her feelings of unworthiness, of hopelessness, of desperation." If she hadn't had Tracey to push her to get counseling and be her support system, who knows what options she might have considered.

"I'm so sorry. I wish I would have known. I would have been there for you."

She could read the regret on his face like yesterday's headlines. "I'm sorry I didn't tell you. I couldn't back then. I could barely function through my own emotions, much less figure out how to share them with people I cared about."

"And now? You couldn't tell me now?"

"I had never known him by any other name than Brayden Colton. Kevin Muller meant nothing to me."

"Wait. What?"

"I didn't know Brayden had given me a false name. I only realized who Kevin Muller was when I saw him on the video Geoff showed you."

"You're saying Kevin Muller and Brayden Colton are one and the same?"

"Of course. Isn't that what you needed me to confirm?" She studied his face. "You didn't know that yet, did you?"

"I knew there was some connection, but to hear you verify that—"

She reached across the little table and grabbed Beau's hand. "I promise you, Beau, I had no idea that Kevin Muller was Brayden Colton. Everything I knew from back then was Brayden, and I had no idea who Kevin was, even after he was murdered."

Her words raced to keep up with her heartbeat. "I know I had every reason to kill him and I did know about the passages and my prints were on the knife, but I give you my word, I had nothing to do with his murder."

"I believe you. I'm trying to figure everything out."

She pulled her hand back and took a shaky sip of water. He could easily charge her with murder. She had means, and opportunity, and now documented motive. A really good motive. Even though he had seen her late Thursday night and had been a form of alibi for her in regards to her prints, with this new information he could surmise that she would have had enough time to stab Muller, then leave through the passage and run up to her room for a quick change before meeting him in Jackson Square.

"I'll talk with Marcel and see what we can come up with."

"So Marcel is going to know about what happened to me?" Her throat tightened.

Beau nodded. "It will be in the case notes."

She wanted to throw up. "You can't keep that out?"

"I'm sorry, Addy, but no. This is a homicide investigation and omission isn't possible. Especially when the information wasn't provided to us."

"I already said I was sorry." Marcel would know. Then more in the department. It was only a matter of time before people outside of the police knew about her past.

"I hate this for you, I really do."

"I know." She couldn't be mad at him. She's the one who kept him in the dark. He had every right to be hurt. If the tables were turned, she'd be hurt.

Just like her father would be when he found out. Because now he would find out. It was only a matter of time. She would have to make sure she told him before he heard it from someone else.

## DIMITRI

"May I speak to you?"

Dimitri looked up from the recipe he'd been adjusting in his notebook. He closed the pad and motioned Geoff inside. "Of course. I need a break anyway."

Geoff sat straight on the edge of the chair in front of the desk, his shoulders squared and jawline tense.

"What's on your mind?"

Before he could answer, Adelaide walked into the office. "I got a message to come to your office?"

"I hope you don't mind, Mr. Pampalon, I asked Ms. Fountaine to join us." Geoff's voice was firm and steady.

"That's fine." Dimitri waved Adelaide to the seat beside Geoff. He nodded at their chief security officer. "The floor is yours."

266

Geoff took in a breath and exhaled slowly. "I need to tell you both something, but also apologize."

Adelaide opened her mouth but Geoff tapped her arm. "Just let me get it out."

She nodded. Dimitri had to admit, he was more than a little confused.

"I had a plan of revenge and carried it out. I'd gone over each and every step and knew I could pull it off without a hitch. And I did." He glanced at Adelaide. "But I made a few mistakes that I hadn't foreseen, and it's put you in jeopardy. My actions have brought suspicion and questions about you." Geoff included Dimitri in his stare. "You too. It's totally my fault, and I see now that there's no way I can remain silent about what I've done. My friend with the police informed me there is substantial reason to bring Ms. Fountaine in for more questioning regarding the murder here last week."

Adelaide looked crushed. Dimitri had a feeling he knew where this conversation was going. There was only one incident that their security officer could be referring to, and if that was the case, Dimitri and Adelaide shouldn't hear any more. "Geoff, I'm not—"

"Mr. Pampalon, I have to tell you both, as my employers and as my friends, what has transpired because you will need to promote someone to replace me in my position with the Darkwater

Inn. I would recommend Sully or Leon. Both are good men and will serve the hotel well."

"I can appreciate your candor and—" Dimitri started to speak.

Geoff ignored him and plowed on. "When my sister was in college at Northwestern, she was raped. About three weeks after, she killed herself by overdosing on sleeping pills. We had no idea why. But I kept digging until I found out why. She'd kept a journal, and in it, she wrote about Brayden Colton raping her. The entries after that date . . ." He shook his head. "She spiraled down into depression to the point where she just couldn't continue."

Dimitri listened to Geoff, but his stare fixated on Adelaide. Her tears couldn't be contained as they slid silently down her cheeks. She grabbed Geoff's hand.

"I checked with the university police, talked to Jada's roommate and friends, until I realized that there wasn't anyone named Brayden Colton. He didn't exist. So I had to really do some searching and digging."

Dimitri had only known about his sister for days, but he couldn't imagine how he would feel if that happened to Lissette. Looking at Adelaide's tear-stained face, rage boiled in his gut.

"I finally found the connection of Brayden Colton to Kevin Muller. It took a while, a long while, but I finally made it. And when I did, I started following him. Tracking his moves." Geoff released Adelaide's hand and gripped his together in his lap. "I found out where he lived, where he worked, what he did on weekends. I researched him until I knew what he ate for breakfast every morning."

Dimitri could see that—the drive and thoroughness was one of the reasons he'd been so eager to have his father hire Geoff.

"I'd planned to confront him, but then I found that his company had signed a contract for their event to be held here at a future date. It was signed three years in advance, so that gave me a great interval to bide my time and plan."

Dimitri held up his hand. "Geoff, you probably shouldn't say anything more." As much as he understood Geoff's emotions, he couldn't hear any more. Plausible deniability.

"It's okay, sir. I'm going to talk to the police after I leave here." He included Adelaide in his gaze. "I wanted you two to hear it from me first. Once I tell the police, I'll be arrested and won't have the opportunity to tell you why I did what I did."

Adelaide laid a hand on his arm. "I understand, Geoff. Brayden Colton raped me in college too. I relate completely to how Jada felt." She wiped away tears. "And I'm so sorry. Had I been more forceful and demanded action, your little sister probably wouldn't have been raped so she wouldn't have committed suicide." Her tears flowed freely down her face.

Geoff turned to hold Adelaide by her shoulders. "I'm sorry that happened to you, Adelaide. I didn't know. I never researched what he did before his assault on Jada." He wrapped his arm around her shoulders and pulled her into a hug. "But you can't take part of the blame. What happened to you and Jada was not only horrible, but was criminal."

Dimitri wanted to take Adelaide into his arms, but he was more of an outsider to the situation that she and Geoff would forever be bonded over.

Moments later, Geoff released Adelaide and looked at Dimitri. "I promise you, I had no idea that the knife I grabbed off the counter had yours or anyone's fingerprints. It looked clean enough, so I didn't give it another thought about someone else's prints being present. I wore gloves but never once considered it might not be clean and print-free."

Geoff turned back to face Adelaide. "But my friend says now that it's come out what happened to you, Ms. Fountaine, you have motive, so some in the department are looking to ask you more questions and run through a timeline on your alibi."

The ticking of the clock on the wall behind Dimitri echoed against his own heartbeat.

Geoff nodded at Adelaide. "If it gives you any comfort, he knew why he was going to die before I killed him."

Dimitri could certainly empathize with Geoff and Adelaide. Kevin Muller had been a horrible person who did awful things to nice people. He deserved to be punished. However, Dimitri also believed that justice should reign and that revenge was ethically wrong.

Yet when he looked at Adelaide's eyes filled with tears and the pain of an abuse he'd never be able to fully grasp the enormity of . . .

"I know I will have to pay for what I did, but I won't apologize for killing him. He killed my little sister, and ultimately my mother; he hurt people I care about. From the research I did on him, he hurt many others." Geoff stared at Dimitri. "Because of his associations and standing in society, chances are he wouldn't have had justice enforced, and then there's the statute of limitations that would make much of what I discovered inadmissible in any criminal charges."

Dimitri nodded. Geoff had done the research.

"Right or wrong, I dealt out the punishment I saw fit for him. Yes, I acted as judge, jury, and executioner, but I won't apologize. In my heart, I know I saved many other women from being a victim of his." Geoff stood. "But now I must confess what I did to Detectives Savoie and

Taton to clear Ms. Fountaine and face my own punishment for my crime."

"That's so wrong." Adelaide stood as well.

Dimitri pushed to his feet. "What can we do? If you need me to speak on your behalf, you only have to let me know." His father would throw a fit, but at this point, Dimitri really didn't know how much he cared anymore. It was time to stand up to his father. To do what was right, regardless of what it would cost him.

Isn't that what Geoff did because of love? Because of his strong sense of justice?

Adelaide nodded. "Me too. I'll even testify in court about what he did to me. How he had a pattern of abuse."

"Oh, *mon ange*, that means the world to me. That you would be willing to relive such a horrible experience to help me—you are a good friend, Adelaide Fountaine." Geoff kissed the top of Adelaide's head. "And I will tell my lawyer." He stopped and shook his head. "I guess I should get a lawyer before I talk to the detectives."

"Let me call my lawyer's firm. Please, it's the least I can do right now." Dimitri had to be on the right side of things for once.

Geoff smiled. "I don't think your father will appreciate that very much."

"No, my personal lawyer." The one he'd recently put on retainer to represent him and Lissette when they would push forward with having Lissette declared a legal child of Claude's. The firm wasn't connected to Claude Pampalon in any way, which gave Dimitri the freedom to be honest. "He's with a great firm, not affiliated with Father's affairs."

Geoff nodded. "I'd appreciate that. If you could call and have him call me so we could talk before I meet with the police, I'd be grateful."

"I'll call him right now. And don't worry about any legal costs. I'll see that they're covered, and I'll hear no argument on the matter either." Finally he could use his father's money for something noble.

If one could call defending a man who murdered an abuser noble.

Dimitri did.

# TWENTY-THREE

## BEAU

"There's a Geoff Aubois and his attorney here to see you and Marcel."

This would be interesting. Beau stood up and snapped his fingers to get his partner's attention. "Thanks. I'll be up there in a minute." He hung up the phone on his desk as his partner stood.

"What's up?"

"Aubois and his *attorney* are here to see us." Beau slipped his jacket on and glanced at the large dry-erase board. "Mark us in interrogation two. I'll bring them back."

He made his way to the front of the station with long strides, ignoring the stares and whispers. The commander had demanded they bring Addy back in today and question her. He'd also assigned another officer to verify the timeline of her alibi. As if Beau couldn't be trusted to do his job. He knew Addy didn't kill Muller, as much as she might have wanted. They just needed to find out who did.

With Aubois here, Beau's gut instinct told him this case was about to be over. He would be most happy when the case was closed and his commander realized Beau had never allowed personal feelings to interfere with the investigation. Surely that would get him marks toward his promotion.

Rounding the corner, he saw the Darkwater Inn's chief of security next to another man. Geoff stood as Beau approached. "Detective Savoie." He offered his hand.

Beau shook it. "You asked to see me?"

"Yes." He gestured to the older man next to him who also pushed to his feet. "This is my attorney, Xavier Kidel."

The older man shook Beau's hand, his flesh cold to the touch and his skin like parchment. Beau resisted the urge to wipe his hand on his pants leg. "Detective Taton will meet us in the conference room." Which always sounded so much better than interrogation room.

He led the way down the hall and into the room, letting them pick which side of the table to sit on. It didn't matter to Beau where each of them sat for the discussion, he knew the information—the truth—that would come out. Those familiar tingles had been dancing on his skin since the front desk called him.

Once they were all seated—except for Marcel, who took up space in his familiar place in the corner, leaning against the wall—Beau pulled out his notebook. He flipped on the recorder, identified everyone in the room, then nodded at Geoff. "Okay, Mr. Aubois. You requested this meeting. It's your show."

Ever so slowly, Geoff Aubois began to confess to the murder of Kevin Muller, aka Brayden Colton. He started with his little sister's diary, describing her attack, then painstakingly detailed his research to find the connection to Kevin Muller. Geoff explained how he'd trailed Muller for months on end, determining the man's habits and patterns, all gained to be used against him.

"It never occurred to you to talk to the Natchitoches police? Or us?" Marcel asked from his place against the wall.

"Why would I talk to you? Kevin Muller hadn't committed any crime in your jurisdiction that I was aware of."

Good point. "Did you try to talk to the Natchitoches police?"

Geoff nodded. "I actually did. After I'd spoken with the university police and realized they'd referred Jada to the police, I did speak to a couple of officers in the department, but to no avail. I had no proof. Jada had filed a report complete with rape kit DNA tied to the name of Brayden Colton. This was before I made the connection between Muller and Colton. They were quick to tell me there was nothing they could do."

Some detectives, some entire departments, wouldn't go out and do any investigation work unless they were almost forced to. Beau glanced up from his notes. "And after you made the connection?"

Geoff shook his head. "By the time I'd made the connection and had proof, the statute of limitations had expired. And the investigator I spoke with told me that if the victim was unavailable to testify, their district attorney wasn't very interested in opening a file on the case. I hadn't thought to look for a record before Jada, which would have given me access to someone who could testify that the two names were the same person. Without anyone to corroborate what I surmised, the DA most likely wouldn't follow up."

Sad, but very true.

"I couldn't accept that Jada's death meant nothing. Kevin Muller had to pay for what he'd done, for the lives he'd destroyed. Just because Jada is dead doesn't mean she doesn't deserve justice."

Beau could understand, especially after hearing Addy's story, but—

"What did you do?" Marcel asked.

"I made a decision that this man would get what he deserved." Geoff described how he planned once he found out Muller would come to the Darkwater Inn.

"Three years is a long time to wait to get justice," Marcel said.

"It's only a slip of time in the big picture." Geoff glanced at his lawyer for a moment. "And it gave me plenty of time to blueprint a very detailed plan that I carried out without a hitch." He shrugged. "Any hesitation I might have felt dissipated as soon as I heard Mr. Pampalon would be out of town during the time Kevin Muller would be at the hotel."

"Walk me through the night of Muller's murder." Beau held his pen over the notebook. "What you did." He should be thrilled getting a full confession, yet he couldn't stop the bad taste from filling his mouth.

"I waited until the last night of the convention because I knew from research that the group would drink and let their hair down. I wanted him relaxed and pliable." Geoff took a sip of the water Marcel had set on the table before they'd come in.

"I'd already gone through the passageway earlier that day while he was in meetings to make sure the door was unlocked and I could get in silently. When it was time, I put on my gloves and grabbed a knife from the kitchen." Geoff included both Beau and Marcel in his look. "Understand, I thought the knife was clean. There's no way I could have known there were any prints on it, much less Mr. Pampalon's and Ms. Fountaine's. I would have never used the knife if I'd known.

"I hadn't expected him to have guests, but I probably should have. No matter, I knew he wouldn't keep them long. He would never let a woman spend the night with him. Not even Sidney Parsons, who was actually in a relationship with him.

"I waited in the passageway, right outside the hidden door to his room. I could hear his words with Ms. Naure. Her raised voice before she stormed out. I heard him pour a drink and sit in the chair. Just as I was about to enter, Ms. Parsons pounded on the door."

He took another sip of the water, then recapped the lid loudly. "She was really mad and let him know it. They had a heated exchange, then she left quickly. Kevin Muller went back to his chair. I knew it was time."

Beau stole a quick glance at his partner, who stared at Geoff almost in admiration.

Geoff continued. "I made my way out of the passageway into the bedroom. I could see his silhouette and knew he was in for the night. I could hear him finishing off his drink, the ice cubes clinking against the glass."

He let out a slow breath. "I slipped from the bedroom into the bathroom. I wanted as clean a kill as possible with the least cleanup. Blood is really hard to get out of carpet, and I didn't want Ms. Fountaine to worry about having to get it cleaned or replaced before Mr. Pampalon returned." Geoff reached for the bottle of water.

Finishing the note, Beau looked over to the security chief. The pain emanating from him was palpable. Beau couldn't help feeling guilty for doing his job. Kevin Muller had been a predator, plain and simple. A man who stalked young women and destroyed innocence and hope. He should have been locked up years ago, saving so many women from his destructive grasp. One man finally stood up and did what many didn't have the strength to do, and it would be Beau's job to put that man behind bars.

It was by no means fair, but it was the job.

Geoff set the empty water bottle on the desk. "He came into the bathroom and, as to be expected, was shocked to find me there. He asked how I got in there, and that's pretty much all I remember him saying, but I think he said more." Geoff gripped his hands together and held them on top of the table. "Just hearing the arrogance and accusation in his voice filled me with a rage I'd never known before. I could only see him over my sister, her tears and pleas for him to stop, and his arrogance ignoring her."

Beau noticed the lawyer was quiet, as was Marcel. All of them were engrossed in the emotions Geoff Aubois felt while murdering Muller.

"I wanted to make sure he knew why he was being sentenced to death. I called him out for what he was—a rapist—then I stabbed him. Each time I stabbed and he still stared at me with those eyes, I stabbed him again." Geoff met Beau's eyes. "He hurt women we both cared about, and many others who have mothers, sisters, brothers, friends who love them and weep for their pain. If these girls could even share their experience with others."

Beau tightened his leg muscles so as to not flinch. He knew that Geoff knew about Adelaide's experience.

"He will not hurt another woman." Geoff's stare remained settled on Beau's face. "I'm here to turn myself in for killing Kevin Muller."

## ADELAIDE

"Two nights in a row . . . what's going on?" Vincent Fountaine sat across the table from Adelaide.

"Do I need an excuse to come see you, Daddy? I thought you liked my cooking." She lifted her plate and took it into the kitchen. Maybe her teasing would lighten the mood enough that she could get through the rest.

Her father followed her with his own empty plate. "You don't, and I do, but I think there's something you aren't telling me." He rinsed his plate and placed it into the dishwasher before doing the same with his glass. "I might not have a degree in psychology, but I do know

281

how to read people. Especially my only child."

Adelaide finished wiping down the kitchen counter and putting the leftover gumbo in the refrigerator. She couldn't put it off any longer. "You're right. I do need to talk to you about something. If it's okay, let's go sit on the back porch." She led the way out the kitchen door.

She'd always loved the backyard of their house. It was furthest from her parents' bedroom, so when her mother was sleeping off her inebriation from the night before, Vincent would set up his laptop on the patio table sitting on the porch that ran the full length of the house. Adelaide would swing on the old tire swing her father made her by cutting half the tire out, turning it inside out, and drilling a hole in the bottom to let water drain.

She loved being outside, partly because her mother couldn't stand being out in the harsh sunlight after a night of heavy drinking, which was practically every night of Adelaide's child-hood. Her mother would leave Vincent to take care of Adelaide, only venturing out in late after-noon.

When her father finished a scene, he'd come out and push her on that old tire swing. He'd rear back and push her so high, he'd be able to run underneath her. She felt like she could fly to the moon.

Even now, her dad made her feel like she was invincible. That's why this conversation would be one of the hardest she'd ever had.

The tire swing no longer hung from the tree, and the patio table no longer held her father's laptop, but there were two cushioned rockers that she and her father sat on. The January wind cooled Adelaide's body as much as what she needed to do cooled her heart.

Her father sat silent, rocking. He had always let her work out things in her head and start their conversations before he'd ask a question. A patient man who loved her. She defied any tears to start.

"Do you remember when I used to write poetry?"

"Of course I do, baby. I kept most of them that you sent me." He smiled. "You're a quite talented poet, if I do say so myself."

Of course he'd remember and of course he'd say that. She smiled back. "And you remember that I used to recite my poems in an open mic venue?"

He nodded. "I do. That one weekend I came to Northwestern, and you took me to that little coffee place and got up on that stage." He reached over and took her hand. "I was so proud of you, honey. You had all those people clapping and some of them tearing up. I was one of those." He squeezed her hand and let it go. "I guess you got too busy with studying and then working to keep doing that, but you sure were good at it."

This was harder than she imagined. She swallowed down the lump in the back of her throat, threatening to block her breathing. "Actually, there's a reason I stopped. I haven't been able to recite my poetry for a very specific reason." She shivered.

"Are you cold? Let me grab you a blanket." He was on his feet before she could protest, ducking into the house.

Maybe she needed the minute. She stared out into the darkness. The quietness. It was here that she came home and healed. Home.

"Here, honey." Her father returned with one of the soft fleece throw blankets and wrapped it around her shoulders.

She noticed he'd slipped on a jacket. "We can go in if you're cold too."

"I'm fine." He settled in the other rocker again. "Adelaide Grace, you know you can tell me anything, right? Nothing you say or do will ever make me love you any less."

She couldn't speak.

"I've known for years that something happened to you in Natchitoches when you came home for that semester. Oh, you hid it and tried to not let me see you were hurting, but I knew. I just didn't know from what. You're as stubborn as I am, so I knew I couldn't force you to tell me. I figured you'd tell me when you were ready." He shifted to face her.

From the light spilling out from the kitchen, she could make out every line of concern etched into his face. "I know, Daddy."

"I'm guessing you're ready to tell me now?"

She nodded, but the words didn't come.

Her father stared at her. Seconds ticked between them. "Honey, you know I love you more than my own life. I've had my wild ideas as to what happened."

"Like what?" Maybe if he knew, she wouldn't have to rip off the bandage keeping her pain inside.

"I thought at first, maybe you'd fallen in love with a boy who'd broken your heart, but then I realized that wasn't your personality. Your determination and ambition wouldn't have been put on hold because of a love affair gone wrong."

If he only knew how close he was.

"Then I thought that maybe you and a boy were serious in love. In a serious relationship and the two of you hadn't been careful and that you'd gotten pregnant and then panicked and had an abortion."

"Daddy!"

"I know, I know. Not your personality either. I have to admit, I was very tempted to research."

Her heart tightened. "You didn't!"

"No, I didn't. I figured I'd just have to stop

thinking all these things and let you be the woman I raised you to be and wait for you to tell me yourself." He grinned. "But I have to be honest, I'm getting to the point where my age is reminding me every day that I'm not immortal and can't wait forever for you to come to me."

"I wanted to come to you, I did." She could barely whisper.

"Yet you didn't, so this must be serious." He reached for her hand. "Whatever it is, I'm here for you. I love you so much."

The tears snuck out before she even realized they'd filled her eyes. "Oh, Daddy, I love you, too."

"Then just tell me."

"I did meet a guy in that coffeehouse where I recited poetry. He came several times to hear me. Told me his name was Brayden Colton and would buy me a cup of coffee. He was charming and flirty and I thought I was so worldly. One night, he asked me to go for a ride with him. I thought he was nice. I should have known better. You taught me better. You taught me not to go anywhere with someone I didn't know well." Her breathing came out labored. Tears spilled down her face.

Her father turned his chair to be in front of hers and took her other hand. "Just breathe, honey. Slowly. In and out. It's okay. I'm right here."

She closed her eyes and concentrated on her

father's instructions. In and out. In and out. Slowly. In and out.

"Okay. Now tell me what happened."

Without opening her eyes, she told him what happened. All the horrible details. The next morning. Talking with the university police. The feelings of everybody staring at her. Feeling worthless. Dirty. Alone.

"So I came home. I thought I could just get away from how I felt by being here, but it followed me. I still felt like trash."

Her father let go of her hands and grabbed her head with a hand on either side of her face. He lifted her face and looked her dead in the eye with tears sparkling in his own. "You, Adelaide Grace, have never, ever been trash. You've never been worthless or alone. I have loved you every day of your life—that precious moment you drew your first breath of air until now and every single moment in between—and I will love you with every ounce of my being until I take my last breath on this earth."

Her tears were overwhelming as her father drew her into his arms. She let herself cry. Let all the pain and embarrassment and shame purge from deep within her very heart. She let her father hold her tightly and tell her he loved her, over and over again. Minutes fell off the clock as she lost her grief and sadness and anger.

Emotionally spent, she pulled back enough to

kiss her father on the cheek. "I love you so much, Daddy."

"I love you too, honey. But now, I need to find this Brayden Colton."

She let out a quick breath. "Well, about that . . ."

# TWENTY-FOUR

## DIMITRI

"Well, it is so nice you finally concluded all your nocturnal activities and have returned home." Claude Pampalon stood in the study, wearing his royal-blue smoking jacket and a disapproving frown.

Dimitri pocketed his keys and joined his father with a sigh. "Welcome home, Father." He crossed the room and sat in the high-back chair. "Did you have a nice trip?"

His father took a sip of the amber-colored liquid in the Baccarat glass. No ice dared clink in Claude Pampalon's brandy. "I had quite a lovely time, right up until you called about the murder in my hotel."

*Don't let him bait you. Don't let him bait you.* Dimitri repeated the mantra to himself. "You needn't have cut your trip short, Father. The police have made their arrest."

"One of our employees, I hear." His father went to the bar and poured himself another drink.

Funny how it was *his* hotel, but one of *their* employees when there was a crime involved. But

Dimitri was prepared—he'd read Geoff's file this afternoon. "Yes, Geoff Aubois, our chief of security. Good man. Outstanding employee. I believe you hired him some seven years ago?"

"So I did." His father tilted his glass to Dimitri before taking a sip. He moved to the couch and sat. "However, I would not refer to a murderer as a *good man* and am a bit perplexed as to why you would."

*Don't let him bait you.* "Because he is. There were mitigating circumstances in that this so-called victim, Kevin Muller, had raped Geoff's little sister."

"So, murdering someone in an act of revenge is acceptable?"

"Acceptable, no. Understandable? Yes."

"Oh, my bleeding-heart son." Claude took another drink. "You are much too easy. People need to be held accountable for their actions."

"Kevin Muller wasn't held accountable for his. Geoff's little sister did everything as she should—reporting the assault, seeking medical treatment, telling the university police—yet he wasn't held accountable. And his little sister wasn't the only one. There were others. Many others. His behavior continued, even up until the day of his death." Dimitri let out a silent breath. He wouldn't tell his father about Adelaide, but the anger he felt over what she'd endured pressed him into defiance.

"You now support vigilantism when the system fails? Is that what you are telling me?" Claude's voice boomed in the spacious room. "That some people are above the law because they are meting out justice on their own?"

*Don't let him bait you.* "No, Father, that's not what I'm saying." For the first time in his life, Dimitri wished he drank. "Geoff confessed his crime to me, then turned himself in to the police. He is in custody and will be held accountable according to our legal system."

Claude shook his head. "Still, that this crime was committed in my hotel, right under the nose of my general manager says a lot." He got up and poured himself another drink. "I think it is time that Ms. Fountaine is replaced."

"No!"

His father's eyes widened as he returned to his seat. "No?"

So much for not letting his father bait him. Dimitri cleared his throat. "Father, I was on site. I've been working in the hotel since I graduated. If anyone is to blame about not foreseeing this possibility, it would be me." He let out a long breath. "However, since none of us are fortune-tellers, there is no way we could know what would happen. Maybe we should do further investigations into possible employees."

His father's frown told Dimitri that Claude hadn't missed the implication. "Perhaps. Possibly the murder was made even worse for the hotel's reputation, being right on the heels of a false fire alarm that brought our city's department here for over two hours, a wasted trip. That was under Ms. Fountaine's purview, was it not?"

"It was, but I was also here for that."

"I understand Ms. Fountaine was with you and Mr. Aubois when the body was discovered?"

Dimitri nodded.

"Did neither of you notice Mr. Aubois acting out of place at the scene of the crime he committed? I find it hard to believe he could be so calm that neither one of you noticed anything amiss."

"Forgive me, Father, but I paid more attention to the dead body than to Geoff."

"Perhaps if one of you had been more observant, the case would have been solved sooner, do you think?"

"I don't, but it doesn't matter. The case is now in the hands of the Assistant District Attorney."

Claude took another sip, then licked his lips. "Yes, about that. I am told he is represented by a firm you hired on his behalf?"

Dimitri nodded.

"But not our firm?"

"I suspected you would feel the way you obviously do, so I hired a different firm so there would be nothing attached to you."

Claude took another sip and set his glass on the table. "I see that you at least thought of how this could reflect on me, even if you do not care how it affects you. My son, you will soon realize that every act you perform reflects on this hotel. As an owner and soon-to-be overseer, you should always look at every possible consequence before you act."

Adelaide was right: it was time to come clean to his father. If she was strong enough to be willing to get on a stand and speak up for Geoff about her horrible assault, he could be strong enough to address his father. "About that . . ."

His father tented his hands and rested them on his stomach. "Yes?"

Dimitri sent up a silent prayer before speaking. "I don't want to be overseer or general manager or even a supervisor at the Darkwater."

Clouds filled his father's eyes as he shot upright, his hands balling in his lap. "What?"

"Please, hear me out." Dimitri held up a finger. He straightened his posture in the chair, even leaning a little forward. "I've never wanted to be in hotel management, Father. I appreciate your desire for me to follow in your footsteps, but that's never been my intent. *You're* the one who has pushed me in that direction, but I've never wanted it."

His father's face wreathed in anger. "Then what, pray tell, do you want to do? I will not continue to support you with no plans, no goals, no income."

"I want to stay at the Darkwater, Father. Just as a chef."

"A chef?" Anger punched those two words until they sounded like an insult.

Dimitri ignored the rage boiling in his father's eyes. "Yes, Father, a chef. I'm a good one. Those rave reviews in the *Times Picayune* that brought in food reviewers from the Travel Channel and Zagat? That was me, Father. Me!" He inched to the edge of his chair. "I love cooking and coming up with new recipes for people to enjoy. And they do." He grinned and shook his head, even though his father's face turned a deeper red than the paint on the walls. "People are coming to the Darkwater Inn just to eat in the restaurant and taste the creations I make."

His father stood, grabbed his crystal glass, and hurled it against the wall. It crashed, amber liquid trailing down to the floor. "A chef? I have given you every opportunity in life, am handing you the reins to one of the most superior hotels in the state, have made sure you are fully equipped to see to the future of the Darkwater Inn for future generations to come, and you want to be a simple *chef?*" He pointed at Dimitri. "I will not accept that."

Dimitri shot to his feet and moved around the table until he stood nearly toe-to-toe with his father. "I don't care what you accept or not. I am never taking over the reins of management of the hotel. You never asked if I wanted any of that, and I don't." He was sure his anger raged just as much as reflected in his father's glare. "If you don't want me at the hotel, fine, I'll find somewhere else to serve as chef, but I am going to remain a chef."

"I will cut off your income."

Dimitri shrugged. "I'll be paid as a chef."

"I will kick you out of this house."

"I'll find an apartment." Adelaide had been right all along—he should have done this a long time ago. It was quite liberating. To be able to do what he loved every day? It made standing up to his father easier.

His father, however, shook with rage. "You will be cut out of my will. You will lose your entire inheritance."

Dimitri gave a snort. "I'm so tired of you holding that over my head. I don't care about an inheritance, never did. So I certainly don't now." He smirked at his father, who, for once, seemed to be at a loss for a viable threat. He softened his tone. "I'm not cut from the same cloth you are, Father. I don't need a lot of money, and I certainly don't need power."

"Yet you used that money and power to provide for Mr. Aubois's legal counsel. How will he feel if you pull it away now?"

Dimitri had always known his father to be ruthless and heartless, but this was even low for him. "Wow, Father. You've sunk to a new low."

Claude stood straight, the rage recessed out of sight. "I do this for you, Dimitri. You were born for great things, and I would be remiss if I did not ensure your proper schooling and training in preparation for securing your future for your children and grandchildren."

The man had done nothing for Dimitri's sake. Ever. "I suppose I will just have to figure out a way to pay Geoff's legal fees myself." He smiled at the shock on his father's face. "What you need to understand, Father, is you can't manipulate me anymore. It's time I do what I want, what I'm good at. I wish you could understand and support me. I wish you could allow me to bring honor to our name and our legacy through my natural ability, but if you can't, there's nothing you can do to stop me from leaving."

Claude Pampalon raised a single eyebrow and smiled. "If you leave, my dear Dimitri, I shall have no other recourse than to fire Ms. Fountaine."

## BEAU

"Am I interrupting?" Beau stood in the doorway of the Fountaine house, staring at Vincent.

Vincent opened the door wider and pulled Beau

into the living room with a shake of his hand. "Nope, I just finished a chapter and need to make some notes for the next. I just made a fresh pot of coffee." He led the way into the kitchen and pulled out another cup.

Beau pulled out his chair at the kitchen table. *His* chair—the one he'd sat in since he was a teen through all the holidays, always welcome at the table like a member of the family. Beau's throat stung with the rawness of betrayal.

"I heard you solved your murder case." Vincent set a mug in front of Beau and one in front of the chair he pulled out and plopped down on. "Congratulations."

"Thanks, but it wasn't just me. My partner and—"

"I know it took a team, but you were a lead part of it, so just take the congratulations."

Beau nodded and took a sip of his coffee, made just the way he liked it, yet bitterness burnt his tongue. He stared out the kitchen window, seeing the tree he and Addy had climbed as children still standing tall and regal, although older and a little more weathered. Would his relationship with Vincent and Addy be like the tree?

"Come on, son, spit it out. You don't just show up here on a Tuesday morning without a good reason. What's got you bugged?" Vincent always did know how to cut through the excuses and silence and get to the heart of any matter.

Once he'd made up his mind that he needed to come clean, he realized how much he loved Vincent Fountaine. The man had been more than just a father figure. He'd been an advisor, a sounding board, and a friend. He'd taught Beau how to stand up for himself and others, helped him grieve when his mother passed away, and loved him even when he was being a rebellious teenager. Because of the love and respect he had for Vincent, he knew he couldn't hold his secret any longer. Not when he had so much to tell Vincent.

All this morning as he got dressed, and on the ride over, he'd rehearsed this conversation a hundred times. Suddenly, he found himself unsure where to start.

"Beauregard?"

"Yes, sir." He wiped his sweaty palms over his pants. "I need to tell you something, sir. Something I've done that I'm not proud of, but even more embarrassed that I kept it from you for such a long time."

Vincent shook his head and rested his elbows on the table. "This seems to be the week for it."

Ah, so Addy had finally told her father. Good.

Now it was his turn. "You have to know how much I love and respect you. How much you mean to me. You've been such a presence in my life, and I would never want to disrespect you in any way. I hope you know that." It was important he understood.

"I know that, and you know that the feeling is mutual. Always has been." Vincent took a sip of coffee.

Beau ignored his own mug. "I can never express how much it's meant to me to have you in my life. You have taught me so much that I can never repay you." He swallowed the lump lodged in the back of his throat. "I look around this house and so many memories wash over me. You taught me how to fire my first handgun." He grinned at the memory. "Even though it knocked me flat on my back, you told me to get up and fire again, this time doing what you told me."

Vincent returned the grin. "I told you it kicked and to widen your stance."

"You can bet I've not forgotten since." Beau stared at the apple-shaped clock on the wall. "I remember the first Christmas after Dad died. You made Mom and me come spend it here. We ate, and you pulled me and Addy out back to show us the matching bikes you'd gotten us."

"Except Addy's had that pink basket and those little plastic things hanging off the handlebars."

Beau nodded. "We raced those bikes for years. At least until she stopped beating me."

"She never did like to lose." Vincent chuckled. "Still doesn't."

"Nope, she doesn't. Do you remember the

Thanksgiving right after Mom died when Addy tried to cook the dinner all by herself?"

Vincent laughed and nodded. "The turkey was still frozen. She was so mad that it hadn't thawed properly."

"Everything else was perfect: the stuffing, green bean casserole, sweet potato casserole, mashed potatoes, and those pies. It was all delicious, but her Thanksgiving was ruined because the turkey hadn't lived up to her expectations."

Vincent sobered and stared at Beau. "Is this about Addy?"

"No, I mean—kind of." Beau ran a hand over his stubbly chin. "Not what you think. Not about what she just told you."

"You knew?"

"No, sir." Beau swallowed hard. "I mean, she told me when it became part of my investigation and I already knew. I confronted her then when I had to take her statement, but when it happened? No, I didn't know. I think only Tracey knew."

Vincent nodded. "So how is this related to Addy?"

Beau felt as if his heart had been spliced open. "I care very deeply for her. I hope you know that. And I have the utmost respect for her. I've been in—er, her friend practically all my life. She's very important to me."

Vincent grinned. "Boy, are you trying to tell me

you have feelings for Addy? Feelings more than friendship?"

Heat raced up the back of Beau's neck and into his face.

Vincent leaned over and clapped him on the shoulder. "Good grief, I've known that for several years now. Was just wondering when you'd work up the nerve to admit it and ask her out. And if you're here to ask my blessing, of course you have it. Nothing would make me happier."

For just a moment, Beau considered not telling Vincent. He looked happy and very pleased with himself. Beau didn't want to hurt the man, but if he didn't speak up now . . .

"Vincent, that isn't it."

"Oh?"

"Do you remember when Angelina was denied being on the national transplant list because of her alcoholism?"

All amusement slipped off Vincent's face. "I do."

"And everyone we knew went and got tested to see if they were a match for possible liver donation?"

Vincent nodded. "What does this have to do with Addy?"

"I was a match."

The room got very still. Very quiet. Even the ticking of the clock seemed to go silent.

"I was a match, but I never told you or Addy.

I'm so sorry. I couldn't. I'd just lost Mom to a drunk driver. I know it was selfish of me, but I couldn't make it right in my head to donate part of me to go into a drunk who had damaged herself by her own choices." He felt like a pair of hands tightened around his throat. "I'm so, so sorry. If I could go back and choose differently, please believe me that I would."

"Son, listen to me and hear me. Do you think, for one second, that I didn't already know that? That I didn't know it as soon as your results were in?"

Wait, what? "But you never—"

"Of course I never said anything. The choice to donate was yours to make. I understood without your telling me, I still do." Vincent leaned over and squeezed Beau's shoulder. "Please don't tell me you've hoarded this secret all these years fearful I would be upset with you."

"I, I . . ." Beau couldn't even think at the moment.

"If that's the case, you can put it right out of your mind this minute. I respect the choice you made."

Relief opened his airway. "What about Addy? Does she know?"

"Ah, so you do really care about her." Vincent grinned. "I don't think she knows. We never discussed it. I doubt it would make a difference to her."

"But I should have told her. Should have told you."

"Maybe." Vincent shrugged. "But it's of no matter now."

Beau took a sip of the now cold coffee and grimaced.

Vincent laughed and stood, grabbing the mug. "Let me get you some fresh coffee now that you don't look like you'll puke if you drink it." He turned and moved to the sink and poured out the coffee. "Then you can tell me all about your feelings for my daughter."

# TWENTY-FIVE

## ADELAIDE

"You wanted to see me, sir?" Adelaide hovered in the open office doorway. "Your secretary isn't out here."

"Yes, come on in and shut the door, please."

Getting summoned to the owner's office always made Adelaide revisit her middle school days when she had to appear in the principal's office. Talk about making her knees go weak, having to face Claude Pampalon did it every single time.

She shut the door and sat in the single chair, a Sanctuary Paris wingback, facing his desk. Anxiety crossed her ankles and tucked her feet under the chair.

Mr. Pampalon's office was, in a word, beautiful. The designer had opted for old-world French elegance with the whitewashed walls and select paintings depicting French landscapes. In the center of the office was the focal point, his massive La Maison Du Travail desk.

He sat in the chair behind the desk, his hands relaxed upon the top. "I have read all of the

304

reports you sent to me. I appreciate your thoroughness and attention to detail."

Adelaide forced the smile to widen. "Yes, sir."

"Am I to assume you have sent proper tokens of appreciation to the fire chief for the waste of his team's time and energy regarding the false alarm?"

Heat filled her face at the implication that she was somehow to blame for drunken idiots' actions and that she didn't know policy protocol. She swallowed hard. "Yes, sir. We sent two large fruit baskets to the station as well as a personal basket to the chief himself."

"The incident was handled by the police department, I understand?"

He'd read her reports so he knew it had been. This was just a calling out on the carpet to keep her in check and make sure she knew her place. "Yes, sir. Those responsible were taken into custody but later released. They have, however, been required to pay a fine instituted by the judge they went before."

"Very well." Mr. Pampalon paused, staring at the papers in an open file on his desk. "I see that room 219 has been adequately cleaned and is back in service."

She nodded. "The crime scene company we hired was very thorough, timely, and discreet. The room has already been utilized with no complaints."

"Very well. I can appreciate the discretion. It would not bode well to have the Darkwater Inn on some haunted tour because a guest had been murdered here."

Was he expecting her to comment? There was nothing she could say, so, as her father had taught her, she remained silent.

Mr. Pampalon glanced back to the paper on his desk. "I see that you have recommended Sully Clements be promoted to chief of security now that Mr. Aubois has been arrested."

"He has tenure here at the Darkwater with an exemplary employee record. He has proven himself to be a viable part of the hotel's security detail."

"I see." Mr. Pampalon smiled, which actually looked more like a smirk. "As I am sure Mr. Aubois's record reveals as well."

Adelaide bit her tongue to not snap that it was Claude himself who hired Geoff many years ago. "Geoff recommended Sully and I concur."

"Pardon me if I do not share your sentiment. It is obvious Mr. Aubois did not always make the best decisions, yes?" He didn't wait for her to answer before continuing. "I would like to see the personnel file on Leon Edwards so that I might make an informed decision of promotion."

Leon was Geoff's second choice. It wasn't worth making a big deal out of it, even though she truly believed Sully would be the better choice. "Of course, sir. I'll have that sent to you immediately."

Mr. Pampalon shut the folder and met her stare over his desk. "It is my understanding that you have provided a statement to the police regarding your relationship to the murder victim, correct?"

Everything in Adelaide went sideways. Her stomach twisted. She balled her hands into fists lying in her lap. This was her job, and she loved it. She took in a deep breath, forcing her expression to remain as neutral as possible. "I've told the police how Kevin Muller raped me, if that's what you mean by *relationship*."

He nodded and narrowed his eyes a little. "Yes. It is also my understanding you intend to testify to this on behalf of Mr. Aubois if needed."

She nodded. "Yes."

He lifted a pen and twirled it through his manicured fingers. "Have you considered how such testimony might affect the hotel? After all, you are the general manager."

This man was unbelievable! And as insufferable as Dimitri claimed many times over.

Adelaide took several cleansing breaths before replying. "I think standing up for injustice, telling the truth, and speaking for those who can't speak for themselves is worth any personal embarrassment I might feel." She drew in another breath, letting it out slowly. "I would think most people would respect that, bringing no dishonor to the Darkwater."

"What about the victim's wife? Do you think she would see your actions as noble?"

He was deliberately taunting her. For what? To see what she was made of, how much she could withstand?

Adelaide wouldn't play this game his way. "I'm not trying to be noble, simply telling the truth." She squared her shoulders and forced her hands to relax. "I'm not sure how his wife would see anything clearly. She was, after all, married to a habitual rapist and sexual predator and was either unaware of his deviant bent, or turned a blind eye to his behavior. Either way, it doesn't matter. I will stand on the truth and no longer hide, ashamed, for the assault on me and many other women, including Geoff's little sister." Adelaide stopped to catch her breath.

"Very well, Ms. Fountaine. Dimitri informed me that you were principled and would not be dissuaded from speaking on behalf of Mr. Aubois."

Her lips tickled to smile. Thank you, Dimitri. To her boss, she nodded and stood. "If that's all, sir, I'll go get Leon's personnel file for you."

"Of course." He stood as well.

She reached for the door, relieved to finally escape.

"One last thing, Ms. Fountaine."

Dejection dropped her hand as she pivoted. "Yes, sir?"

"I would appreciate it very much if you would refrain from encouraging my son to not take his rightful place in the Darkwater Inn and to pursue the notion of becoming a chef."

"Sir?" She didn't quite know how to respond. Had Dimitri talked to him, finally told him what he wanted to do?

"I spoke at length with my son about his proper place in the Darkwater. He understands that now and will be taking a much more active role here, outside the kitchen." Mr. Pampalon smiled the smile of a snake oil salesman. "I would appreciate you keeping your opinions on the matter to yourself and not encourage him to be distracted."

No way had Dimitri let his father talk him out of being a chef. The man had to have held him over a barrel.

"That is all, Ms. Fountaine." Claude Pampalon gave her a nod of dismissal, then turned back to his desk.

At least it wasn't a job dismissal.

## BEAU

"Detectives." The officer approached Beau and Marcel.

"What do we have, Officer Williams?" Beau

asked as he and his partner slipped their vests on, then slammed the trunk shut. Indigestion roiled in his gut right under his ribs on the right side as he cinched the bulletproof vest. He'd have to find some antacids after shift.

The young officer shook his head. "This one's a mess. Neighbor called in reporting gunshots. When we arrived onsite, we found a victim under the carport. Before we could call it in, the possible shooter came out through the side door, fired at us, and pulled the body back into the house."

"And we're the lucky ones who got the call?" Marcel checked his gun, then re-holstered it.

"Sorry, man." Jon Williams shook his head. The man stood less than six feet, but he'd been a huge asset to the department's softball team last spring. Beau liked the man who was proud of his wife and kids to the point of being that annoying guy who just had to show off pictures on his cell to anybody who would stand still and talk to him for longer than five minutes. There was something to be said for a husband and father who put his family first.

Beau studied the house with the tall weeds marring what could be a nice lawn. The house itself was nice enough, but needed a little TLC. "Anybody tried to talk to the shooter?" His chest tightened. He wasn't apprehensive about the call, so it had to be his body regretting the tacos he had for lunch.

"Yes, sir. He's not answering us."

Beau glanced around at the spectators lining the street. "Any idea who the victim and shooter are?"

Williams nodded. "Neighbors say it's a couple who often have loud fights. George and Cali Hinson. Both African American, both in their late twenties, no children. Both live in the house. It's a rental and the owner lives in Baton Rouge."

"Lovely." Marcel glanced at Beau. "My turn to take point?"

Beau nodded. "I'll head around back." He ducked as he made his way into the back-yard.

The brown grass stood even taller in the back. A three-legged, rusted barbecue pit leaned against a tree. An old birdbath lay crumbled in an ant bed. A dog barked from the fenced yard two doors down.

His breathing accelerated on its own volition as a shooting pain stabbed into Beau's chest through his back, right between his shoulder blades. The pain stole his breath. His legs gave out from under him as the pain intensified. It felt as if a large vise twisted in his chest.

Was this a heart attack?

He couldn't move. The pain held him hostage, twisting him on his back as he curled into the fetal position, bowing his back around the pain radiating out, causing his eyes to water.

Definitely had to be a heart attack.

Beau tried to reach his radio comm, but the agony pulled his arm back down. He rolled, his body no longer paying attention to any of his commands.

A man appeared over him, holding a gun. Seconds passed, but they felt like an eternity before the man ran off.

Beau couldn't breathe. Death had to be imminent, the unbearable pain so intense.

"Beau? Beau? Are you okay?" Marcel dropped to his knees. "Hang on, buddy. I got you." He clicked his radio. "Ten-double zero at this location. We need an ambo immediately."

Beau never thought he'd be the officer down. "I-I think . . . I'm having . . . a heart attack."

"Just hang on, partner. Help is on the way." Marcel held his hand tightly. "Just stay with me, man."

"I l-let the guy . . . g-go. I couldn't . . . d-d-draw."

"It's okay, man. The uniformed tackled and cuffed him. We're good."

Sirens wailed. The dog two doors down barked louder.

Beau closed his eyes. He could hear people talking. Knew his partner had taken custody of his service gun. Could feel himself being moved about, but he couldn't do anything. The pain. The pain.

The ambulance ride brought agony with every bump. He was going to die from a heart attack. He worked out, ate pretty healthily, got plenty of exercise, but he was going to die from a heart attack. Just his luck.

The hospital nurses were quick to attend to him. They kicked Marcel out of the room, and an EKG was hooked up immediately. An ultrasound wand passed over his chest and abdomen. Minutes passed. A nurse came in, giving him a little cup of medication, which was one of the nastiest things Beau had ever tasted.

Just as quickly as the pain had come over him, it disappeared. Had he survived the heart attack? How much damage had been done?

He sat up on the examining bed slowly, testing the pain. Soreness remained, but nothing like he'd felt before. Wires connected him to the machine beside the bed.

Beau ran his hand over his chin. He could have been shot and killed by that man tonight. Worse, he could have put his partner in danger. And Jon Williams. Marcel was younger than him, and his life could have been cut short because Beau had been unable to back up his partner.

Jon had a wife and two kids who could've

been widowed and orphaned today because of Beau's inability to do his job. Beau knew how that felt. His dad had died in the line of duty, leaving him and his mother alone. While Beau had always been so determined to follow in his father's footsteps—being a hero—he hadn't taken the time to consider the mortality of the job.

"Detective." The doctor entered, clipboard in hand. "Good news, you aren't having a heart attack."

"Whew." It was a relief, but then— "What caused the pain? I promise you, it was the most intense agony I've ever experienced."

The doctor smiled and nodded. "Oh, I understand completely. I had the same attack two years ago."

But he was fine now, so that was good news.

"You had a gallbladder attack."

"A what?"

"A gallbladder attack. According to the ultrasound results, you have over thirty large gallstones, which caused the attack."

"A gallbladder?" Beau had been sure he'd been having a heart attack. Or a punctured lung. He'd never considered a gallbladder could cause such pain.

The doctor grinned and nodded. "For a little organ, it can cause severe pain. Some people display minor symptoms like nausea, indigestion, fever. For others, like you, it comes on fast and furious, fooling many into believing they're having a heart attack."

"So what do I do about it?" Images of the man standing over him with a gun in his hand filled his mind. "I can't let it happen again." It could put him, and others, at risk.

"You have many options: zapping the stones, surgery, doing nothing. Some people have one attack and nothing again. Others get up and walk outside and have their gallbladder rupture." The doctor scrawled on the clipboard and then put his pen in his white jacket pocket. "The internist on call is on his way to review your chart and talk to you."

A nurse entered and began removing the wires from his chest.

"What did you do when you had an attack?" Beau asked the doctor.

"I had mine removed laparoscopically. Surgery on Friday, back to work on Monday." The doctor shrugged. "But the internist will discuss your options and expected results with you when he gets here."

"Thanks." That sounded like a good option.

"He'll be here soon." The doctor left.

The nurse removed the last connection and wiped his chest with a tissue to remove the clear gel. She smiled at him. "There's a man in the waiting room who I assume is your partner,

Detective. He's quite adamant to see you. Shall I send him in?"

Beau nodded. "Please. And thank you." He smiled at the nurse as she left.

He knew he couldn't have foreseen a gallbladder attack, but he still felt awful about putting Marcel and Williams at risk.

"Hey, partner." Marcel grabbed his hand. "How're you doing?"

"I'm fine. Gallbladder attack. Waiting for the internist to get here."

"Gallbladder?"

Beau grinned. "I know, man, but I'm going to get it removed so it won't be an issue again. I'll be back within a week and backing you up." He watched his partner's face for any microexpression of wariness on that comment.

There was none. "Good thing, bud, because I don't want to be assigned to some arrogant jerk I can't deal with." Marcel grinned. "Or worse, someone who eats pickles on their burgers. You know that smell gags me."

Beau grinned. "Well, we can't have that, can we?"

The nurse came back. "Detective, there's a lady at the nurses' station asking about you."

Beau frowned.

Marcel snapped his fingers. "Adelaide."

"What?" Beau stared at his partner.

"I called her."

"Why?"

Marcel shrugged. "I'm not really sure. For some reason, I just thought I should call her." He stood. "I can go get rid of her."

"No, it's fine." She'd shown up when Marcel called. He didn't know if that was because of concern or obligation. Maybe it was time to find out. He nodded at the nurse. "Send her back, please."

Now or never.

# TWENTY-SIX

## ADELAIDE

What if he didn't wake up?

Adelaide stared at Beau's still body lying in the sterile hospital bed. After what her mother put her and her father through, she avoided hospitals like the plague. The doctors and nurses were nice enough, it was just the place itself. They all smelled the same: strong disinfectant trying to mask the stench of death.

His chest rose and fell with every breath, but he hadn't woken up from surgery yet. Shouldn't he have by now? The doctor said everything went as expected, but what did that *really* mean? If the patient was still breathing, was that an acceptable result?

She reached out and took his hand in hers. His skin was cooler to the touch than usual. Was that something she needed to tell the doctor about? She'd ask the nurse who seemed to come in to check on Beau every ten to fifteen minutes. Well, the nurse probably already knew what temperature his skin would be.

Wake up, Beau.

Seeing him lying there, so still and lifeless, did strange things to her emotions. He'd always been there for her growing up, watching over her like a big brother, but there were times, just every now and again, when a different emotion would sneak up and surprise her.

Like the first time she noticed how hypnotic his eyes could be in candlelight. Her dad had been in New York meeting with his editor and was late landing because of the storm that had rolled in. The electricity had gone out, and Beau had come to the house to check on her, knowing her father hadn't returned. He'd helped her light candles, and they'd made peanut butter and jelly sandwiches and had eaten them while telling jokes until her father made it home. Beau had caught her attention as a man, not a friend.

Or the time she'd seen him out on a date with a very beautiful woman. She'd smiled, wanting him to be happy but experiencing her first stirring of jealousy. She couldn't explain why, only that for those few fleeting moments, she'd felt some sort of unexplainable ownership of him.

And like the time after her mother died. Well, after the funeral, when everyone kept bringing over casseroles and cakes. She'd been so sick of having to smile demurely, thank them, then listen to their lies of how lovely her mother had been. Beau had shown up with individual bags of peanut M&Ms, her favorite. At that moment, she'd never known anyone more thoughtful or handsome as Beauregard Savoie.

She rubbed his hand between hers. What would she do if something happened to him? She didn't know if she could face it. Maybe he'd been a part of her life for so long that she took him for granted.

Wait . . . what was she thinking? Was she actually considering thinking of *Beau* as more than a friend? That just . . . was it wrong? Weird? Their lives were so entwined that they seemed to be part of each other sometimes. Maybe all that she'd been through lately had started to catch up with her. Maybe she—

"Addy." Beau's voice croaked.

She smiled. "Hey, you. How're you feeling?"

"Like I got run over with a truck." He grinned at the line she'd given him the first time she'd had a hangover.

"Well, you look better than that," she replied with the retort he'd given her back then. "All kidding aside, the doctor said everything went as expected."

"Good, then."

The nurse entered. "Look who's up." She checked his chart, then moved to his side and pushed the button to activate the blood pressure cuff on his arm. "Would you like some water? You can't have anything to eat for a few hours, but ice chips and little sips of water will make you feel better." She jotted down his blood pressure.

"I'd like that. Thank you."

She smiled at him again. "I'll get you some. The lab will be in momentarily to draw some blood for discharge tests."

"Okay, thank you."

The nurse winked at Adelaide. "You can come get the cup of water. I'm sure he'd rather you help him out than me."

Adelaide didn't know how to respond, so she shrugged at Beau, then hopped up and followed the nurse from the room.

"I'll get the ice water for you. Be sure and don't let him gulp it because it can make his stomach upset, and after abdomen surgery, we sure don't want that, do we?"

"No. No, ma'am."

The nurse filled a large insulated mug with ice chips and then filled it halfway with water before putting the lid on it, jamming the straw through the hole, and passing it to Adelaide. "Try to get him to suck on a couple of the chips. It's better than drinking too much water."

She nodded, then carried the cup back to the room.

The technician was there from the lab, setting up. "If you've got a weak stomach, honey, you'd better wait outside."

"I'm fine." She smiled as she let Beau take a

small sip of water, pulling the straw from his mouth before he finished. "Your nurse said to let you have only little sips."

"I'm thirsty."

"Hello, have you met your nurse? I'm following her orders, bud." Adelaide laughed.

"Okay, let me see that band of yours to make sure you're the right patient." The lab technician grabbed Beau's bracelet. "Beauregard Savoie, yep, it's a match. Time to draw the blood." He sat down and tied the rubber strap above Beau's elbow, then tapped his arm. "There we go, a nice juicy one."

Adelaide didn't have a weak stomach, but if this guy kept talking about juicy veins . . .

"See, it's not so bad." The tech might be chatty, but he was quick, that much was for certain. He removed the strap and finished filling the vial, then removed the needle and put a cotton ball over the puncture. He wound a stretchy bandage wrap over the cotton to hold it in place. "Keep a little pressure on that so it won't bruise."

Beau smiled at Adelaide. "All done. Can I have another drink of water now, please? As a reward for my good behavior?"

She grinned and shook her head but held the straw so he could take a sip.

"Okay." The tech stood and grabbed his supplies. "I'm done. Oh, do you happen to know off the top of your head if your blood type is positive or negative?"

A little bit of color fled Beau's face. Probably the blood draw was a little more than usual. He did, after all, just have surgery.

"I'm negative," he told the lab tech.

The lab tech grabbed a pen and wrote on the vial. "Good deal. O negative. Got it." He left with a rattle of his cart.

Adelaide looked back at Beau. He was paler than pale. What on earth was wrong with—

Had the tech just said his blood type was O? That couldn't be possible because that's what her mother had needed a living liver donor to have, and Beau had been tested and wasn't a match. There had to be some mistake.

"Addy."

But as she looked into his eyes, she knew there wasn't a mistake.

Beau had lied to her.

## DIMITRI

The stars filled the night sky, dancing around the half-moon like revelers around a Mardi Gras float. Soon January would segue into February, full carnival season. Even the temperatures complied and had dropped into the low forties. A beautiful night, but Dimitri couldn't enjoy the evening. Ever since his father had threatened to fire Adelaide if he didn't give up his desire to be a chef, Dimitri had worked on formulating a plan to pull the power from Claude Pampalon.

Tonight was the night to execute his plan.

"I think it's time we talked, Father." Dimitri stood in the middle of the downstairs study, facing the chair his father sat in.

His father neatly folded the newspaper he'd been reading and set it on the coffee table. "Then by all means, young Dimitri, please talk."

The condescending smile wouldn't stay on his father's face for long. Not if Dimitri had anything to say about it. He sent up a silent prayer for wisdom and guidance, and especially for peace.

He'd rehearsed his speech many times over, but standing before his father now, it was harder than in front of a mirror. Still, he would get through this. "You've told me my entire life how the Pampalon name means something. Our reputation is everything."

Claude nodded. "It is." As expected, his father took lead in the conversation. "It is not always easy to keep the hotel forefront in our minds, considering the result of every single one of our actions, but we must. While others can dally in both private and public, Pampalons are to be better. We are to hold ourselves to a higher level of respectability."

This couldn't be any more perfect if Dimitri

324

had written his father's monologue himself.

"I know you are disappointed that you must take your rightful place in the business, but every Pampalon is required to make sacrifices for the family name and legacy."

Dimitri couldn't stop his grin. "I agree. Completely."

Claude didn't smile. He straightened in the chair, probably feeling like a deer in a hunter's crosshairs, but not knowing where the danger would come from. "I am glad you agree. I only want the best for you. I always have."

"Speaking of sacrifices made by every Pampalon for the family name and legacy—"

"Yes?"

Footfalls echoed in the hallway, then Lissette walked into the room.

Claude stood, smoothing his slacks. "You did not tell me we had company, Dimitri." He moved toward Lissette and extended his hand. "I'm Claude Pampalon, Dimitri's father."

She stared at his hand as if it were a two-headed snake. "Lissette Bastien, your daughter."

He stumbled two steps back, caught himself, then glared at Dimitri. "What kind of prank is this, son?"

Dimitri pulled the envelope from his back pocket and handed it to his father. "It's no prank. These are the DNA results proving Lissette is your biological daughter."

Claude sank onto the chair, his posture not nearly as rigid as he pulled the results from the envelope.

Dimitri nodded at Lissette. He'd warned her Claude would blow. He'd tried to prepare her for every outburst his father would launch. Together, they would stand firm and prevail.

"Please, sit down." Claude's calmness was unnerving.

Lissette glanced at Dimitri before she eased herself onto the couch. Dimitri sat beside her as she asked, "So you knew I was your daughter all this time?"

Claude slowly nodded. "Odette kept no secrets from me."

"Yet you never claimed me." Lissette's upper lip went stiff.

"I was not able to do that. You heard what I just told Dimitri. I could not claim an illegitimate child. It would have destroyed the Pampalon name."

"Perhaps you should have thought of that before you slept with another woman while still legally married to my mother. After all, you're the one who said we must live in a way to bring honor and respectability to our name. Having a child out of wedlock in no way does that." Dimitri took Lissette's hand and squeezed. They knew they had to break Claude, and it might sound as if they were against each other, but that's the way they had to come across.

Claude's Adam's apple bobbed.

"You left my mother destitute with your child. We barely had food to eat and often times had the electricity cut off because we couldn't pay the bill. Yet you claim you had to uphold your honor and reputation? It's disgusting."

"Your mother explained all this to you, yes? Odette assured me she had expounded the situation to you."

"You mean how you told her it would only destroy her reputation if the truth came out? That she'd never be able to work in New Orleans again? That I should have never been born?"

Dimitri tightened his grip on her hand. He barely knew her, but he was so proud of her for standing up for herself.

"Yes, Claude, she told me that you wanted her to abort me. That eventually, that's what caused you to leave her, that I was a visible reminder that you were human. You made a mistake. You gave in to your desires while denying everyone else theirs."

"That is enough." Claude's voice sounded like a low roar.

"No, I'm just getting started. I've spent my lifetime being denied by you, and you won't shut me up this time. I am your daughter, your flesh and blood as much as Dimitri, and I will *not* be denied any longer."

Claude stiffened his back and squared his shoulders. "What are you saying?"

Dimitri recognized the stance of his father—Claude was in predator mode all the way. "Lissette deserves as much of the Darkwater Inn as I do, Father. She's just as much your child as I am."

His father turned his glare on him. "So you think?"

"I do." Dimitri lifted his chin. "With that in mind, we have a proposition for you."

"You have my full attention." The loathing rolled off Claude's tongue as easily as the words he spoke.

"You're well aware that I have no desire to be the active CEO of the Darkwater Inn. I love the hotel, Father, I do, but I don't like the business side of it. I love cooking for our guests." Maybe now his father would understand.

"We've been over this, Dimitri."

No such luck. The man was too narrow-minded to accept things he didn't want to. Only he didn't have a choice any more.

Lissette looked down. He knew he had to stand up not only for himself, but for Lissette and Adelaide too. "Cooking is my passion, and if you didn't deny yours, I don't see why you're trying to force me to deny mine."

Claude's eyes widened.

Dimitri pressed on. "You've lectured me for as

long as I can remember about the importance of the family name and legacy. You've taught me by your example how important it is to get what you want, even resorting to blackmailing your own son." Dimitri let go of Lissette's hand and reached for the DNA results Claude had dropped onto the table. "I learned well, Father. Better than you can imagine." He waved the envelope. "But you can't blackmail me any longer. You have the biggest secret that can destroy our precious family name and legacy."

Not that Dimitri cared one whit about the Pampalon name or legacy, but his father did. If playing into his father's mind-set would help him get what he wanted, what was best for everyone, he'd use their reputation as a way to open his father's eyes.

If that was even possible.

"How dare you speak to me in that manner and tone?" Claude's voice boomed.

"How dare you deny me all my life? How dare you live in this mausoleum of a mansion while my mother and I survived on leftovers thrown out by others?" Lissette stood, trembling. "I'm in no mood to play, *Daddy*. This is it. This is your reckoning—that pivotal point in your life where your decision matters for the rest of your life. What you do now can affect the rest of your days, so I would suggest you listen very carefully to what Dimitri proposes."

Claude's face had paled when she called him *Daddy,* something Dimitri had never been allowed to utter. Ever.

Dimitri tugged Lissette's hand to bring her back to sitting beside him on the couch. He faced his father, and spoke with calmness. "What we propose is actually a win-win situation for everyone. Lissette will begin learning every aspect of the Darkwater Inn, just like you demanded of me. She'll learn from the bottom up, under the guidance of Adelaide Fountaine. When she's learned everything, she will assume the position of CEO of the Darkwater Inn, as you intended for me. I will stay on as well, as head chef, but avail myself as needed to assist Lissette and Adelaide, who will continue as general manager."

His father didn't respond, so Dimitri continued. "No one has the desire to embarrass you, so no one need know that Lissette is your daughter, unless you wish to publicly claim her. You will, however, include her in your will as an equal heir as I am."

"And if I choose not to accept this ridiculous proposition?" Claude glared at them both.

All of Dimitri's hoping that his father would see reason fell short.

Lissette cleared her throat. "Then I shall go public with my life story, including all the dirty little secrets my mother told me about you."

# TWENTY-SEVEN

## BEAU

"Good morning." The nurse pulled back the curtains. "The doctor will make his rounds soon, and I expect he'll discharge you."

Beau sat up in the bed and took inventory of himself. The grogginess had dissipated, and while his abdomen was sore, he didn't feel any pain.

"Let's get you up and into the shower, why don't we?"

He swung his legs over the side and realized sometime during the night, his IV had been removed. That must have been some pain medication they'd given him.

Twenty minutes later, showered, shaved, and teeth brushed, Beau sat comfortably in his bed awaiting the doctor to make his rounds.

A knock sounded on his door, then his captain's head popped through. "Okay to enter?"

"Of course." Beau pushed himself up higher in the bed. "Come on in."

"Good to see you up, Savoie."

"Thanks, Captain." What was he doing here?

Beau didn't know if the captain made hospital rounds if anyone in the department was hospitalized. Especially for something like a gallbladder removal. A gunshot wound or injury in the line of duty, sure, but this?

"I just wanted to come by and let you know that as soon as you're back, we'll give you a desk until the doctor clears you for active duty."

"I'm sure it won't be that long, sir. I'll be back active as soon as they tell me I can." No way did he want to ride a desk for the rest of his career. Sure, he'd be more cautious now that he realized how he could affect others, but he wouldn't sit on the sidelines.

"Good to hear. Good to hear." The captain nodded. "And as soon as you're back active, I'm putting you up for your promotion as planned."

"Thank you, Captain. I won't let you down."

"I know you won't."

The door opened and the doctor entered, the nurse right on his heels.

"Well, I'll get out of the way. See you at work, Savoie." The captain nodded at the doctor, then rushed out the door.

"Something I said?" The doctor smiled. "How're you feeling?"

"Fine. Good." As long as he could get out of here today, he felt magnificent.

"All your labs are in line and the nurse says she's ready to kick you out of here. Do you have any questions?" The doctor handed the clipboard to the nurse, who grinned.

"Just want to know when I can go back to work."

"I'd recommend you take a few days off to rest. I'll clear you to return to work on Monday." The doctor smiled. "Follow up in my office a week from today, next Wednesday. If all looks good then, I'll release you from care."

Music to his ears. "Thanks, doc."

The doctor shook his hand. "The nurse will be back in with your discharge papers. Call my office if you have any problems." With that, he was gone.

"I'll be back in a few minutes with your prescriptions and appointment for next week. Do you have someone who can pick you up?"

Maybe he could get Addy to answer his voice mail if he told her he needed a ride. She hadn't answered any of his messages so far. There was always Marcel if Addy refused. "Yes, ma'am."

"Go ahead and call them, honey, while I'm getting all your paperwork together." She winked at him and left.

He dialed Addy's cell again. It went straight to voice mail. "Addy, it's me. Please listen. I need a ride home from the hospital, and I was hoping you would come get me. We need to talk. I need to explain. To apologize. Please call me back."

Beau waited five minutes for her to call back. Ten. Fifteen.

She wasn't going to return his call or pick him up.

He dialed Marcel's number. His partner answered on the first ring. "You good, Beau?"

"Interested in springing me from this joint?"

"Doctor says you can go?"

Beau chuckled. "Well, I'm not running away."

"I'm on my way."

The nurse came in with a stack of papers. "Your prescriptions," she said, then flipped to the next page. "Appointment for next Wednesday morning at nine." Flipped another page. "Dietary restrictions and recommendations which I strongly advise you heed so you aren't back in pain with vomiting and diarrhea."

Beau nodded. Definitely didn't want to go there.

The nurse continued flipping through papers. "Wound care instructions. Signs to look out for and to call immediately if you see. Information about what living without your gallbladder looks like." She came to the last several sheets. "I'll need your signature on the highlighted lines on these three sheets. You're stating that I went over these items with you."

Beau heard blah, blah, blah as he reached for the pen and scrawled his signature where she indicated.

She handed him the papers. "These are your copies. Your clothes are in the closet. You're free to get dressed. When your ride is here, have them pull up to the front doors, and I'll take you down in a wheelchair."

He slipped to his feet. "Is that necessary?"

"Not really, but it's policy, so I have to do it. Buzz me when you're ready." She grabbed her papers and left.

He quickly texted Marcel to pull up front and call when he was there, then went into the bathroom to get dressed. He was more sore than he realized once he had on his pants, but it wasn't painful. Putting on his socks and shoes was more of a challenge as he bent at the waist.

Before he put on his shirt he ran a finger along the four stapled incisions: three diagonally along the bottom of his right ribcage and one right above his belly button. The nurse had told him the scars would be about the width of his thumbnail once they healed. Odd to think that these were the first scars he would have. He'd never really thought about scars before.

His cell phone rang. Marcel. "Hey, are you here?" He pulled his shirt on and pressed the nurse's call button.

"Sitting out front waiting as instructed."

"Be there in a sec."

The nurse opened the door and pushed in a wheelchair.

"I really can walk down, you know."

"Yes, I do, but this is policy, so get your behind in the chair and let's go."

He shook his head but obeyed the nurse's orders. They made their way down the hall and into the elevator. Seconds later, they were approaching the front door. Beau could see Marcel leaning against the car, arms crossed, and grinning.

After getting Beau settled into the front passenger's seat, Marcel slipped behind the steering wheel and took the car out of park. Beau looked over his shoulder to wave at his nurse, but someone else walking into the front door of the hospital caught his eye.

Adelaide.

## DIMITRI

"Adelaide, can we talk for a moment?"

"Of course, come in." She stood from behind her desk.

"I came by earlier, but you were out. Is everything all right?"

She nodded as she made her way to the settee to sit. "Beau was released from the hospital this morning."

"How's he doing?" He sat beside her.

"Okay, I guess. I just missed him." She crossed her ankles and relaxed back on the loveseat.

Dimitri noticed she looked more than disappointed that she'd missed Beau. Had he misread their relationship? He didn't know how to process that. Was it just friendly concern, or was there something more between them?

"Have you heard anything from Geoff?" she asked.

He nodded. "He and his attorney are working on a negotiated plea agreement with the state. His lawyer, Mr. Kidel, has asked you and me to both give affidavits and character statements on Geoff's behalf."

"Of course. Any time." She tilted her head. "Dimitri, I need to ask you something. It's not really my business, but in a way, it is."

His heart hiccupped. "Ask away."

"Your father confronted me yesterday morning. We discussed my reports of the hotel while he was away. Just before I left, he said a few things that led me to believe you'd told him about your desire to be the chef here."

"I did." He smiled. "I finally got up the courage to tell him."

She frowned. "But the way he spoke . . . the things he said implied you had given up the notion and would be stepping into the role of CEO as he'd originally planned."

Dimitri shifted in his seat on the loveseat. "That was his hope."

She shook her head. "No, he spoke with more

certainty than hope. It was as if you two had discussed it and he'd won."

He hadn't wanted to tell her all the dirty details, especially the ones that would expose his feelings for her. Maybe he could sidestep. "He attempted to blackmail me into moving into the CEO position. He threatened to cut me out of his will, make me move . . . all his usual noise."

"And you agreed?"

"At the time, he threw in several new threats that I needed to consider because they weren't about me." He didn't want to give her time to question anything. "So, I bided my time because I knew the DNA results would be in yesterday. Lissette and I confronted him last night and made our own demands."

Adelaide lifted her eyebrows. "Really?"

"The sad part is he knew he had a daughter and had done nothing." Dimitri shook his head. His father was a real piece of work. "When he was confronted with the test results and Lissette put him in his place for abandoning her and her mother, he couldn't bully us any more."

"I can't imagine."

"I never thought I'd see it either, but once we pointed out how hypocritical he was by lecturing me about my place in the family legacy and the sacrifices required of Pampalons, all the while knowing he had a daughter he didn't claim nor take responsibility for, he didn't have a viable argument left."

"Very true."

"And that's what led me to come speak with you."

"Oh?"

Dimitri nodded. "Lissette will start working at the Darkwater Inn very soon. She'll start in housekeeping and move her way through the departments, just as Father had me learn. Once she gets to the point of management, I'd like to ask you to take her under your wing and teach her. I know it's a lot to ask you to train your boss-to-be, but she likes you and is eager to learn."

"Likes me?" Adelaide gave a little start. "She doesn't even know me."

"But she wants to know you better. She is, after all, my sister." So much of his and Lissette's plans hinged on Adelaide's cooperation. He'd never considered that she wouldn't comply.

"Of course I'll teach her." She flicked imaginary lint from her slacks. "Should I start preparing my resumé?"

What? "Why would you do that?"

"If she is going to take my place . . ."

Dimitri reached over and grabbed her hand. "Oh, no. You aren't being replaced. You'll stay on as general manager. Lissette will eventually step into the role of CEO, and I'll get to stay as chef."

"Oh."

This silly, precious woman. "No way would we think of letting you go. I wouldn't allow it. If I could stand up to Father to not fire you, I wouldn't—" and just by the look on her face, he knew he'd said way more than he'd intended.

"Your father wanted to fire me?" Her voice wobbled. "I do a good job here. This place has part of me in it. I've never called in sick, never taken more than two vacation days at a time, I'm never late. The things that happened lately would have still happened had I not been the general manager. They would've still happened if your father had been here running the place himself."

How could he have been so stupid as to let it slip? "It wasn't your work performance at all, Adelaide. It was only to keep me in line."

She searched his face, then her eyes widened. "That's why you originally agreed to move out of the kitchen into the CEO position? Because he threatened to fire me?"

The lump in the back of his throat nearly blocked his words from getting out. "Yes, but that's just the way he is. Manipulation is his first language. He can be ruthless, even with his own child, apparently—"

The rest of what he was going to say got lost as she leaned over and hugged him. Tight enough that he could feel her heart beating against his chest. Her warmth seeped into him, settling deep within him.

He wrapped his arms around her and closed his eyes, inhaling. The delectable scent that was uniquely Adelaide wafted into his senses.

Just as fast as she was in his arms, she moved out. Tears glistened in her eyes. "I'm so sorry he did that to you, but I've never had anyone besides my dad stand up for me like that. To be willing to give up what you really want to do to let me do what I love—" She shook her head and smiled. "Thank you."

He wanted nothing more than to yank her back against him and kiss her thoroughly, as he'd wanted to for months. But now, knowing her history and what she'd been through, he would never move so fast as to frighten her. She was a lady who would require a delicate approach—time and attention.

It would be worth it to gain her trust, and perhaps one day her love.

"Adelaide, would you go out to dinner with me sometime?" The question was out before he could stop it.

She jerked straight. "You mean, like on a date?"

# TWENTY-EIGHT

## ADELAIDE

"That was some delicious jambalaya, sweet-heart." Vincent Fountaine finished separating the leftovers into two containers.

Adelaide smiled. "I'll let Dimitri know you enjoyed it. He added some new spices and I think it makes it really stand out." She slipped the last fork into the dishwasher, then shut the door. She should've probably brought Dimitri with her to meet her father. He'd asked before, and now . . . well, she probably should introduce them. Especially since Dimitri had asked her out.

She hadn't given him a straight answer, just told him she'd think about it. She still didn't know what to think about that. She needed to talk to Tracey to get her input and advice. Right now, Adelaide's mind was too crowded.

Her father poured two cups of coffee and slid one to her. "I'm still finding it hard to believe Claude Pampalon has been bested." He shook his head as he carried his coffee to the kitchen table and sat in his well-worn chair.

"According to Dimitri, his father really had no

choice." She sat down in the chair across from her father. "Mr. Pampalon didn't fire me, so there's that."

"He'd be stupid to fire you." Her father took a sip of his coffee. "Still, I'd be careful. Claude Pampalon isn't a man accustomed to not getting his way. I'd bet he's working an angle to turn the tables. It's what he does. Who he is."

"That's what I told Dimitri and Lissette." Adelaide took a sip of her coffee, savoring the familiar blend that she'd grown up on. "They feel confident he'll continue to play by their rules. Dimitri said they have an appointment tomorrow with Mr. Pampalon's lawyer to add Lissette to the will."

"I don't know that I'd trust that if I were Dimitri, but that's none of our business as long as it doesn't affect your job." He stared at her over the rim of his cup. "Don't go getting messed up with the Pampalons more than as an employee. You see what type they are—how that poor girl and her mother were just ignored." He shook his head.

"Dimitri isn't like that, Daddy. He abhors the way his father has behaved."

"Maybe so, honey, but he was born with that silver spoon in his mouth and raised by his father alone. People like that are usually self-centered and focus on their own needs before anyone else's."

Was her father actually judging Dimitri because of who his father was? "Dimitri is nothing like his father, and I know it. His father threatened to fire me unless Dimitri stayed at the Darkwater Inn and moved up into the CEO position. Dimitri agreed to it. He was willing to sacrifice his own happiness so that I could keep the job I love."

Her father ran his finger along the cup's rim. "And yet it's Lissette moving into the CEO position, and you're still the general manager. He's still cooking, so he didn't sacrifice much."

"Daddy! That's not fair. It worked out the way it did because Dimitri demanded Mr. Pampalon treat Lissette as he should as his daughter. Many would have wanted to protect their own interests and inheritance, but Dimitri cared more for doing what was right."

"You haven't considered that maybe he really didn't have a choice, since she truly is Claude's daughter? If Dimitri hadn't been her advocate, she still would have gone to Claude and demanded he acknowledge her."

"You don't know him. Dimitri is a good man, despite who his father is. He didn't have to let his father manipulate him even for a day by taking up for me, but he did." Why was her father trying to turn her against Dimitri?

"Yes, I'm asking myself why he would do that for you."

"Gee, thanks! I am a good employee, you know.

Or maybe Dimitri did it because we're friends. Maybe because he likes me."

"Does he? Like you, I mean?"

"Of course. He wouldn't have made me the jambalaya to bring over if he didn't like me."

"You know what I'm asking, Adelaide."

She swallowed. "He did ask me out today."

"What did you say?"

"That I'd think about it."

Her father nodded. "Ahh, so you're not sure about him either."

"That's not it." She stood and carried her cup to the dishwasher. "He's been one of my bosses basically since I started at the Darkwater, so it's a little hard to switch that mind-set so quickly."

"He'll always be Claude's son, a Pampalon. Demoting himself to work in the kitchen doesn't change that."

"No, it doesn't, but it does change our position now that he's no longer my boss." She opened the refrigerator and slipped one of the leftover containers inside, then reached for the other.

Her father stopped her. "Leave that one out. I'm taking it to Beau." He poured himself another cup of coffee before returning to the table. "Or maybe you could drop it off on your way home."

She shut the fridge and leaned against the counter. "Daddy, did Beau tell you that he was a match for donating to Mom?"

"Yes."

"When?" How could her father not have told her?

"We talked about it this week, in fact. That boy's been letting guilt eat him, thinking it was some big secret."

What? "I don't understand. I didn't know. He never told me."

"Oh, honey, I knew back when he was tested."

"You never said anything."

"Why would I? It wasn't your business. Wasn't really mine, to be honest."

"She was my mother. He was my friend. I had a right to know."

"No, darlin', you didn't." He took a drink of coffee. "You were fourteen years old and it was your mother. You two had a tentative relationship from the day you were born. Your momma did her best to destroy every relationship she ever had. She was an embarrassment to you, and there were times you wished she wasn't your mother."

How did he know? "I never said any of that."

"You didn't have to. Your momma didn't just hurt you, she hurt everyone who ever cared about her. But she hurt me most when she chose the bottle over you every single time. I hated it. Hated her for doing it more times than I'd like to admit, but that's the truth."

"You never said a word to me."

"I couldn't. She was your mother and I kept

hoping and praying she'd change. That she'd stay sober and be the mother you deserved. That's the only reason I let her stay—the hope that she'd turn her life around and it would benefit you."

Adelaide went to her father and hugged him. "I love you, Daddy."

"I love you too, sweetheart." He released her. "And you shouldn't be so hard on Beau either. It was his decision to make, and at eighteen, he made the decision he felt at the time."

"It's not that he chose not to save Mom that hurt me. It's that he lied to me about it for so many years. And I found out by accident."

"You should talk to him. Give him a chance to explain."

Adelaide chewed her bottom lip.

Her father stood and hugged her. "The boy's been part of your life forever. Let him tell you what happened." He nodded at the container on the counter. "And you'll save me a trip out to boot."

Was she ready to hear what Beau had to say?

## BEAU

Knock! Knock! Knock!

Beau pushed himself off the couch and made his way to the front door, trying not to trip over Columbo, who seemed to think he was Beau's nursemaid. "Get from between my feet,

Columbo!" Marcel was on duty, so he'd probably sent a uniform over to check on him.

The cat meowed twice, then ran back to the couch and curled up on Beau's blanket and glared.

Typical Columbo.

Beau shook his head and opened the door, then froze. He hadn't expected to see Addy on his step. For a moment, he didn't know what to say.

"Dad wanted me to drop this by on my way home." She held up a plastic container. "Do you want me to put it in the kitchen?"

"Sure. Yes. I mean, I can take it, but if you want to." He opened the door wider and let her in.

"Have you eaten tonight?" She headed toward the kitchen. "Fridge or do you want to heat it up?"

"Marcel made me eat earlier."

"Then fridge it is."

Columbo jumped off the couch and followed her into the kitchen, meowing pathetically.

"Hey, boy. How're you doing?" Her voice wafted into the living room.

"Don't let the little monster fool you. He's eaten too!" Beau hollered as he sat back on the couch and waited until she came back. His heart thudded, echoing off the pain medication in his head.

"Are you okay?" Addy stood in front of him, her hands on her hips.

"Will you sit down, please? I want to talk to you, but I can't stand for long without getting tired." Maybe he used the sympathy card.

She took a seat in the chair adjacent to the couch. Columbo jumped into her lap, settled, and purred.

Little traitor.

"Do you hurt?"

"It's more sore than actual pain. Or maybe the pain pills dull that enough. I don't know, but it's bearable."

"Well, that's good." She ran her fingers through Columbo's thick fur. The treacherous cat leaned into her touch, purring louder.

Beau took in a slow breath. "I understand why you left and why you wouldn't answer my calls."

"I did come to the hospital, but you were already gone. I hope you know I wouldn't have left you stranded."

"I know. Marcel came and got me. I actually saw you as we were leaving, but it was too late to turn back."

She nodded, her lips pressed tightly together.

Columbo's tail twitched and he opened one eye to stare at Beau, as if daring him to upset Addy.

Beau let out a burst of air. "I need to explain about why I didn't donate part of my liver to your mom."

"You don't owe me an explanation."

"I do. I'm not sure how much you remember

about my mom, but she was everything to me. Especially after Dad died."

Addy smiled, her fingers buried in Columbo's gray striped fur. "I remember your mom's gingerbread at Christmas. I loved to come over when she was baking because the whole house smelled so good."

He smiled too. "She was a great cook. Loved to bake." If he closed his eyes, he could still smell how the house welcomed him home during the holidays after she'd spent the better part of a day in the kitchen.

"I remember she hemmed one of my dresses for me because Mom had forgotten to take it to be altered. I was so upset that my play would be ruined because of Mom's drunkenness, but your mom just took the dress and hemmed it without a word."

Yes, he remembered. He remembered even more that she did for Addy—like making Vincent take her to the makeup counter to have the ladies show her how to apply her makeup. Or how she told Vincent a lady needed a special shopping trip to get *unmentionables* when she became a certain age, and took Addy herself. He smiled and nodded. "She was like that. She loved you and appreciated how your dad took me under his wing after my dad died. It worked."

"It did." Addy still wore the smile.

"I loved her with everything I had. Then in

one moment, she was just gone. I don't know if you remember, but she died instantly, which I'm grateful for so she didn't suffer. But I didn't get to tell her goodbye. I didn't get to hold her hand and tell her what a wonderful person she was, how much I would miss her, and how much I loved her." Tears burned his eyes, but he didn't care.

Addy moved to sit beside him on the couch. Columbo's ears flattened as he stared at Beau, then readjusted himself next to Addy, who took hold of Beau's hand. "I know. I'm so sorry."

"But you see, I was only eighteen. I was so bitter that some drunk had gotten behind the wheel and taken her from me."

"You had every right to feel that way." The warmth from her touch crept deep into his bones.

"I did, but when the time came after that to be tested for possible liver donation for your mom, I was still so angry. When I came back as a match, at first I was shocked. Then I was angry. I couldn't save my mother, my world, who was killed by a drunk, but I could save a drunk?" He glanced at Addy. "Sorry."

"No, she was a drunk. That's the truth, no matter how ugly it is."

"I thought I could donate, Addy, I really did. I never wanted you to lose your mom. But I couldn't. Every time I looked over the paperwork, I could only see Mom's coffin. It was messed up, but in my mind, donating to your mom was like giving a seal of approval to a drunk. I just couldn't do it."

Tears seeped out of Addy's eyes. "I understand."

"I hated myself for not being able to go through with it. I didn't want to hurt you or Vincent, but I just couldn't. So I lied. I told you both I wasn't a match. You both accepted my word without question and it was okay. Until your mom did die. Then I felt like I'd killed her."

"Oh, Beau, you didn't kill her. She did that herself with every drink she took." She grabbed his other hand as well, holding both as she stared into his eyes. He saw no judgment or condemnation in them, only pain and pity.

"In my immaturity, I hadn't realized how awful I would feel."

"You shouldn't have. Daddy never asked the doctors to let me be tested, even though they would have made an exception to the minor rule as her daughter."

"I didn't know that."

She smiled. "I didn't either until Daddy told me. I was okay with it because, well, you know Mom and I didn't have the best relationship."

"I'm so sorry." He wanted nothing more than to hold her, but he couldn't.

"I'm not upset that you didn't donate, I was hurt you lied to me."

He opened his mouth to apologize again, but she put her fingertips against his mouth. "No. I understand now. It's okay. We're okay." She dropped her hand and smiled. "Just no more secrets, okay?"

He nodded. "No more secrets. I promise."

"I promise too."

"You're pretty amazing, Adelaide Fountaine."

"So are you, Beauregard Savoie."

Emotions filled the moment. Beau ran a finger along the side of her face, cheekbone to jawline, then he cupped her head with both his hands. Slowly, he lowered his mouth to hers. A soft graze of his lips against hers. Warmth. Sweetness. He tilted his head to deepen the kiss.

Brrring!

She started, then jumped to her feet. "I need to go. We'll talk soon."

He stood. "Addy, don't go."

Brrring!

"I'll check in on you tomorrow. Good night, Beau." She slipped out the front door so fast, there was no way his sore body could have stopped her.

Brrring!

The one moment he'd dreamed about for years, gone. Why hadn't he put his stupid cell phone on silent?

# TWENTY-NINE

## ADELAIDE

"What do you mean, he *kissed* you? Back that truck up and spill the tea, woman!" Tracey pulled her hair up into a messy bun and plopped down onto the couch.

"You know what kissing means. He kissed me." The back of Adelaide's neck grew warm just remembering how it felt to have Beau kiss her. She still wasn't sure how she felt about it, emotionally, but physically . . .

Tracey groaned and pulled a throw pillow into her lap. "Girl, did he peck your cheek or kiss you, like really kiss you?"

Maybe it'd been a mistake to tell Tracey, but Adelaide had needed to tell somebody or she'd go nuts with the myriad emotions bubbling inside her. "It was a real kiss."

"Wow. After all this time. It's so about time."

"What?"

Tracey shook her head. "Don't tell me you didn't know that man's been hung up on you since we were in high school. Everybody knows that."

"I didn't. I mean, I don't." Adelaide shook her head. Her best friend had to be messing with her. "He hasn't."

"Oh, yes, he has. Ask anybody, or better yet, start paying attention. Beau has always been soft on you."

No, she would have known.

Adelaide thought back to all the times Beau was there for her. Opening doors, always being super nice. The way he looked at her.

She took the other throw pillow from the couch, covered her face, and screamed. How could she have been so blind?

Tracey laughed. "Girl, it's okay. I'm just glad he finally made a move." She pulled the pillow away from Adelaide's face. "This is the first time a man's touched you since . . . yes?"

"Since I was raped? It's okay to say it. I'm not ashamed anymore. Finding out what all he did, not just to me but to so many others, made me realize I'd done nothing wrong. It was not my fault."

"You know I told you that very fact years ago."

"I know. I just needed to learn it for myself."

Tracey grinned that toothy grin of hers. "Go ahead and say it. Come on, you know you gotta."

Adelaide shook her head. "You were right."

"Ahh. Music to my ears." Tracey closed her eyes and leaned her head back on the couch.

Adelaide threw the throw pillow at her.

"All kidding aside, were you okay with him kissing you?"

"You know, I've turned down a lot of dating opportunities because I was worried that if there was any physical contact, I'd freak out."

"But you didn't?"

Adelaide shook her head. "I didn't even think about it, to be honest."

"That's awesome." Tracey stretched a leg out and propped it on the coffee table. "What did you think?"

"At first I was shocked, but then it was . . . nice." Heat blasted across her face.

"Nice?" Tracey giggled. "I'm not sure Beau would appreciate his kiss being referred to as *nice*."

Adelaide giggled herself. "I mean, I enjoyed it. More than I thought I ever could." She'd felt connected to him. "But it was Beau, so it was familiar. I trust him."

Tracey smiled. "That's really good, Ads. I mean it. I was so worried that you would never let a man get close to you."

"Gee, thanks for the vote of confidence."

"Don't misunderstand, I wouldn't blame you if you felt that way. Some women who go through assaults like yours never get over the physical connection to their experience. It's totally logical."

Adelaide shrugged. "I get that, but you know what? Now that I've told people about what happened to me, hard as it was, I feel as if I've been set free. I don't want to give that piece of trash even a sliver of power over me anymore. I refuse to let what he did to me define who I am."

Tracey leaned over and hugged her. "I'm so proud of you. And I love you, my bestie."

"As I love you. I don't know if I ever thanked you for being there for me and forcing me to go to therapy, but you saved my life."

"I got you, girl." Tracey gave her a final squeeze, then pulled the throw pillow into her lap. "So where did you leave it with Beau?"

"He got a phone call and I said I needed to go, so I left."

"Ran away?"

Adelaide grinned. "No, I walked out the front door, but man, my heart raced like I was running."

Tracey chuckled. "You should be glad he just had surgery or he'd have followed you."

"Don't I know it. I just need a little time to assimilate my emotions. They're swarming."

"I can't believe he hasn't called you."

Adelaide pulled her phone out of her purse and showed her welcome screen to Tracey.

"Eight missed calls? You need to call him back and put him out of his misery. He's probably terrified he's upset you and that you're angry or traumatized."

"I did. I called him back and told him I was okay, but that I just needed a little time to think. He said he understood."

"Good. I'd hate for him to think you were upset. That man's waited on you for years."

"Mmm-hmm."

Tracey narrowed her eyes. "What aren't you telling me, Ads?"

"Well, Dimitri asked me out today."

"What? And you're just now telling me?"

"This day's been really crazy."

"Sounds like it. How did Dimitri ask you out? I've always thought he was so handsome."

Adelaide smiled. "He is handsome. Very."

Tracey flashed her a cheesy grin and winked.

"He confessed the reason he'd originally told his father he'd give up his dream of being a chef was so his father wouldn't fire me."

"What?" Tracey shook her head.

"Claude had threatened to fire me if Dimitri didn't agree to give up being a chef and give in to his father's wishes to become CEO."

"Wow, that man's a piece of work. First-rate jerk. How can you stand to work for him?"

"You know that I love my job. It's what I always wanted to do with my life. And the Darkwater Inn is in my blood, strange as that sounds."

"I know, but still. Claude Pampalon is a jerk."

Adelaide laughed. "You'll get no argument from me on that, but he won't be hovering for much longer."

"Do tell."

"According to what Dimitri told me, after proving to Claude that Lissette Bastien is his daughter with a DNA test, Claude agreed to let Dimitri stay in the kitchen and train Lissette to take over as CEO."

"Hold up. You're telling me that they come up with DNA results and Claude Pampalon just rolls over and agrees to what they propose?" Tracey shook her head. "That doesn't fit. Claude Pampalon, by all accounts, is accustomed to getting his way. And a control freak."

"I know, but Dimitri assures me that it's all settled."

Tracey kept shaking her head. "I don't know. I know you want to believe that—heck, I do too, for you, but really? Do you honestly believe Claude's going to let this go?"

Adelaide let out a low breath. "No." She shocked herself to admit it. "And I have to confess, I'm really uneasy about Lissette's involvement in voodoo. I know Dimitri doesn't believe in that because of his faith, but it concerns me that she had been putting binding curses on him."

"Casting binding spells." Tracey automatically corrected her wording.

"Whatever. I'm just not comfortable with it all."

"I don't blame you. From what I learned, she's not just a dabbler but is very active in the practice."

"Dimitri won't tolerate that."

Tracey shrugged. "It's not something you just stop."

"Yeah, it makes me uneasy."

"You just be careful, girl. Watch your back."

Adelaide nodded. "I will."

"And Dimitri asked you out."

"He asked me to dinner sometime. I asked for clarification, as in a date, and he confirmed." Adelaide bit her bottom lip. "It made my heart skip a beat."

"What did you tell him?"

"That I'd see."

"Let me get this straight. In one day, the handsome guy you've become friends with over the last several years asks you out. Then the sweetheart of a guy who's been sweet on you since high school decides to kiss you. On the same day?"

"I know, right?" Adelaide couldn't stop the smile from spreading nor the warmth that reached her toes.

"It's like somebody cast an attraction spell on you."

"That's not even funny."

"Sorry." Tracey nudged her. "But that's really something, you know?"

"Yeah." Was it a fluke?

"What are you thinking?"

"I don't know. That's just it. It's been an emotional week. I've had to process a lot. I just don't know what I think. What I feel. Or what I should." Adelaide looked at Tracey. "What does that say about me?"

"That you're a normal person who survived a traumatic experience and are dealing with a lot of emotional crap at the moment." Tracey put her arm around Adelaide and hugged her. "Want my advice?"

"Of course."

"Take it easy on yourself, Ads. Give yourself space. Take it day by day, and don't let anybody rush you. Do what you want. Go out with Dimitri *and* Beau. Nobody says you have to jump into a relationship. Or don't go out with either of them. Go out with whoever interests you." She hugged her harder. "Do what's best for you."

If only it was that easy. "How do I know what that is?"

"Only you can decide that, sweetie, but there's no rush. You take your time and do what *you* want, when you want."

If only she knew what that was.

# DIMITRI

"Are you okay?" Dimitri stood as Adelaide stepped into the hall.

She smiled. "I'm fine. Mr. Kidel said he'd take us to see Geoff in a few minutes." She sat in the chair beside Dimitri.

He reached for her hand and squeezed it. "Everything okay?"

She nodded. "I gave my statement of what Kevin Muller did to me, how he lied about his name and everything."

His heart stood still. "Are you sure you're okay?" He'd only given a statement of Geoff's character and outstanding employment history, but Adelaide . . . she had agreed to give a statement of the vileness of Kevin Muller.

She let go of his hand. "I am. It was actually quite liberating to do something useful with what happened to me." She smiled slowly, her face brightening. "To be honest, I felt empowered. At first, I was very apprehensive, but as Mr. Kidel asked me questions and led me to tell the details, I felt . . . I don't know, it just felt like every time I tell my story, a weight lifts off me."

Before Dimitri could say something stupid like a stammering schoolboy and embarrass himself, Mr. Kidel opened the door and joined them in the hallway. "It's all set. Let's go see Geoff."

They followed him as he led the way. "I'm sorry we had to meet in this place, but it's convenient when visiting someone in the jail. I do, however, appreciate you both coming and giving statements."

"Of course, anything for Geoff." She hugged herself as she followed Mr. Kidel. "How's he holding up?"

"He's doing well, considering."

"Do you think the plea offer will come like you thought?" Dimitri hoped so.

Mr. Kidel nodded. "I do, with all the evidence against Muller. Especially with both of your statements. I'll meet with the ADA this afternoon and see what they're open to."

He led them through the process of checking in to visit at the jail, and they were led to a room. "Since I'm his attorney, we get to use the room instead of the common visiting area. It affords us more privacy."

"We certainly appreciate it, Mr. Kidel." Dimitri pulled out the chair for Adelaide before sitting beside her at the table.

"We can't visit but a moment, but I know you both are Geoff's friends. It'll do him a world of good to see y'all and know you stood up for him."

"Of course." Adelaide nodded.

A few minutes later, a uniformed police officer led in Geoff.

Adelaide stood and hugged him. "How are you doing?" she asked.

"I'm good. You didn't have to come visit me. A jail is no place for a lady like yourself."

"Oh, please." She let him go.

As soon as she did, Dimitri shook Geoff's hand. "Do you need anything?"

"I'm good, Mr. Pampalon."

"They can only stay a few minutes, Geoff," Mr. Kidel said, reminding them.

He nodded. "I can't tell you how much it means for you both to come here and to give statements on my behalf. I'm grateful."

"Of course. And as I told Mr. Kidel, I'm happy to testify in court if you need it." Adelaide's warmth projected from her smile.

"I appreciate that. I really do."

The officer opened the door. "It's time."

Mr. Kidel nodded. "Sorry, but y'all will have to leave now."

Adelaide stole another quick hug. "Stay strong. We're here for you."

Geoff smiled and nodded.

Dimitri shook his hand and gave him a side hug before taking Adelaide's elbow and leading her out.

"He looked good." Dimitri led her the way Mr. Kidel had shown them the way to exit.

"He did. I'm glad we got to see him for a minute, at least."

Dimitri opened the door and let her precede him. A blast of cold air cloaked them as they made their way to his car. He settled Adelaide into the passenger's side before sliding behind the wheel. "It's gotten colder."

"Weather said there was supposed to be a cold front pushing through. Guess it made it."

He started the engine and turned the heat on. The silence fell between them like a rock. Had asking her out caused such confliction? He needed to find out and make a course correction, if possible. He didn't want to risk their friendship. "Adelaide, I hope my asking you out hasn't made things awkward between us. I'm in no way rushing you, of course. I just wanted you to know my intent, but only if and when you're ready."

She twisted in the front seat to face him. "I appreciate that, and when I'm ready, I'll let you know." She smiled. "But I do need to talk to you about something important."

"All right."

"I don't want to offend you, but you know how much I care about you, so I only bring this to your attention because of that."

"Okay." His gut tightened in anticipation. Or dread. He wasn't sure which.

"I know Lissette is your half sister, but Dimitri, she practices voodoo. I know that goes against your faith."

He let out the breath he'd been holding. "It

does, but Lissette assures me that she's finished with that."

Adelaide pressed her lips together.

"What?"

"She's apparently been very active in the practice, and it's not something you just quit." She leaned over and took his hand. "I just want you to be careful, Dimitri."

He squeezed her hand. "I am. You'll see. Lissette's turning over a new leaf. She's even coming to church with me on Sunday. She and Elise both." He released her hand and grinned. "Want to come as well?"

She laughed. "Need a gaggle of ladies on your arm, Mr. Pampalon?"

"I wouldn't mind."

Adelaide sobered. "I'm not quite ready. I'm starting to talk to God again and listen, but it's personal for now."

His heart nearly burst out of his chest. *Thank You, Jesus!* He contained his delight. "Of course. I understand."

"One other thing."

"Yes?" he asked.

"Your father. Do you think he really is going to step aside and let Lissette take the CEO role? Seriously?"

She'd voiced what had kept him up a lot last night. "I'd like to think he would, I pray he does, but like you, I'm realistic. I've taken every precaution I can think of to ensure that's what happens, but I'm also being watchful."

"Good. I didn't want you to be unaware. I don't trust your father to just let it go. It's not in his nature."

He shook his head. "No, it's not. But I can't live in fear of what he might do. All I can do is move forward, doing the best that I can, and handle whatever he comes up with to throw my way."

"Well, I'll be here to help you with whatever he does."

Her smile did crazy things to his heart. He'd better get them going before he really stumbled over himself.

# THIRTY

ADELAIDE

"This is going to look fabulous on you." Tracey laid the dress over Adelaide's bed. "It's perfect for you."

Adelaide stared at the dress she knew she would never buy for herself. The tag alone, Mardi Gras Couture House, screamed of money and position in society that Adelaide had never belonged in. Yet here she was, staring at the most beautiful dress she'd ever seen.

The off-the-shoulder Mikado trumpet gown was deep crimson with contrasting black embroidery and heat-set stones, a deep plunging neckline with an illusion modesty panel, a keyhole back, princess seams, and contrasting hem. Tracey was right: it was a perfect dress.

"And look at the mask I found. It matches as if it were made to go with the dress, yes?" Tracey laid out the elaborate Mardi Gras masquerade mask and set it on the bed beside the dress. It was a Venetian Carnival–style mask. The gold half-face was bordered with red finely tatted lace and ornate with swirls that hosted a dozen ruby insets. The black and red feathers extended at least six to eight inches from the mask itself.

"Oh mercy," Adelaide breathed. "I love them."

Tracey laughed. "I figured you would. Come on, let me do your hair and makeup. I've been looking forward to tonight for forever."

Adelaide giggled and let her best friend lead her into her dressing area. Despite everything, all the upheaval of the last couple of weeks, Adelaide looked forward to dressing up and attending the Mardi Gras ball with Tracey.

"I decided your hair should be half up, half down." Tracey played with Adelaide's hair. "What do you think?"

"I don't care. Do whatever you think will look best."

"Yes!" Tracey grabbed the brush and bobby pins. "You know, you could join our krewe, and I bet you'd be queen in a year or so."

"No, thank you. I enjoy the balls, but I remember all the work you had to put in when you were queen. I don't have time."

Tracey laughed. "Yeah, but it was fun." She kept brushing, then braiding. "So, did you talk with Dimitri about his sister?"

"I did." Adelaide didn't really want to discuss anything very heavy. Tonight was going to be fun. "He said he'll watch out for any signs. Apparently, she's turning over a new leaf. Even going to church with Dimitri."

"That girl's got a serious crush on him. He should watch her too. I wouldn't be surprised if she put a binding on him to make him fall for her."

Adelaide snorted. "Like that would ever happen."

"I wouldn't be surprised. Look down so I can get this line straight."

Bending her head, Adelaide considered how she felt about someone having a crush on Dimitri. Did she mind?

Strangely enough, she found that she did. The thought that he would like someone else too really bothered her. Did that mean she was ready to date him?

No, just because another woman—girl, really— found him attractive wasn't a reason to start dating someone if she wasn't sure she was ready to move into a romantic relationship. It wouldn't be fair to Dimitri.

Or Beau.

"Okay, look straight."

She automatically obeyed Tracey's instructions. Her friend grabbed the curling rod and went to town on the length left hanging down her back. "What about you and Chuck, Trace?"

"What about us?"

"Are y'all getting serious?"

Tracey smiled as she curled more hair. "I think so. He definitely does."

"Do you think you'll marry him?"

"Marry?" Tracey laughed, full and throaty. "I guess. One day."

"But not soon?"

"No. I'm still too young, at least to my way of thinking. So is he, although he likes to think he's older and more mature." Tracey wound another section of hair around the rod. "Why do you ask?"

Adelaide shrugged. "You seem happy with him, but you're still your own person. Like tonight, you're going out to a ball without him."

Tracey laughed again. "Yeah, but he's working. It's hard that he got promoted to captain, which means he's at the fire station a lot more than I'd like, especially during the carnival season, but overall, yeah. I get what you're saying. A lot of women seem to lose themselves when they get serious with a guy. I'm not one of those women." She stared into Adelaide's face. "And neither are you, Ads. Don't you forget that."

"I won't." She smiled.

"Good." Tracey stood back and stared at her. "It's good, but it's missing something." She tapped the tip of her nose. "Pearls."

"Pearls?"

Tracey ran back to the bed and grabbed her bag and rummaged through it. "Yes, pearls." Triumphant, she held up a string of little fashion pearls.

"I thought you brought that big fake ruby necklace for me to wear with the dress."

"Yes, silly. These are going in your hair."

"Um, okay."

Minutes and a couple of hard pulls and scalp scrapes with bobby pins later, Tracey turned her to the mirror. "Ta-da!"

Adelaide stared. A single braid lined her face, about an inch or two from her face, ear-to-ear, with the bulk of her hair hanging in ringlets down her back. The pearls were woven into the braid, looking both natural and sophisticated at the same time.

"Wow, you should've been a hairdresser."

"Wait 'til you see what you look like after I do your makeup." Tracey laughed. "You know I always wanted a living doll."

"And to think I managed to escape your clutches in school when you were still perfecting your trade."

"Shh. Don't tell anyone about those days." Tracey reached for the hairspray. "I am going to set this before I start your makeup."

Adelaide closed her eyes. "Go for it."

After the cloud of hairspray finally cleared, Tracey applied Adelaide's makeup. Heavier than Adelaide usually wore, but masterfully applied so she looked beautiful, even if she did think so herself.

"Thanks, Trace. I needed to feel special. You

always seem to know how to do that."

"Don't you dare cry, Ads. I'll kill you if you mess up that eyeliner!" She grinned. "But I do love you, and I'll always have your back. No matter what." She clapped her hands loudly. "Now, let me get myself ready, and we can put on our party dresses and paint the town red!"

Before Adelaide could reply, Tracey snapped her fingers. "You know what we need up in here? Some tunes!" She grabbed her cell and opened her playlist. "Here we go."

Familiar notes of a popular zydeco band belted out from the speakers. Both Tracey and Adelaide danced around the dressing area. Tracey grabbed a roller brush for them to use as a microphone as they sang.

Adelaide savored the moment. Almost like she was back in high school getting ready for homecoming or prom. Excited and unencumbered by memories of pain and shame. Tonight, she was young and free and happy.

All very hard earned.

## DIMITRI

"I can't believe I'm actually going to a Mardi Gras ball. Are you sure I look okay?" Lissette sat in the front seat of Dimitri's car, smoothing her dress while checking her reflection in the lighted visor mirror.

"You look lovely." Dimitri smiled as he drove. He'd made sure his assistant sent over a proper dress and mask for his sister to wear to her first ball.

"Tell me again what'll happen." She practically bounced in her seat.

"Once everyone has arrived, the hosting krewe will introduce its court, saving the king and queen for last."

"And once they're introduced, then the dancing begins, right?"

He nodded. "Right."

"I told you I can't dance well, right?"

"I've prepared my toes to be stepped on." He chuckled. "You'll be fine, Lissette. You look beautiful and you'll be graceful. Just enjoy yourself."

"I've never attended a ball. I mean, I always wanted to, but I was never invited." The wistful look on her face twisted Dimitri's heart. He made a mental note to ask his assistant to have the Pampalon family join one of the krewes for next year.

They pulled up to the estate hosting the krewe's ball. Many of the older, established families opened their homes to host balls during the season. Dimitri figured it was just a way to show off their status, but regardless, it was what it was. Tonight's ostentatious display of wealth was courtesy of Malcolm Dessommes, the most eligible bachelor in New Orleans. The

Dessommes family was old money, older than the Pampalons even. Dimitri had been pitted against Malcolm many times during school, which should have made the two of them enemies but hadn't. Neither wanted to compete on the level that their fathers demanded, and that made the two instant and fast friends.

Lissette nearly burst out of the car when the attendant opened her door. The deep emerald dress shimmered, a fine contrast to her dark hair and mesmerizing eyes. Dimitri would have to watch her tonight with all the suitors sure to come out of the woodwork when they caught sight of her.

The wide set of concrete stairs up to the twelve foot front door were lit with little white lights. All the shrubs and the trees wore them as well. Gas lamps flickered along the walkway, decorated with streamers of green, purple, and gold. By all appearances, Malcolm had spared no expense with the decorating company. Dimitri was sure the feast would be just as ample and sumptuous.

He secured his black mask over his eyes before offering his arm to her, then escorted her inside, allowing the mock jester to announce them as Lady Lissette Bastien escorted by her brother, Sir Dimitri Pampalon.

A collective gasp reverberated against the walls of the main room as Dimitri led Lissette down the interior staircase.

"Why are people staring?" she whispered.

"For one, you're quite lovely."

She narrowed her eyes at him. "Truth."

"Because no one knows I have a sister."

She grinned. "They do now."

He nodded. "So they do."

They'd barely made it off the stairs when Dimitri felt the clap on his back. "My friend, what have you been up to?"

Dimitri smiled and turned. "Just keeping it real. How about you?"

Malcolm took a sip of champagne and stared at Lissette over the rim of the glass. "And did I hear the jester correctly that this lovely vision is your *sister?*"

He grinned. "Allow me to introduce you. Lissette Bastien, this is our host for the evening, Malcom Dessommes. Malcom, this is my younger sister, Lissette."

Malcom bowed low before offering his arm to Lissette. "My dear, you simply must come with me and tell me the details of your relations with my friend."

She looked at Dimitri, practically glowing.

"You take care of her, Malcom," Dimitri said with a wink at Lissette, who took Malcom's arm.

"But of course, my friend." Malcolm led Lissette toward the food tables. Dimitri knew he would watch out for her too, or he'd have to answer to Dimitri.

The jester continued to introduce guests. Dimitri checked his watch. In less than fifteen minutes, the krewe would begin introducing the court, and the dancing would start. He'd promised Lissette the first dance.

He wove his way to the bar and grabbed a sparkling water. Leaning against the railing, he watched the people mill about. Many were familiar, but some wore their masks and were hard to recognize. Dimitri shook hands with several business owners and accepted hugs from their wives or girlfriends.

"Hello, Dimitri."

He turned, smiling. "Hello, Elise. Don't you look lovely!"

She smiled and ducked her head. "Thank you. You look handsome as well."

"Would you like a sparkling water?"

"No, thank you. Lucien is getting our drinks."

Ah, now that he thought about it, he realized a ball wouldn't be a place the young Elise would normally attend. "Lucien?"

She tilted her head to the young man grabbing two champagne flutes from the server's tray. "My date for the evening."

The man made his way to them, thrusting a flute at Elise. "Who are you?" he asked Dimitri.

Dimitri snorted at the young man's rudeness, but kept his eye on Elise. "I'm Dimitri Pampalon, a friend of Elise's family." He stared at Elise, then at the glass, then at young Lucien.

"Oh, well, nice to meet you." Lucien took Elise by the arm. "Come on, Niall and Sondra are saving us seats on the balcony."

"You take care," Dimitri told Elise, watching her walk away.

He made a mental note to check on her in an hour or so and make sure she was okay and still sober. Tilda would have his hide if he knew Elise was drinking and didn't watch over her.

The jester beat his stick on the marble floor twice and announced, "Lady Tracey Glapion and Lady Adelaide Fountaine."

Dimitri turned and almost choked on his sparkling water. He couldn't take his eyes off Adelaide as she floated down the stairs. His mouth went dry. As he came to his senses and glanced around, he realized that the women seemed to have the same effect on most of the men watching them enter.

Dimitri made his way to offer his arm to them as they descended. "Ladies."

"Hello, Dimitri. You remember my friend Tracey?"

He offered his other arm to Tracey. "I do. Both of you ladies look absolutely stunning this evening."

He spoke to them both as he led them toward the spread of food, but his heart pounded as Adelaide smiled at him. As beautiful as she looked right now, it was hard for him to remember she wasn't ready for romance. He'd agreed to wait, but the way she looked . . . his work was certainly cut out for him.

"I see a friend I need to speak with before they introduce the court," Tracey said with a nod toward a masked man in the corner. "I'll find you soon," she said to Adelaide before heading off with a swish of her skirt.

"Adelaide, I have to say, you look more beautiful than ever tonight. That dress, even that mask—"

She giggled. "It's all on loan from Trace. We figured we deserved a night out on the town. It's been a long time since we were able to have a girls' night."

"You do deserve a beautiful night. I do hope that you'll save me a dance?" He'd promised to be patient, but that didn't mean he couldn't stay in the game.

She blushed along the bottom edge of her mask. "Of course. I'd love that."

Maybe this would be their new normal. Flirting, smiling, sharing, and staying friends until she was ready for more. As long as he could hold her in his arms on occasion, like he'd get to do later tonight for a dance—maybe two—he'd be okay.

They would be okay. And for now, that was enough.

# THIRTY-ONE

BEAU

He kind of hated these things, yet every year he went because when you wanted to make an impression with the political side of the New Orleans Police Department, you went to at least a couple of the Mardi Gras balls you were invited to. He'd be back at work next week, and he'd meet with the captain regarding his promotion.

Beau wanted it badly.

So he put on his fresh-from-the-cleaners tux, dusted off the Phantom of the Opera mask he always wore, and made his way to the Garden District to attend a Mardi Gras ball he really cared nothing about. He couldn't even remember which krewe this ball was for.

The attendant who parked his car looked offended at having to get behind the wheel of a regular Dodge. Like he was insulted the Charger wasn't a Benz or Cadillac. Beau didn't really care. He'd put in an hour or so, make sure he saw the mayor, then make a quick getaway.

He waited in line behind a couple who clearly were attending for the first time. She fidgeted, he kept patting her hand to calm her. New money.

The jester announced them, then took Beau's invitation. He pounded his baton on the floor twice before announcing, "Detective Beauregard Savoie."

Beau descended the stairs quickly. It was all pomp anyway, but the food was usually worth the trip. Last year, fresh oysters and shrimp overflowed from the tables at almost all the balls, each host hiring the best chefs for preparation and display. Every host wanted their tables to be the best, the most remembered and talked about.

Beau spied the tables and made his way to the food. The one good thing about the overabundance was that the city's homeless kitchens were kept supplied during the carnival season. It made him feel less guilty about attending.

He reached for a plate, then froze as a vision moved in the corner of his eye. Even though she wore a mask, there was no mistaking her.

Addy.

She wore a red dress with black that fit her like a glove, outlining every curve. The neckline plunged, and he meant *plunged*. Her hair glittered and glistened. From behind the mask, her eyes shone like diamonds, or like the ruby hanging around her neck.

A man stood beside her, talking to her, and in that moment, Beau had never wanted to rip another person's throat out as badly. Unless it had been Kevin Muller. The man turned . . . Dimitri. Beau's insides seized as he forced himself to cross the few feet between them.

"Hello, Addy."

Her smile lit up her eyes peering from behind the extravagant mask. "Hi, Beau. I didn't expect to see you here."

He couldn't stop his gaze from traveling back to Dimitri. "Apparently."

Her eyes clouded for a moment. "What?"

No, he wouldn't be that guy. He grinned. "Nothing. You look exquisite."

She twirled. "You like? Tracey did it."

Dimitri held out his hand. "Detective."

Beau shook it. "Pampalon."

"You can call me Dimitri, you know."

"Yeah." He resisted the urge to wipe his hand on his pants leg, having a strong feeling Addy wouldn't be amused.

Had she come with Pampalon? Every muscle in Beau's body went rigid at the thought. Surely not.

"Where's Marcel?" she asked.

"Oh, he skips these shindigs. He's not yet on the promotion ladder where seeing and being seen is important."

"Oh, but you are a sight for sore eyes." Tracey strode to the group and gave him a gentle hug. "How're you feeling?"

"Quite well, actually." Beau studied her. "You are a vision."

Tracey struck a pose, grinning.

"Where's Chuck tonight?"

"Working, as usual, so Ads agreed to be my date." She looped her arm through Addy's.

Addy tilted her head toward Tracey. "Some date. She brings me, then runs off to talk to someone else."

"But I love you more than my luggage." Tracey tugged on Addy's arm. "We need food." She glanced between Dimitri and Beau. "Hmm. Could you gentlemen please grab us a couple of bottled waters?" Without waiting for a reply, Tracey dragged Addy to the tables of food.

Even though the main floor of the estate was spacious and flowing, the room felt small and stuffy as Beau and Dimitri stared at one another. Without a word being exchanged, Beau knew Dimitri was attracted to Addy, and he was pretty sure Dimitri knew he was as well.

"There you are." A young woman appeared at Dimitri's side. "I thought I'd lost you."

Dimitri had a date? Maybe Beau had been wrong about his interest in Addy.

"Lissette Bastien, meet Detective Beau Savoie." She smiled. "Hello."

"Detective, this is my sister, Lissette."

It took a minute for the words to register in Beau's head. Sister?

Dimitri nodded. "She'll be working at the Darkwater Inn with Adelaide and me."

So, he'd been right about Dimitri's interest in Addy. Beau cleared his throat. "I'll grab the ladies' water while you tend to your sister." He didn't wait for an answer before heading to the bar, grabbing two bottles, then heading over to the small table Tracey and Addy had chosen.

"Where's Dimitri?" Tracey asked, but her eyes locked with Beau's, and he saw the real questions lurking there she dared not ask in front of Addy.

"He's seeing to his sister."

"I don't trust that girl." Tracey glanced over her shoulder at them. "You be careful of her, Ads."

"We've had this conversation already, Trace. No more seriousness tonight. I want to have fun."

"You got it, sistah!"

The krewe began to make its court introductions. Tracey stood and looked at Beau and Addy. "I'm going to go watch the grand march. Either of you want to come?"

They both shook their heads. Tracey winked at Beau, then was gone.

He always did like Tracey.

He leaned close to Addy's ear. "I meant what I said, you do look breathtaking."

Addy smiled and lowered her chin, the blush spreading across her cheeks visible under the mask.

The music started, and groups of people made their way toward the dance floor.

Beau wanted nothing more than to have Addy in his arms again. He stood and made a sweeping bow, then extended his hand to her. "Shall we, milady?"

She took his hand, grinning.

Once he had her in his arms, they swayed in time to the music from the live band. The space on the floor became more crowded, so he pulled her closer to him.

"Your dad dropped by to check on me."

"What did he have to say now?"

He chuckled. She knew her dad well. "He invited me to Thursday supper."

She shook her head. "That man is incorrigible."

He hadn't considered that she might not want him there. Fear prompted him to speak. "But if you don't want me to go, I won't. And I won't be offended."

Addy shook her head. "Don't be silly. It's just he can be so obvious sometimes—" She stopped moving to the music and stared at him with wide eyes. "You didn't tell him about our, um, kiss did you?"

"Of course not." It hurt a little that she thought he might.

She began dancing again. "Good. I mean, it's none of his business."

He wouldn't lie to her, though. No more secrets

between them. They'd promised. "But he knows how I feel about you."

Her steps faltered. "You told him?"

Beau tightened his hold on her waist. "He asked. I didn't lie."

"Oh." She stared at Beau's chest.

"Addy, look at me."

She lifted her gaze.

"It doesn't matter. What matters is your happiness. You know how I feel about you, at least I think you do, but you are in charge of our relationship, whatever that means. Friends, more, whatever. It's all in your hands and in your timing. No matter what I or your dad or Tracey or anybody else thinks. Okay?"

She stood on tiptoe and planted a kiss on his cheek. "You, Beauregard Savoie, are a true gentleman."

He could barely keep time with the music as she beamed up at him.

"Excuse me." Dimitri appeared at their side. "May I cut in?"

## ADELAIDE

"That was a little rude, yes?"

Beau had been gracious in allowing Dimitri to cut in, but Adelaide had seen the confliction in his eyes before he released her.

"All's fair in love and war, right?" When

Dimitri smiled, it was hard to stay upset with him.

"I don't think we're discussing love or war, are we?"

"Touché." He dipped his head.

She'd made her point, time to move on. Tonight was for fun. "Is Lissette enjoying her first ball?"

Dimitri glided her across the floor, all grace and fluidity. "She is. I do believe Malcolm Dessommes has taken a liking to her. I'll have to keep an eye on that."

Adelaide chuckled. "How does it feel to suddenly be a big brother?"

"Odd, but"—Dimitri twirled her—"also very good. I always wanted a sibling."

"Me too." She'd often wondered what her life would have been like with a brother or sister, but then she realized she had a sibling in Tracey. A sister she chose for herself, which was the best kind.

"Isn't Detective Savoie like your brother?" Dimitri's eyes twinkled.

"No. He's important to me, and we share a past, but he's not like a brother."

The twinkle in his eyes dimmed. "Oh."

The song ended and everyone clapped. The band started the song for the second line dance, and everyone fell into step.

Tracey came and swept Adelaide along. "Come on, we're going to dance out into the streets."

Together, she and Tracey danced along with the crowd. Adelaide glanced around and one time saw Dimitri with the young Elise close behind him. Another spin and she spied Beau talking with the governor.

They spilled out into the courtyard, then the streets, the band leading them all like modern-day Pied Pipers. Adelaide didn't care. She'd never felt freer or more alive. Everything seemed brighter, bigger, better.

Or maybe Adelaide's perspective had changed. Either way, she didn't care. She was going to enjoy the ride.

Tracey pulled her out of the line, breathless. "I need to catch my breath. You good?"

"Better than ever."

"I saw you dancing with Beau and Dimitri."

"Yep."

Tracey waited, then shoved Adelaide's shoulder. "Come on, Ads, spill. What's going on? What are you thinking? Feeling?"

"I'm feeling alive, for the first time in a really long time. I decided I'm not going to date either, or anyone else, for now. I want to take some time to get to know myself, really know myself. I want to figure out what I want out of a relationship. I don't want to play games, I'm too old for that, but I'm so young in relationship matters. I want to be fair but not waste time or energy. I've already done enough of that."

"Well, look at you, Ads. You go, girl. I'm proud of you."

"Me, too. I'm proud of me." Adelaide grinned because she *was* proud of where she was in her heart, in her mind, and in life at the moment. It'd been a long time coming, but she was plain happy, and that was a good place to be.

# EPILOGUE

## ADELAIDE

"All rise. Court's in session, the Honorable Judge Robinson presiding."

"Be seated." The judge in his black robe took his seat behind his massive desk up on the pedestal of the courtroom, peering down at everyone below him.

Adelaide sat on the front row behind Geoff, flanked on one side by Dimitri and Lissette and Tracey on the other side.

"I understand the parties have reached an agreement?" the judge asked.

"We have, Your Honor." The assistant district attorney on the case, Pam Lion, stood. "We have agreed to a guilty plea to manslaughter with a recommended sentence of two and a half years."

The judge tossed his glasses onto his desk and stared down at her. "A murder, reduced to manslaughter with a recommended sentence of two and a half years?"

The ADA looked flustered as she flipped through papers. Her second chair handed her a specific one. "Yes. Oh. Your Honor, there are mitigating circumstances in this case to which the state feels this is a just and adequate charge and sentencing recommendation."

"I see." The judge himself flipped pages, making little noises every so often.

"Is he not going to accept it?" Tracey whispered.

Adelaide shrugged. Mr. Kidel had told them that the state made the deal and that with a two and a half year sentence, Geoff would likely be out in two years. He hadn't mentioned anything about the judge questioning the charge or the sentence.

Geoff seemed to be wondering the same as he and Mr. Kidel huddled together whispering.

"I've finished reading the case notes, counselors." The judge's voice boomed. "How do you plead to the charge of manslaughter, Mr. Aubois?"

Mr. Kidel held Geoff's elbow as they both stood.

"Guilty." Geoff's voice seemed to bounce off the walls of the courtroom.

"You understand by accepting this plea agreement, you are waiving your right to a trial, yes?" the judge asked.

"Yes, Your Honor."

"And your attorney has discussed this agreement with you in detail?"

"Yes, Your Honor."

"Then I accept this plea agreement, and in accordance with the recommendation of the state, as well as documents provided, I hereby sentence you, Geoff Aubois, to twenty-six months at the Elayn Hunt Correctional Center in St. Gabriel, Louisiana." The judge hit his gavel. "Court is adjourned."

"All rise." The bailiff stood.

Those in the courtroom stood as the judge left the bench.

Mr. Kidel turned to Geoff. "He even lowered the sentence."

"Thank you." Geoff shook the lawyer's hand.

"Elayn Hunt Correctional Center? I thought he'd be sent to the state prison," Dimitri said as he reached across the space and shook Mr. Kidel's hand.

"I'd requested the correctional center since Geoff had been security. It's a lower security, so he'll have more freedoms."

The uniformed officer came to Geoff. "It's time."

Geoff turned quickly and gave Adelaide a big smile. "Thank you, for everything."

She leaned over the rail and gave him a hug. "I'll come visit you."

He shook his head. "You don't need to do that."

"I want to, so you'd better put me on your visiting list."

"I will." Geoff shook Dimitri's hand. "Thank

you too, for everything. I can never repay you."

"Oh, but you will when you get out. You'll be back to work at the Darkwater Inn."

The smile slid off Geoff's face. "I won't be able to have a firearm, Mr. Pampalon. I won't be much use to the Darkwater."

But Dimitri shook his head. "You don't need a weapon to oversee the digital surveillance and monitoring system." He held up a finger. "No argument. Your job will be waiting on you as soon as you get out."

Geoff's upper lip trembled. "Thank you, sir. Both of you." He looked and included Mr. Kidel in his gaze. "All of you."

"Time to go." The officer put handcuffs on Geoff's wrists and led him out the door.

Adelaide blinked back tears. Tracey grabbed her hand and tugged her from the courtroom while Dimitri and Lissette were still talking with Mr. Kidel.

"What's the rush?" Adelaide asked as Tracey nearly jerked her arm out of its socket.

"Come on, I want to show you something." Tracey led her to the elevators.

"What?"

"Just wait and see because you wouldn't believe me if I told you." She punched the *down* button.

Adelaide shook her head, but grinned at her best friend's antics. No telling what Tracey had up her sleeve. Her unpredictability was one of her most endearing traits.

As soon as they stepped out of the courthouse, Adelaide understood. She looked to her best friend, grinning. "Snow? It's snowing?"

"I know, that's why I knew you wouldn't believe me unless you saw for yourself. It's really snowing."

Adelaide walked along the square, her face toward the sky. Snowflakes lit on her face, planting little icy kisses.

She spun slowly in circles, watching the flakes come down. There was already a good dusting of snow over the surfaces outside . . . sidewalks, streets, benches. The stark white seemed to wash the city in newness, like a fresh start full of hope and promise.

Just like Adelaide was starting her life afresh. Anew.

Full of hope and promise.

Dear Reader,

Welcome to one of my most favorite cities of all time—New Orleans. The city itself seems to hum with vibrancy of life and expectation. I love my time spent in the Crescent City and hope that you've enjoyed getting to taste a little of the flavor of Cajun country. Creating the Darkwater Inn was so much fun, and even though the hotel itself isn't real, I pulled in many aspects from some of the beautiful and charming hotels of the area.

I'm always amazed as my characters take on their own personalities, and with these three main characters, that was certainly true. Adelaide, Beau, and Dimitri are so different, but they have some similar traits. Their strong hearts and passion for those closest to them pushed me as a writer. It is my hope that I've done them justice as I tell Adelaide's story, which involves both Beau and Dimitri, not just for this book, but for the books to follow.

As a Christian, I often struggle with forgiveness—of others and of myself—and these characters certainly had to deal with this, each in their own way. Some of their faith journey is also my own, and it's an honor to be able to share this with you.

I hope you'll enjoy reading the Darkwater Inn series, and I would love to hear from you. Please visit me on social media and on my website: *www.robincaroll.com.* I love talking books with readers.

Blessings,
*Robin*

# ACKNOWLEDGMENTS

With every book I turn in, I'm simply amazed at the many hardworking folks behind the scenes who work their magic to make the final product a story that awes me. I can't thank the team at Gilead Publishing enough for their attention to detail while allowing me to tell Adelaide's story. Special thanks to my editor, Becky Philpott, for her input and direction. Thanks to copyeditor Jamie Chavez for her many catches. Thanks to Dan and Jordan and Katelyn and so many others who made this book possible. My most humble gratitude.

I can't express enough how in awe I am of the AMAZING cover Kirk DouPonce (DogEared Design) created for *Darkwater Secrets*. Thank you, Kirk, for your vision and talent that always brings the perfect design.

I'm so grateful for my agent, Steve Laube, and his willingness to share his wisdom and experience with me. It is a privilege, sir, and one I appreciate.

This book was brainstormed with some pretty amazing writers at a private retreat. My thanks for their input and excitement: Colleen Coble, Carrie Stuart Parks, Ronie Kendig, Lynette Eason, and Michelle Lim. I had a great time hanging out with y'all and always look forward to being able to brainstorm with you.

Every writer needs a circle of prayer partners, beta readers, and those people who will push and stretch you. I'm eternally grateful for mine: Pam Hillman, Heather Tipton, Tracey Justice, Cynthia Ruchti, and Cara Putman. You ladies don't let me get away with anything or take any shortcuts, and I appreciate each of you for that!

I'm beyond blessed to have my family who is always willing to brainstorm, come up with plot twists, and walk me through some scenes. I love y'all and wouldn't be able to do any of this without you, Casey, Remy, and Bella.

Lots of love for my extended family's encouragement. I can't tell you how much I appreciate your continuous support: Mom, my grandsons—Benton and Zayden, Bubba and Lisa, Brandon and Katie, Rachel and Thomas, Justin & Baby G, Robyn—Rebecca—and Rion, and Wade (because you are more family than not).

I realize every day how fortunate I am for the man who blesses me every single day. Casey, it is an honor to be your wife, and I'll never be able to tell you how much it means to me for you to walk beside me in chasing this dream. It's because of you that I'm not afraid to try to fly. I love you.

Finally, all glory to my Lord and Savior, Jesus Christ. I can do all things through Christ who strengthens me.

# ABOUT THE AUTHOR

"I love boxing. I love Hallmark movies. I love fishing. I love scrapbooking. Nope, I've never fit into the boxes people have wanted to put me in." ~Robin Caroll is definitely a contradiction, but one that beckons you to get to know her better.

Robin's passion has always been to tell stories to entertain others and come alongside them on their faith journey—aspects Robin weaves into each of her published novels.

Best-selling author of more than twenty-seven novels, Robin Caroll writes Southern stories of mystery and suspense, with a hint of romance to entertain readers. Her books have been recognized in several awards, including the Carol Award, HOLT Medallion, Daphne du Maurier, RT Reviewer's Choice Award, and more.

When she isn't writing, Robin spends quality time with her husband of twenty-eight-plus years, her three beautiful daughters and two handsome grandsons, and their character-filled pets at home. Robin serves the writing community as Executive/Conference Director for ACFW.

# Connect with Robin!

Website:   www.robincaroll.com
Facebook: facebook.com/Author.RobinCaroll/
Twitter:   @robincaroll
Instagram:@robin.caroll
Pinterest:  @robincaroll

**Center Point Large Print**
600 Brooks Road / PO Box 1
Thorndike, ME 04986-0001 USA

**(207) 568-3717**

**US & Canada:**
**1 800 929-9108**
www.centerpointlargeprint.com